BROKEN

A FEMALE-DRIVEN NOVEL
MATTHEW LIBURDI

Love has a special place in the heart

For some, it will guide them

For others, it will betray them

This is a work of fiction. Names, characters, businesses, places, events, and incidents are either the products of the author's imagination or used in a fictitious manner. Any resemblance to actual persons, living or dead, or events is coincidental.

From the Author Matthew Liburdi

I would like to thank everyone who read my novels.
Please pass each book on and ask your friends to write a
review as you did. Your words, especially your reviews,
inspire me to continue writing.

CLICK LINK TO VISIT AUTHOR WEBSITE

Please enjoy BROKEN

Editor - Matthew Liburdi

Front cover design - Matthew Liburdi

Marketing videos - Matthew Liburdi

Media content - Matthew Liburdi

Other novels by Matthew Liburdi

CRUMBLING KINGDOM

YA / Family Novel - Suspense - Thriller

DECEPTIVE TIMES

Four-book Action/Adventure series

Deceptive Times 1

Deceptive Times 2

Deceptive Times 3

Deceptive Times 4

WOLLOH

Psychological/Horror

WOLLOH 2 – BROKEN 2 – DECEPTIVE TIMES X5

CRUMBLING KINGDOM 2

coming soon

BROKEN

PART 1

Chapter 1

INTRODUCTION

THE HEROINE

Tamara Hudson was born and raised Texas-tough and was damn proud of it. She knew her path early on, not discounting the guidance from her warm and loving parents. Tamara valued her education, excelled in sports, categorized herself as a social butterfly, and participated in after-school activities. By the tenth grade, she had already picked her College. Texas A&M, which she credited to her Grandfather, Thomas. A European immigrant who came to America on the dream of riches. Thomas settled in East

Texas and hit it big wildcatting. He invested his last nickel in a well that became a gusher. Thomas soon inherited the rank of oil baron and married Adela, his Latino sweetheart, who sadly passed, giving birth to their tenth child, her sixth girl. Thomas always bragged about how blessed he was and how his kids transcended in life. Of fourteen grandchildren, his two favorites were from his youngest son, Thomas Junior. Samantha was fourteen months older than Tamara, yet he always told them they looked like twins.

Nothing could compromise her strong bond with her older sister, Samantha. The day she went missing, inner turmoil tore at her soul. Tamara questioned the police report, especially the private detectives her dad and the other family hired. Even though they found no proof of foul play, Tamara understood that her sister did not compose the poorly written goodbye message. In her heart, Tamara knew Samantha did not run away for love and would never resurface.

Tamara listened to her intuition, and with support from her father, she went undercover. She transferred to Brown University and enrolled under her mother's maiden name. Right out of the gate, the sisters unanimously vetted her as the number one pick out of the other ten applicants. Stunning beauty, offset with her smooth mulatto skin, gave her a unique sex appeal. Not discounting her excellent grade point average and being a top-seeded tennis player.

The first few months were disorienting. Not a single clue surfaced. Equally disturbing, the second in command, the sister named Amanda, insisted she resembled Samantha. "Pure coincidence," Tamara declared. Before long, Tamara started to believe Samantha did run away with her boyfriend until a tip surfaced. A fraternity brother supposedly heard Derik, her boyfriend, shagging in his room a few days before they went missing. What sparked her interest, even though he did not physically see the girl, he swore her moans sounded like Amanda Manchester, not Samantha. He had slept with Amanda a few weeks earlier.

Tamara dug deeper. She questioned professors, even the sisters from other sororities, targeting the ones Amanda had burned—slept with their boyfriends. The list was longer than she could have ever imagined. At any rate—though based on hearsay rather than solid concrete evidence—everyone believed Samantha would have never quit school to chase love. They also thought Amanda had something to do with their disappearance.

To prove her theory, Tamara befriended Amanda. She understood that earning her trust would require trickery and sacrifice. She would have to even the playing field by lowering her standards—a deception far outside her natural tendencies. To help, she bribed the most ruthless person she knew, Phil Macrevice. He was fresh out of College, and she knew one of his dirty secrets. Phil wholeheartedly agreed, finding the challenge exhilarating. Over the next six months, he redefined her mannerisms by exposing her frailties while cultivating her fears.

Interestingly, she conquered her iniquities naturally, which Phil found paradoxically deceptive. Tamara found the final lesson in the art of duplicity sinful. She mastered how to use her sexual prowess to tempt and seduce. Phil completed her education by coaching her in the virtues of barroom talk and bedroom sex, which he, being the beneficiary, enjoyed. Tamara was not a virgin, yet she had minimal sexual experiences. Still, she found his skills satisfying. Phil, well, he found her graduation gift cruel.

Over the next few years, an ugly transition occurred. Tamara rummaged through the cobwebs and discarded her old self. She distanced herself from her parents and relatives until a wolf emerged—a hunter eager to conquer.

Tamara found her place in the sorority addictive. Her dominance, guided by treachery, earned her legacy as the protege of Amanda and the trust of Pricilla, the leader. She became number three on the totem pole.

It took until their senior year for Amanda to accept Tamara as a reliable friend. She admitted never having someone so close to confide in, except, of course, her father. Amanda finally opened up, revealing some of her deepest and darkest secrets, always careful to dodge the duplicity and hidden agendas regarding her family. Tamara dug further and befriended her father, Randolph. He insisted that their friendship would end if Amanda discovered even a hint of rumor. Amanda did not share well, especially with her father.

Together, they dominated the campus. Their atrocities, ranging from verbal squashing to lurid tales of perversity and lust, were unmatched, even within the fraternities. What Tamara found the hardest to control was her fondness for the pursuit. She secretly confided with her family priest to balance her emotions and keep herself in check. She would never wholly jeopardize her actual values.

Pricilla and Tamara become best friends. Even Beatrice, her mother, found Tamara stimulating. Out of the thirty-six members within the sorority, she, like Amanda, earned rank in the Felines—an elite club owned by Pricilla, which by definition conveyed the Destroyers of Men. Ten hand-picked intelligent young women—wealthy, dependable, and self-sufficient with high extroversion. Some were predators, others traditionalists, yet all believed in the code. Women were the governing species. They vowed secrecy, eternal friendship, and to stand by each other, in life and for life, through thick and thin, no matter the circumstance.

Tamara found the group singular but hive-minded. In a sense, it was like marriage without divorce. The only way out was to die or get voted out in exile.

Graduation came and went. While most of the chapter redefined careers, enrolled in graduate school, and married, the Felines kicked post-sorority life into high gear. For them, the revolution began. The world was indeed their oyster. Amid their distractions, revelries, extravagant travel, not to mention wild sex parties and challenges, they continually tested each other. Games dare and experiments involving everything mischievous, naughty, even malicious, until tragedy. Beatrice passed away.

Not discounting her grief, a gainful direction transpired. Because Amanda found her demise more painful than

Pricilla's, Tamara was one step closer to uncovering what happened to her sister. It happened after multiple tequila shots at her uptown apartment. Amanda accidentally revealed a secret to her dark past—a reflection of her genuine cruelty. She had a childhood sweetheart. A man of impeccable virtue and loyalty wrapped around her finger. James Rawlings, a virgin male in his late twenties who devoted his life to her from the moment they met as kids. What Tamara discovered was that Amanda would never marry him. She was incapable of sharing. Her agenda was to see how long she could keep him engaged. Her fuel was his submission. She insisted if James ever found another lover or married, she would kill her.

Tamara finally found a strategy to pierce Amanda's soul.

Chapter 2

AMANDA MANCHESTER

Amanda was born six minutes past the hour of midnight on July the fourth in the upstairs bedroom of the Victorian. In the same room, her father, Randolph, was born twenty-seven years earlier by the same doctor, except two minutes earlier. Amanda remained hairless for the first eighteen months and below average in growth. She was a chronic crier during this period until they removed her tonsils. By five, she was deemed an American princess, a materialistic spoiled brat, not by her parents.

Amanda took after Randolph. Like his father, he was born into nobility. Unfortunately, during his final year of college, his parents mysteriously died on an expedition deep into the Amazon. The diagnosis from a rare form of cardiac failure spawned from mosquito bites. Six months later, Randolph met Veronica Boyd: a medium-height, well-endowed, curvaceous, starving Broadway actress. Within weeks, they were on their honeymoon to Tahiti and conceived Amanda.

Always well dressed and clean-shaven, except for a thick dark mustache below an ambitious Roman nose, which covered what he considered a narrow upper lip, women of all classes judged Randolph Manchester, like his grandfather, dashingly handsome. Not tall to speak of but lean and strong-chested, he used his gifted and energetic tongue prolifically to every advantage in his celebrity lifestyle. Randolph earned a Ph.D. in business and law and kept a history of dark and dirty secrets hidden from his friends and Veronica. His most egregious was his carnal love for Amanda, his precious little angel.

Amanda acquired Randolph's traits early on. She discovered that questioning authority was advantageous, which made the game all the more enjoyable. Amanda also had a fondness for extravagance, especially birthday parties. Even though she had everything she could desire, she wanted more. For her fourteenth, Randolph hired Teresa—a working girl from the other side of the tracks. What Amanda found exciting was that he watched Teresa go down on her and give his angel her first orgasm.

Over the next few years, her appetite for flesh turned sinful. Amanda preyed on the overly-producing testosterone types hungry for their first taste of the female desire. It was also when she developed her alternating personality disorders, which she asserted was due to Randolph watching her have sex with other women. He ended it on her sixteenth birthday, maintaining he could no longer further her learning.

One morning, between breakfast and stepping out the door, she persuaded Randolph that private school stunted her mental growth. The following day, she was walking the local public high school hallways. Amanda joined the student council and bribed her way onto the cheerleading squad. Not content being a subordinate, she took over as captain within a month. Controversy flared. To keep the scandal under control, Randolph bribed the school board. Amanda labeled herself the queen and named the squad the Untouchables. She demanded compliance. Those who broke the rules were banished and humiliated, and no one could maintain relationships for more than three weeks, male or female. She would prey on ripe young men with low self-esteem. Charm them with kindness and end it with cruelty only she could inflict.

Randolph spared no expense for her graduation party. Showing her true colors, she complained, preferring the Maserati over the Mercedes Benz. Her college of choice was Brown University, where her alternate personality and cruelty developed to the next level.

Chapter 3

COLLEGE

Amanda Manchester found university life gratifying. She quickly out-flanked the other sisters, earning the reputation as second in command, even in the secret club, the Felines. She held the pecking rights on the long line of douchebags waiting for an opportunity to bang the elite women on campus. She had many acquaintances but no true friends. The reason Randolph taught her love was a two-edged sword. He maintained her mother knew about his roaming desires, but she did not know of him watching her sexual acts. That was their dirty secret.

Amanda believed she was God's gift to the male species. Though never divulged, Pricilla, the queen of the sorority and the president of the Felines, was the thorn in her side. She stood in the way of her rightful place as the true leader.

It was during her sophomore year her hereditary character matured. Randolph knew this would happen. It was also when the nightmares began. Amanda believed they were a byproduct of her father's carnal misdirections during her teenage years. Even though they were infrequent, they were always the same, which pushed her ferocity toward the outer edge of extreme.

KARMA

It happened early one Sunday morning. She woke out of a slumber. Or was it unconsciousness? Amanda tried to focus, but absolute darkness punished her. The only actuality was that she was lying on a bed, and the backside of her head felt like something blunt struck it.

To her right, she hears a wheeze and then another one.

"Who's there?"

There is no answer, yet despite the limited ambiance, the outline of a woman standing a few feet ahead becomes clear. Suddenly, the contusion on her head made sense. She woke from unconsciousness, which meant she was in a fight. Her left shoulder ached, and she was gripping a blunt object in her right hand. "Who are you, and what do you want?"

Only silence.

Behind the woman, Amanda can make out the faint outline of a threshold. Further right, a window, a lampshade, and a digital clock. Amanda realizes this is her room. Another wheeze, this one laborious, could only mean the stranger was injured. The hardened object in her hand fits perfectly within her palm. A cold chill radiates, and her index finger rests on a curved mechanism. For her life, it remained distant. Could it be amnesia set in from her head wound?

The stranger shuffled her feet and raised what looked like a baseball bat. "You fucking bitch." She roared. "You made me kill him! It's now your time for you to die!"

Amanda instinctively raised her right hand and squeezed. What sounded like a cannon followed by a flash in the dead of night could only be the discharge of a gun. Amanda watched the woman drop the object and fall heavy to the floor.

Not sure why she was yielding a gun, she turned on the light and gasped. Bleeding profusely from two wounds to her chest, she glared at one of her sorority sisters. As alarming, her boyfriend, Derik, was lying on the bed in a pool of blood. Suddenly, the gun made sense.

The mid-term party was Greek-themed, mixed with fire and ice—the biggest bash of the year. Samantha invited her four-month-old boyfriend, Derik, whom none of the other girls in the sorority knew about, except, of course, Amanda. She was keen on her trickery months ago but waited on the sidelines for the right moment. Samantha broke a commandment: No sister shall engage in a relationship longer than three weeks, which they swore to uphold with a proud and common bond.

To keep her secret, Amanda blackmailed Samantha. Derik must sleep with her at her off-campus apartment. Unknown to Amanda, Samantha had hidden secrets. She was born in Texas and raised cowgirl tough. Her father taught her never to back down and, if pushed, to defend herself ugly. She also took medication to control anger issues. It was time to even the playing field because Amanda had already victimized most of the other sisters. Dressed in black and armed with a baseball bat, she followed Derik. She intended to scare him, not kill him. What she discovered turned out to be her worst nightmare. Derik was a two-faced liar. He had already slept with Amanda multiple times. Samantha could barely hold back her rage, listening to him joke about how naïve she was. The first swing connected with his skull. He fell bloodied to the floor. She continued the assault, bashing Amanda multiple times while screaming obscenities.

Derik stood. "Sweetheart! Baby, what're you doing?" He gasped and toppled forward.

Not aware of who attacked her, Amanda collected the small caliber pistol from the bottom drawer of the nightstand and fired.

Even though shot, Samantha remained standing. The agony seemed to lessen with each wheeze. She heard Amanda plead, but her mind could not respond. A few moments later, she regained her senses and raised the bat. Another piercing ache penetrated deep into her soul. Samantha dropped the bat. A moment later, her world went dark.

"Daddy!" Amanda sniffled into the phone.

"Angel, what's wrong?" Randolph demanded.

"Daddy, I need help."

"Are you OKAY!"

"I'm hurt, but I can manage. Something terrible happened. Two people are dead. Daddy, I'm scared."

"Where are you?"

"The apartment in the city! I don't know what to do."

A slight pause. "Angel! I understand. Do not say another word. Lock the front door. Do not answer it for anyone."

"Okay. It's locked."

"Listen. I'm sending Thomas. Once I hang up, take the battery out of your phone. Do not use your computer. Do not email or text. If you aren't already, get dressed. Something simple and clean up as much as possible. Do you understand?"

"Yes, please hurry. I'm scared. I'm so scared."

Within the hour, Thomas cleaned the apartment. After fabricating emails and texts, he wrote a goodbye love message on her notepad and buried the bodies below a footing at a construction site. Supposedly, they ran away to Europe to elope. They wanted to start a new life far from the corruption of American upper-class society.

Amanda soon forgot. Her alibi worked perfectly. Multiple people confirmed she left the party alone. Even though their parents searched everywhere, even hired private detectives, the trail went cold. Nobody ever saw Samantha and Derik again.

ONE YEAR LATER

Randolph summoned Amanda to his Rhode Island mansion. She had come of age, and it was time to educate her about the family, specifically their enigmatically dark and controversial past. The secret elevator stopped at the lower level basement. Amanda marveled how the door to the passageway, which Randolph explained extended far below the garage, blended perfectly with the wall. He opened a concealed panel, entered a code, and they stepped into a sculpted and very drawn-out wood-paneled room. The lights automatically activated.

Amanda had a basic understanding of her heritage but found herself spellbound. Rows of inlaid bookshelves filled with ancestral ledgers and writings. Portraits, paintings, and antiques, some of which he categorized as priceless treasures. They entered a lightly ornate drawing room. Oak paneled and textured with exquisite crown molding. They sit on two Baroque-style upholstered armchairs in front of a life-size portrait of a man. Randolph placed her hand on top of an inscribed leather book, and together, they recited a sacred oath. A pledge of secrecy privy to only a few select family members. Randolph proclaimed this would bond them for eternity. She completed the ceremony by vowing never to disclose what she would learn except to her offspring and only if they proved their worthiness.

Randolph clarified. "Killed."

Chapter 4

JAMES RAWLINGS

CHILDHOOD YEARS

His nurturing was painfully difficult. His mother, a big-boned German born in Scranton, Pennsylvania, during the height of the Vietnam War, openly believed in God through the strict denomination of Jehovah's Witness. Yet, after her parents died in a freak car accident on her twenty-second birthday, she abandoned Him. For years, she crawled in and out of the bottle, finding it difficult to keep faith when everything around her, contradictory to her upbringing, seemed to multiply to the negative. Her longing for self-absorbed satisfaction led her to Jerry, her ex-con alcoholic drifter husband. Together, they rode an emotional pendulum. On the eve of the second blue moon in March, at nine-forty-six in the evening, Brenda Rawlings gave birth to a robust twelve-pound six-ounce boy. At eleven months, he was walking, and by three, he was reciting the alphabet. At five, he played chess and the piano and wrote poetry and music. James Rawlings preferred mathematics to sports and reading to television. Emotionally, he found it difficult to interact with other kids, especially females. His mother blamed this on the abusive nature of his part-time father. By Kindergarten, his father disappeared from his life.

James Rawlings wholeheartedly loved his mom. He idolized her. She was the only person who understood him.

HIS ANGEL

James Rawlings knew she was the *one* the moment he saw her. It was the summer before Kindergarten. A time when his mom was battling the first stages of her sickness. On this particularly long and scorching summer day, while lying in the sand on his back under the monkey bars. Not from falling; he hated climbing due to the callouses associated with this exercise; a shadow caught his attention. To his left, staring from outside the bars, he locked eyes with Amanda Manchester. An angel of beauty dressed in a pink skirt and white tennis shoes with her hair pulled back into ponytails. She clasped her hands and looked up as a passing cloud blocked the sun. As if prompted by thought, she climbed to the top, laid belly down on the bars, and gazed upon him with a stone-faced expression.

"Hi," he said. "My mom named me James Rawlings. What's yours?"

She slightly bent her head. "Amanda! Amanda Manchester! My dad was born from nobility, which makes me rich in heritage. Does your mom have a rank?"

Her words had no meaning, especially to his young mind. Her voice, however, was virtuous. "Sure! My mom was in the war, too. Now she's just a mom." He wiped some sweat from his head. "Man, it's hot today."

"Yeah, I know. My dad told me it was going to be another scorcher."

"Scorcher, huh? What's he a weatherman?"

"No! I told you he was from the nobility."

Even though no more words were said, as the sweltering sun reemerged, he swore the reflective haze illuminated her like an angel. At that very moment, James Rawlings knew Amanda Manchester was his angel.

His Second Encounter

On the first day of Kindergarten, James watched Amanda and her father arrive. She was wearing a white dress with ankle-high socks embroidered with pink flowers. Similar to the day they met at the park. As important as she stepped into the sun shining through the window, she glistened like an angel.

"What're you waiting for?" His mother nodded.

James wiped his clammy hands on his jeans and walked over. Before he could say a word, his mother stopped him. She held out his Speed Racer lunch box and the yellow dandelion.

With the stem between his fingers, he tapped her shoulder. As her eyes found the flower, he handed it to her and recited the poem.

The moment my eyes found yours

There was no pretending

How your stare dug

Your lips spoke

Together

I offer this golden trill as a token

To our kindled friendship

Love

My flower blossomed

You are my Angel

Amazed he remembered the words, he drew a breath and glanced up at his mom. Her grin acknowledged his bravery.

"Umm! Wow, holy cow. A poem and a flower!" Her eyes showed amazement. Amanda cocked her head sideways and inserted the stem above her right ear. "How'd you know? I love Dandelions."

"The park! I've watched you pick them."

"Really?"

"You prefer them over the daisies and the four-leaf clovers."

"I know, but they're too hard to find."

"The clovers?"

"Yeah."

"You only need to know where to look."

"Where's that?"

"My backyard! Would you like to come over sometime?"

That began James Rawling's adolescent love affair with Amanda Manchester.

A mild-mannered voice asked, "Young man, your chivalry's gratifying!" Randolph ruffled his hair. "Brenda, it's good to see you. We must have you over for cocktails."

HIS HEARTBREAK

James Rawlings turned eleven two days ago. He did not go to school. Through the open window of the hospital, nine church bells ring. He looks back at his mother and weeps. A few moments later, her eyes closed. Without question, his world had turned dark.

James Rawlings found the second set of foster parents acceptable. Through thick and thin, mainly when heartache manifested, his strength came from the memories of his mother and Amanda. On his tenth birthday, he presented Amanda with a ten-line poem and a single long-stemmed red rose with the tenth thorn trimmed. For James Rawlings, this ceremony consummated their eternal love.

Her remembered words. "*I love you, James! I know you love me. Promise me you'll be my first. Promise me you'll wait, no matter what.*" She sealed her love with ten simple pecks on his lips. For James Rawlings, his heart was forever hers.

PART 2

Chapter 5

PRESENT DAY

James Rawlings does a double-take. His gut tells him the smoking hot young woman setting up her picnic fits the profile of his childhood sweetheart—*his angel?* The obvious was the premise of her walk. Specifically, how her hand nicked her hip with each sway and how she discerned the rose, the wine bottle, and the two glasses in the basket positioned on the corner of his blanket. Adding to the difficulty, she chose a spot a few meters ahead of him out of all the open areas. The problem is that he can only imagine what she looks like—so many years separated them.

Interestingly, as she steps from her sandals onto the blanket, she looks his way and smiles. His heart flutters. Does she recognize him? Her remembered words ring.

James, I will love you forever, I promise.

A disturbance to the right pierces the park. Everyone within earshot watches a cumbersome woman wearing a bright orange summer dress declare war on her man. Apparently, he spilled his beverage on the blanket. Without a word, he empties it and walks away. James chuckles as she swiftly packs and chases him.

Looking back, he finds himself suspended. She removed her baby-T, exposing a pink bathing suit top that barely covered her voluptuous chest. She peels her skintight shorts over her slender feet, neatly folds them, and places them into an oversized shoulder bag adorned with ten studded diamond emblems circling the number ten. Without question, she fits the mold—a goddess of perfect proportion—*his angel.*

James thinks back to his youth. Her remembered kisses. At the time, ten harmless pecks. He lowers his sunglasses. Even though he dreamt about this scenario multiple times, he felt derailed, not particularly on her beauty or acknowledgment but on the surrounding landscape and the picnickers enjoying the warmth of the summer sun. He grabs the squeezable Bota bag and takes a chug—a vodka, gin, club soda concoction. The heat stimulates him. With renewed focus, he glances her way. She has angled her body towards the sun and appears to be taking a second glance at the single red rose resting within the white vase.

Does she remember the significance?

After walking her fingers over her tanned thigh, which kindles his spirit, she makes eye contact and smiles.

James returns the gesture.

At this point, he cannot discount the obvious. *It must be her!* Inspired, he removes the rose, places it near his nose, and inhales. James imagines inserting the stem into her long, flowing ebony hair. Looking back, she broke eye contact. His stomach tightens. He wipes moisture from his forehead and places the rose in the vase.

His mind wanders. James can hear the words of his late mother.

Son, true love is pre-ordained like *a vivid story in your memory. If you're lucky enough, love does find you; don't be shy. Be bold. Take it by the reins and hold it. Cherish it.*

If you don't, you'll lose it, and regret will haunt you for eternity.

His heart felt heavy, knowing she was preparing him for this moment.

Inconspicuously, he watches the woman open a paperback titled BROKEN. A red rose highlights the cover. She places it on her lap and begins stroking her hair. The way she twirls the ends and then starts over suggests she, too, is deep in thought. Or could she be flirting?

A barking dog draws his attention. James combs back loose hair and watches a shepherd jump high into the air and catch a floating yellow disc. The dog returns it to an older man wearing a baggy T-shirt and calf-high white socks. Oddly, he looks his way and nods as if telling him not to be afraid. A comfort embraces James Rawlings.

From behind, runners, primarily female and wearing matching pink t-shirts—run for the cause—weave their way through the maze of picnickers. Two women split from the group and waved as they neared. James acknowledges, only to realize they were gesturing to her.

Embarrassed, he lowers his hand. His posture reminds him of when he was a kid trying to find refuge after being bullied. James watches her stand, adjust her bathing suit, and wave. She looks lankier than he remembers but attractively curvaceous, especially in her slinky two-piece.

Uncertainty confronts James. Could this woman be her, the love of his life?

James catches the last glimpse of the runners before they enter the wooded area. The elderly couple arrived. They prefer to sit on the park bench in the shade of the tree line. Typically, they seem content. They don't talk much, but he knows they genuinely love each other. Their secret lies within their gaze and how they hold hands. It shows earned respect. He looks at the Middle Eastern couple to his left. In his ledger, he labeled them the singing love birds. They look barely twenty and arrive like clockwork every Sunday. They, too, are deeply in love. How does he know? The way they make goo-goo eyes, kiss, and continually lip sync—*I Love You*—as if in their bubble.

James looks back and gulps. A tan, dark-haired, muscular man wearing a ridiculous pair of skintight yellow shorts, matching yellow flip-flops, and sunglasses is talking to her. How his hands flail while speaking bothers him. He tries to listen, but the ambiance washes their voices.

A surge of relief purges as she folds her arms. What James finds attractive is that she looks his way, slightly nodding and smiling.

With an agonizing groan, he straightens his legs. The oxygenated blood returning to his thighs from sitting Indian-style tingles. As a kid, he imagined this exceptional sensation temporarily gave him superpowers. James stands, adjusts his shorts, and notices the man is staring his way. He glares back. Strangely, he nods.

Nervously, he looks down, brushes a blade of grass from his shorts, and stares at the two wine glasses inside the basket. Glancing back, he watches the man shake her hand, pick up his backpack, and walk toward him.

Chapter 6

James purposefully avoids eye contact. In the backdrop, he watches her refold her arms across her chest. Interestingly, she has a cheery sort of grin.

The man stops a few feet ahead of his blanket in the exact spot that blocks her completely. His eyes dart from the basket to the vase. He sighs, bends down, and rudely plucks the flower. James Rawlings drops his jaw. Up close, he appears shorter, and his skin much lighter.

"A red rose may say I love you," the stranger says, "but she'll never know your true feelings unless you present it to her."

James feels thunderstruck.

"But don't worry," he says calmly. "Honestly, I think she's crazy about you."

James looks stunned. "Really?" He wrinkles his forehead. "About me?"

"Yeah, you, Sherlock!" He looked towards her. "Can I give you some advice?" He offered the rose. "Walk over, present the flower, and start a conversation."

His logic was close to the truth. The flower was for her. James snatches the stem and punctures his thumb on the tenth thorn, which he carelessly overlooked to clip. He switches hands and sucks the prick. "You mean you're not her boyfriend?"

"Who—Amanda? God no! I was making my rounds through the park and came across her. She's by far the hottest."

A relieved sigh vents, yet his throat tightens as James processes her name.

He called her *Amanda!*

Could this woman be his angel?

"Have we met before?" James asks as his eyes dart to her and back.

The stranger does not reply. Instead, he opens his backpack and pulls out a pair of black shorts and a faded pinkish T-shirt. He quickly dresses and shoulders the bag. From time to time, his brown eyes connect. "Amanda insisted you wouldn't recognize her."

James gulps. Again, he finds himself speechless. He shakes his head, accepting that maybe she is his childhood sweetheart. A deep breath separates reason from doubt. "What were you two talking about?"

The man looks curious. "Look, Romeo. I'm only the messenger." He glances at the massive metallic watch strapped to his wrist. "Really! Two-thirty-seven! Duty calls!" He installs his yellow-rimmed sunglasses. "Take my advice. Wipe some of that sweat from your face and mosey on over. You'll find Amanda interestingly attractive." He inserts his thumbs under both shoulder straps. "I've seen you here before. The rose is perfect!" A slight smile highlights his face as he turns and, with a quick pace, slogs his way through the maze of picnickers.

James inhales deeply and makes eye contact. Amanda has adjusted her stance. This time, her stare seems distant. Could she be lost in a fading memory? He wipes his forehead and twirls the rose.

The squawking of geese catches his attention. James looks up at a flock of birds flying in a perfect wedge formation. A straggler desperately tries to rejoin. Suddenly, a distinctive noise tears at the very fiber of his awareness. A cry so dispelling he cringes. In shock, James watches an unusually low-flying jumbo airliner roar by overhead. It is so low it feels like he can reach up and touch the tubular fuselage, four jet engines, and massive wings with extended landing gear. Combined with the piercing whine from what sounds like failing engines, he covers his eyes as a rush of hot turbulence slaps his face. In a heartbeat, the tranquility of the park turns chaotic. The rose he was so carefully holding tumbles through the air, along with blankets, clothing, and branches. James cowers to the unforgiving wind. A few seconds later, he watches the landing gear clip the tree tops, and a second later, the plane disappears.

James locates Amanda. She has her hands covering her ears, and her expression displays terror. She reaches down and removes the crumpled blanket around her legs. His mind freezes, listening to the cries of the other picnickers.

James casts a deep exhalation while staring at the boundary between the blue sky and the trees. The exhaust plume, darker than usual, wafts skyward. The thought of the plane falling out of the sky terrifies him.

For he knows the airport is twenty miles in the opposite direction. Making the situation all the more harrowing, the strenuous cry of failing engines, which only moments ago challenged his deepest fears—resonates.

Time seems to stop as James waits for the inevitable. The sound of an explosion! The tree line has surrendered, yet the smell of jet fuel lingers. From behind, a hand grips his bicep. Startled, James turns and stares at Amanda. Her eyes are big and full and glazed. She has her mouth slightly open.

"Do you think, I mean, is it going to crash?" Her hand trembles.

James peels away her digging fingernails. Her skin feels soft and damp. He can sense her panic. She breaks eye contact and stares in the direction of the descending aircraft.

"I hope not." He grips her hand. "Let's go see."

Amanda quickly dresses, and they sprint across the grass. James knows they will have a clear view of the valley below at the top of the hill.

They pass countless people—some crying, holding each other, while others stare into the sky as if waiting for certainty. The elderly couple looks horrified. James guides Amanda through the sparsely wooded hillside and stops beside a fallen log. Together, they gaze across a sunken valley—a metropolis blanketed in a spectacle of color and haze. Like a twisting river, what stands out is the twelve-lane freeway flowing through the center.

Chapter 7

Tension builds as they search the basin. Miraculously, the plane landed on the oncoming side of the interstate. Scattered vehicles litter the sides and the meridian for miles in either direction. Some are sideways crumpled and stacked, while others are spread out in a terrible array of destruction, proving they averted catastrophe. In a sense, they look like matchbox toys someone kicked about on a giant game board.

They stare in shock as a massive fireball on the far side rises precipitously. Amanda squeezes his hand as a thunderous shock wave booms. Sirens, from every angle, stifle the calm. The broken aircraft lists sideways and nose down to the pavement. The white airframe, one wing partially damaged, stands out amongst the multitude of multi-colored vehicles. Another explosion, this one smaller, startles Amanda. She tightens her grip. Tears roll down her cheeks.

In silence, they watch passengers, who look like ants from their perch, begin sliding down evacuation ramps. Echoes of grief, laden with terror, resonate. Helicopters hover over the wreckage. Amanda tightens her grip. A fire engine cradling a long ladder begins spaying a curtain of water. A sense of relief purges as two more arrive, along with a handful of ambulances.

James releases her hand and grips her shoulders. Her eyes are full and glossy. He hangs his head and sniffles. "I feel so helpless. I mean, watching from up here."

"I hope everyone's OK?" She tapers away.

"It's a miracle it even landed!"

"Should we—I mean, go help?"

"We'd never get close enough."

Along with other spectators, they watch the drama unfold. Remarkably, the plane does not explode. They keep track of the rescue with their phones. So far, there are only two casualties, none of them passengers. The news media hails the Pilot, one of the seventeen seriously injured, a hero for landing in a stretch of road light with vehicles.

James finally guides Amanda back down the hill. The sun below the tree line casts a daunting shadow across the grassy meadow. Blankets and personal items are scattered. Even though they have not talked much, he feels a connection formed. The anguish has left her frail, and he finds himself with similar emotions.

"Where'd you park?"

"Behind the white four-by-four on the far side." She points, working her way through the half-empty parking lot.

For whatever reason, she barely says two words. James feels his confidence turning timorous. He wipes his sweaty palms and helps her load the supplies into the trunk of her black Jaguar.

"Wow!" She shuts the hatch. "What a bazaar day!"

"Crazy for sure!" James tries to find something more sophisticated.

Amanda grins. Her gaze seems to penetrate right through him. "Did we just witness a miracle?"

James nods. "The angels were working overtime."

Amanda grins. She covers her mouth. "Thank God! You know what's weird?" She pushes her hair back behind her ears.

James crunches his shoulders. *Does she notice his perspiration?*

She tilts her head slightly. "I don't know your name! I'm not sure, but I think you're someone I used to know."

James clumsily looks down. "Umm—really!"

Her eyes probe. "What'd Luke, the Italian guy, say?"

For whatever reason, her soft voice gives him confidence. "He told me your name was Amanda. And yes, it's me—James Rawlings. Full grown!"

She furrows her brows. "The same James Rawlings who lived on Teaberry Street, four houses down from my two-story colonial with the apple tree in the front yard?"

"You remembered! Those were good times, especially how we loved eating the green ones."

"Ugg! They made me so sick."

He makes a sour face. "To this day, I can't eat them."

Amanda wraps her arms around him. "God, James! I missed you. Your mom, is she?"

His eyes water.

"I'm so sorry." Amanda steps back. "I remember how sick she was. How long, I mean, after I left?"

"A little shy of a year. One day, she was fine, and the next—"

Amanda gently places two fingers over his mouth. "I'm so sorry. She was always so kind to me."

James wipes a tear. "Yeah, she liked you. Do you remember how old you were when you moved away?"

"Sure, I was ten. We were in the fifth grade, right?"

His heart flutters. "Do you remember Mrs. Garner?"

"Heck yeah! Her red hair and those blue eyes were always in a tight bun. Remember how she would always click her tongue?"

"Like humming a tune."

"You had a crush on her?"

"Come on. I was a kid. Besides, it wasn't real. She was my favorite teacher, that's all."

Amanda grins. "Is she still teaching?"

"Yup."

"Really! How does she look?"

"The same, I guess, but a bit older! She still lives in the house on Tacoma Street."

"Wow!" Amanda snatches the vibrating phone out of her purse, buries her head, and starts typing.

James nervously pockets his hands. "One day, you were there; the next, you were gone." His face shows longing.

Amanda looks up. "God! I'm sorry. Work. Did you say something about the day is long?"

James grins. "No, no, no! I was referencing the morning after Thanksgiving. I remember it like yesterday, especially when the moving truck pulled up in front of your house. My heart sunk, realizing the day finally came."

"You wanna know something." A smile highlights her face. "I've never stopped thinking about you. I cried for months, threatening to run away every chance I could. I wouldn't say I liked the city, the people, the cars, and the concrete. It suffocated me."

"New York City?"

"Yeah, The Big Apple! The melting pot, my dad would say." Amanda sighs. "James, you look amazing. I knew it was you the moment I saw you."

James feels his face blush. "Same here," his scratchy voice longs. "For me, it was your walk."

Amanda slants her head. "Really! How so?"

"How your hands nicked your hips as they moved forward."

Amanda bites her lower lip. "You remember that?"

"Like it was yesterday. What about you?"

Amanda looks surprised.

"How'd you know for sure it was me?"

She pauses. "Easy! Your boyish looks."

"Really!" James grins.

"Well, almost. Truthfully, it was the rose. James, you haven't changed. You still look at me as if I were the last woman alive."

James looks down at his feet. "You noticed?"

"At first, I was concerned. You know, a strange man ogling. But when I saw the rose, it solidified my fears."

"You remembered."

"Of course! You gave me one with two green leaves and the tenth thorn trimmed with a ten-line hand-written poem on the tenth day of every month until the day I moved."

"Two years, six months to be exact. I still have a shoebox full of them."

"Poems?" Amanda looks curiously.

"I continued writing, hoping you'd return."

"James, you're so sweet. I don't know what to say."

"I had no choice. The love of my life vanished. The truth was when I found out you were moving, I was so devastated, I put a spell on you."

Amanda frowns. "Really?"

James clams up, realizing he made a monumental mistake. "It was harmless. More or less unspoken words, I considered them charming at the time. Truthfully, I couldn't bear the thought of losing you."

"I knew you liked me, but, holy shit. We were only ten. We had no idea what was going to happen in our lives."

James raises his hands and shrugs. "Kid stuff. What can I say?"

She grins.

"So, are you back home for good? Is that why you came to the park today?"

Amanda bites her lower lip. She breaks eye contact, retrieves her phone, and briefly plays with the screen. She looks up, preoccupied. "I have to go." She tilts her head, inhales, and forces a pressed teeth smirk.

James feels his heart freeze. Amanda recited, in the near exact insincere tone, with the same God-awful wretched smirk, her goodbye she delivered to him over sixteen years ago.

Chapter 8

Sometimes, life throws roadblocks. When you finally weave through the layers and find the clear path, another one sideswipes you. Today was one of those days. James wants nothing more than to run after Amanda, open-armed. Yet, as her car disappears around the corner, in a way, he feels better than he has felt in years. He keys her number into his phone.

The evening air suddenly feels bitter cold. James folds his arms and walks to his car. His damp shirt only adds to the agony. He inhales deeply to cleanse his mind —the emotional shock of how his angel appeared and disappeared from his life again. James can smell her scent on his shirt. Sweet, like the blooming garden rose flowers at home.

Two days pass before James finds the courage. He opened her contact information multiple times, only to find his mind hopelessly vacant. For the umpteenth time, he reads over the scribbled notes. Nervously, he presses the number and activates speaker mode. James places the phone on the table and counts four rings.

"Hello!" A soft voice finally beckons.

His mind wrestles with a single word. "Amanda!"

"James, is this you?"

"Umm, yes, yes it is, hello!"

"I'm so glad you called. How are you?"

"Good, I'm good. And you?"

"Your voice sounds rough. Are you sick?"

"No, no! I mean, no, nothing like that. How's it going?"

"Oh gosh, rushed and edgy, not to mention overworked. My boss has me running through hoops. That's why I left so abruptly last Sunday. James! I'm so sorry. You probably think I'm such a bitch, especially after seeing me for the first time in all those years."

"No, no, no, what are you saying!" He shakes his

head. "Don't say that. I would never!"

"You're so sweet. By the way, did you read about the plane? I mean, the verdict? Birds got sucked into the engines."

Her words registered loud and clear, but her voice triggered the sweet memory of holding her hand in the park. James visualizes her smooth skin and how her long fingers perfectly intertwined with his, how she pressed her boobs buried under the thin fabric of her t-shirt to his chest, which only further beckons his desires. Suddenly, he finds himself aroused.

"Are you still there?" Amanda asks, which only increases his desire.

"Umm, yes, yes, I'm here. Sorry, it must be a poor connection," James replies. "Birds?"

"Can you believe it?"

"It is frightening that something so simple could have such a horrific impact. Do you want to know something? I can't believe I'm talking to you. I thought I lost you again."

"James, you haven't changed a bit. You're still the

biggest sweetheart on the planet."

His ticker feels like a beating drum.

"The problem is, I'm no longer the sweet little innocent girl you knew. James, life has changed me."

Even though her voice registers loud and clear, James finds himself lost. He hates the fact he lost his charisma the day Amanda moved. Even though he categorizes her as the love of his life, he knows she needs time. He clears his throat. "I know what you mean. I've changed too, especially after my mom passed."

A profound silence follows. James begins to think the signal was lost.

"Amanda! Amanda! Are you still there?"

A few seconds later, a muffled voice replies. "Yes, James, I'm so sorry about your mom. Hey, listen!" This time, a deep sigh follows. "I have to cut our conversation short. Please, please, please, don't be mad. I enjoy talking to you." This time, a deep sigh follows. "Your voice, it's so soothing. It reminds me of my innocence when the world was a dream. James, let's talk tomorrow

—okay."

James hears muffled moans for the next few seconds, almost as if Amanda lost her breath. "Umm, yeah, sure, of course, I could never be mad at you. I'll call you tomorrow. How about we meet for coffee or a drink?"

James swallows a dry lump, relieved that she answered his call. What worries him is that a dreadful silence follows. "Amanda! Amanda! Are you still there?"

Chapter 9

Four weeks have passed. James must have called Amanda fifty times. Not once did she answer. Adding to his frustration, after a few rings, it prompted to voice mail. Deep down, he wonders if she ditched him.

"Hey, butthead!" A familiar male voice beckons. "Snap out of it. You're starting to worry me."

The ambient sounds of the office, the beeping and clicking of computer keypads, and the fragrant mix of stuffy office air combined with voices snap him back. James focuses on the phone in his hand. The words *call failed* below her name blink. He flinches to a slight ping on the side of his head.

James looks up. "What the fuck!" He stares at Randy, his co-worker in the neighboring cubical.

"Get a grip, lover boy!" Randy throws a second crumpled paper.

James easily swats it.

Randy sighs. "Casanova! Put the phone down and get back to work."

"No, I mean, was I?" James raises his hands.

Randy shakes his head, "Listen, bucko, you're starting to freak me out."

Five o'clock could not come fast enough. Minutes turn to hours, making Friday seem like Monday. They enter their favorite watering hole, the Swing Door on 5th Avenue. While Randy hits the head, James claims their usual chairs, the furthest from the two-saloon style doors and closest to the restrooms. He orders beers and two shots of Don Julio Tequila from Rebecca, the voluptuous brunette bartender. Today, her man killers are bounding from her slinky white halter.

Randy slaps James on the head and holds the shots high. "Here's to swimming with bow-legged women, being single, and drinking double."

They shoot the golden fluid, slam the glasses, and hoot.

"Two more!" Randy signals Rebecca. "Buddy, you won't like what I'm about to say, but I will say it nonetheless."

James raises his hands. "Forget about it. I don't need another lecture about my love life. Besides, who made you the authority?"

"Easy! Me, myself and I!"

"That's what I thought. Last time I checked, you've never been in love. You've never had a relationship last longer than two days! So, quit with the Dr. Ruth poor lover boy pity shit. You're not qualified."

"Maybe so, but whatever spell this Amanda chick cast on your dick sure is a doozy. Let me tell you something." Randy folds his arms. "The only way to break it is to hook up with someone else."

"He's right." Rebecca intervenes, pouring two shots.

James stares at her tits, ready to bust through her halter. Combined with the first shot and weeks of depression, his dick pulses. Without question, she epitomizes the word babe. James swallows hard, vulnerable to her sex, yet looks away, knowing he could never cheat on Amanda. Besides, her six-foot-eight boyfriend could crush him with his tree trunk-sized biceps.

"Deep down, I know you're both right." James pounds his fist on the bar. "But I'm a prisoner of my past."

Rebecca smiles while purposefully squeezing her arms snug to her chest. "These puppies have a way of breaking shackles."

"God damn, I love the way they jiggle!" Randy jokes.

Rebecca wrinkles her nose and strides away. "Yeah, I do have nice tits!"

James wholeheartedly agrees, staring at her tight ass.

No matter how you roll, Randy loves to be the center of attention. He is a clone of his father, the founder of the brokerage firm. Randy came aboard fresh out of college four years ago. He is a natural trader!

Randy grabs his package. "My Peterbilt would fit perfectly in her trailer."

"I hate to bust your bubble, but she's way out of your league."

"That only makes the hunt all that more interesting." Randy peels a few C-notes from his roll and places them on the bar. "I'll bet these would even up the odds!"

James laughs.

Rebecca turns, licks her fingers, and slaps her ass.

Honestly, for the first time in years, James feels free. Could it be the rejection combined with the alcohol? His insides tingle as Rebecca stoops her possessions on the bar.

"He's got a point," she says and blows Randy a kiss.

James drops his mouth. "Seriously!"

Randy grins. "That's what I'm talking about. Rebecca, your tits are awesome." He hoots and stuffs a bill deep inside. Randy addresses James. "Now pick up your shot and down some liquid courage. Tonight, you're going to experience the world I live in."

Five shots, four beers, and two thick steaks later, they exit the cab. James follows Randy through a dimly lit hallway and down two stairs. Randy slips a C-note into the pocket of the bouncer, and they enter the sultry establishment. Two women, no hookers, immediately proposition. The one sporting giant boobs with thick dark nipples stops James. She grabs his crotch.

"OH, MY GOD! Your cock is massive."

James cringes as she presses her tits to his chest. Admittedly, even though her odor chokes him—a mixture of sweat, perfume, and sex—her warmth, combined with her talented hand, arouses him.

Quick on his feet, Randy intervenes. "Slow down there, tootsie. We'll be flexing soon."

James gulps as she releases her grip.

"I'll be close by, big boy." She blows him a kiss and walks away.

They enter the hollow of the club. Randy stops at the heart-shaped bar. Mirrors line the back wall. The black lights above highlight a curvy redhead disrobing on an elevated floor. He spreads two fingers in a V. "Two shots of your best tequila and beers!"

They admire the attractive and very naked bartender. The white tassels covering her nipples rotate as her tits bounce to the movement of the martini shaker.

His plan to self-medicate is working. Two gorgeous vixens sporting nothing but skin eye them. "Follow me!" Randy signals.

With beers in hand, they find a table three back from center stage. On cue, the two strippers approach. The blonde straddles Randy. Her tits are small, comparatively to the brunette who aggressively mounts James. He finds her broad shoulders and narrow waist appealing. Her roaming hand quickly cups his crotch. She squeezes and skillfully fluffs her tits across his face. James wonders if he will break the chains tonight, not discounting the Mexican grog pulsing through his veins.

Randy flexes, and the private dances in the back room begin. Candy and Breeze are nothing but impressive. The music enhances the show. James can barely think straight as Candy again straddles his legs. His shy hands finally grip her narrow waist. Candy responds skillfully and positions them on her breasts. Her gyrations increase, and a few moments later, his body spasms and a wet spot appears. Candy smiles.

Chapter 10

Randy insists harmless pre-mature ejaculation—including masturbation—does not count. He categorizes self-pleasure as a God-given right. A harmless hormonal act promoting safe sex helps keep a man in check. For James, paying strippers, no struggling young women congregating in strip clubs to dance naked can only be duplicitous!

TWO MONTHS LATER

James climbs the lightly wooded hill bundled in his winter coat, cashmere scarf, and leather gloves. Halfway up, he looks down through the pines. The setting sun has cast an orangish shadow across the green meadow. At the crest, he rests his back on a fallen log. A few months back, he stood near this very spot with Amanda. He remembers the image of the jumbo jet and how its massive fuselage smoldered on the interstate. They removed the final section a week ago. Rumor has it they are going to build a memorial.

James sighs, wondering if Amanda remembers. Emotionally, he feels derailed, especially at work. Fortunately, his portfolios are stable, yet his turmoil lies in the unknown. Why did she say the things only to disappear into thin air? Could she be married?

Dusk settles before he ventures down the hill. An eerie fog hovers. The leather seats in his Mustang are chilled. James locks the doors, exhales deeply, and presses his forehead to the steering wheel. He closes his eyes. This time, instead of visualizing Amanda, the distinct image of the Italian man surfaces. Could he be the reason Amanda vanished?

The drive home proves grueling. He scours the sidewalks around every corner and stoplight, hoping to glimpse Amanda. Instead, he only finds blank expressions —reflections of his inner soul. James wakes to darkness. He can make out the faint tint of the yellow tennis ball nudged to the windshield. James reaches for the keys but finds them in his hand. Twice this month, he woke in a similar slumber. While staring at the boxes filled with the hoarded rubbish his mom collected, a transparent reckoning surfaces. With a disgusted sigh, he marches into the living room and grabs one of three framed pictures from the fireplace mantle. Even though James has stared at this particular image a thousand times, some nights waking up with it on his lap, something different stands out tonight.

James and Amanda hug his mom in front of her 'Queen of the Garden' single-stem rosebushes. She cared for them like siblings until the cancer consumed her. The rosebushes stand five or even six feet tall. Each one bears a single thick blossom of incredible color and vibrancy. She named them Lincoln Double Delight and Turnpike Tea. The shadow of a man stretched across the lawn took the picture—Joe Petronni, who lived next door but has since moved.

James extends the leg-rest on the Lazy Boy and stares at his mother. She looks exhausted—a mixture of horror, love, and fear. Below her three-hundred-dollar wig, her glossy eyes show the anguish of the horrible chemotherapy her doctor routinely administered. He looks scared, a frightened fatherless boy, afraid of the future. Amanda, however, looks drab, similar to her look while staring at the crashed jumbo jet. The same expression she delivered to him while driving away.

Suddenly, a haunting truth surfaces. Amanda Manchester, the love of his life, has a cold heart. From this point forward, James will push her out of his thoughts, similar to how he discarded his vacant father.

Two weeks have passed since purging his bleeding heart. Does James Rawlings still love Amanda Manchester? Of course, with all of his heart and soul. The difference is that he has consciously established a boundary. Until Amanda comes to terms with her own life, he refuses to cross it.

The office feels different today. The whirring of the computers, the drum of the machines, even the aroma of the potted coffee and pastries, which in the past irked James, amazingly, smelled inviting. James smiles as he strides down the narrow corridors separating the egos of his narrow-minded co-workers. He rests his elbows on the compartment.

"What's up, buttercup?" James stares into Randy's bloodshot eyes. "Did you forget Sunday fun days are for the young at heart? Not the wannabe rock stars."

Randy sips the steaming broth from the twin-busted mug. "Your so right, this coffee sucks, and my head is killing me."

"Sorry bro, how about two extra strength aspirin!"

Randy follows James to his compartment and greedily swallows the medicine. All the while, James replaces the picture of Amanda with one of his mom—the one she gave him for his sixth birthday.

"Wow!" Randy shakes his head. "Did you get laid?"

Chapter 11

The week breezes by. His portfolios are soaring above office averages. His body feels toned and defined from hitting the gym. James Rawlings even started reading again. His aura feels elevated, and his mind clear.

Friday never felt better as James entered the Swing Door. Happy hour always rocked. He signals Randy, already perched at the bar. Tonight, Tamara, the petite, half-Spanish, half-American beauty, and Rebecca are tending. Without question, they turn heads. Honestly, he feels attracted to Tamara. Tonight, her risqué costume leaves nothing to hide. She has concealed her offset brown eyes behind emerald contact lenses and her short curly hair under a full-face banged bob-cut white wig. The extra tight white mini-shorts hug her perfectly formed ass. The black belt with an extra-large chrome buckle extenuates her exposed belly button, which makes her cream-colored mulatto skin and slender waist appear tapered. Her white boots climb past her knees, and a yellow bikini top barely holds her above-average breasts.

Tamara welcomes James with a smile. "Looking good, Rawlings!" She winks. "You're two behind Randy! You ready to get it on?"

"Locked and loaded." James blows on the tip of his index finger, representing the barrel of his fake gun, and removes his jacket.

Tamara double-flips the Tequila bottle, catches it, and pours two extra full shots without spilling a drop. Randy whistles and hoots.

Due to the fourth landing on a Monday, the long weekend had begun. Portabella mushrooms, broccoli, and a medium rare sirloin, all washed down with mugs of broth, set the stage. Tamara cleared the plates and poured two more.

"I'm off at eight!" She hints.

Randy punches his shoulder. "Dude, what're you waiting for?"

"Cool it, bucko. I'm still digesting."

The ambiance heightens. At the end of the bar, a group of overzealous stock brokers performs a typical weekend pre-function. They chant, and down the row of shots, Rebecca lined up.

Tamara places her elbows on the bar before James and squeezes her chest. "This might be a bit forward, but what the hell." Her voice elevates. "You've heard about Pricilla Wellington, right?"

James perks up. "You mean the pistol from California who inherited all those cool millions?"

"None other!"

"What about her?"

"She's throwing a fourth-of-July weekend bash at her mansion at the lake. I have an invite: fifty rooms, unlimited fun, boats, skiing, party, party, party, and guess what."

Randy shrugs. "What?"

"I have an invite."

"I call Bullshit. It's the party of the century."

"Rules are, I bring two hot guys. And I'm staring at them right now. What do you think? You two in?"

Randy hangs his jaw. "You're shitting me, right? I tried to get on the list, but—"

Tamara squeezes her man killers with her biceps. "You're not packing the right equipment."

"Goddamn, you're telling me!"

James looks perplexed and buries his face in his cell. "Didn't her mom burn through five husbands building her fortune?"

Tamara sighs. "You're searching the wrong site, seven. Rumor has it she was a Black Widow!"

"Was?"

"Yep! She passed away a few months ago."

"How?"

"In her sleep. Verdict: a heart attack, but I don't believe it."

"Why not?"

"She was only fifty-four and in better cardio shape

than a thirty-year-old Pilates instructor."

"Are you saying someone snuffed her with exotic poison?"

"The autopsy didn't reveal foul play, but it doesn't add up. I think someone gave her a dose of her own medicine!"

"How so?" James asks.

"Think about it. Six of her seven husbands mysteriously croak similarly a few years after she marries."

"What happened to number seven?"

"Get this. He drowned while scuba diving in Bali."

"Fuck. Talk about karma!" Randy taps his knuckles on the bar, pretending to shed the negative energy.

"That's why they never convicted her of murder. Autopsies confirmed they all died of natural causes."

"Eighty mill, right?" James asks.

"Not even close. Try in the range of one-fifty, not counting the jets, helicopters, trains, cars, and a real estate portfolio. Don't quote me, though."

"Remind me to keep clear of this, Pricilla." Randy

pounds his shot. "Like mom, the daughter might be twice as deadly. Are you reading me? Even her name scares me."

"Trust me. Pricilla is harmless and prettier than a Fairy Tale Princes."

"How'd you know?"

"Sorority sisters."

Randy slaps the bar. "You're full of surprises but hot as hell!"

Tamara giggles. "So, what's the verdict? You two in?"

"Absolutely! The three amigos!"

James stands and stink-eyes the both of them.

Randy pats his back. "What's wrong, buttercup? Scared!"

James raises his hands and sighs. "Why not! I had no real plans for this weekend."

Randy hoots with delight. "Good man, but I'll bring a few doses of anti-venom for protection."

The mansion sits on a parcel of wooded land, encompassing two-thirds of the lake's twelve-point-seven-mile waterfront. A ten-foot-high cement retaining wall with a single guard gate surrounds the periphery. A paved runway, private jets, a few helicopters, and a small city houses the workers. An armed militia-type guard checks their identification while a second one walks around the vehicle with a German Shepard.

"Can't be too careful nowadays." Tamara jokes while waiting for the Iron Gate to swing open.

"Yeah, for a second there, I thought we would have to bend over for a cavity search."

Laughter breaks.

Tamara swiftly navigates the two-mile illuminated paved drive winding through the heavily wooded property. Every tenth of a mile, they pass another life-sized pallid statuette. In this one, two naked men intertwined and mounted to a squared support structure.

"It appears clothes are optional this weekend!" Randy happily announces.

James opens the welcome kit and takes a sip from the miniature bottle of tequila. He glances at Tamara. "I'm not good at naked, especially in public."

Tamara reached over the center console and caressed his leg. "Clothes are optional, but don't worry. Play it the way you see it. Besides, you have an amazing body." She winks.

As they exit the timbered acreage, the road, stretching hard right, opens into a vast meadow. Manicured bushes, lonesome pines spotted with peculiarly shaped water fountains, and even more statuettes. In the midst, they feast upon a modern five-story and well-illuminated structure. Tamara winds down an easy slope and pulls under a sweeping terrace. Skimpily clad in white, servants suggest they pulled up to a casino, not a house. The scope alone dwarfs the car.

Tamara waves at the ripped, well-groomed man dressed in skin-tight white shorts and flip-flops. His sparkling teeth glow under his bright green Elvis hairdo. Randy eyes the attractive Asian attendant sporting a slinky two-piece white bikini with white pumps as she opens the trunk. He senses a hint of seduction as she winks. While she loads the luggage onto a wheeled cart, the eccentric man greets them.

"Tamara, it's so good to see you again. As always, you look ravishing."

"Dorian!" Her eyes drift past his chest, stopping for a moment above his thighs. "You look as sinful as ever."

"Pricilla's pleased you made it." Dorian opens the doors. "My, my, who are your friends?"

Tamara points. "This hunk of a man is James Rawlings, and this big boy is Randy. Boys, Dorian!"

Randy looks curiously. "As in Basil?"

Dorian smiles and caresses his facial skin, suggesting he, too, has a painting guarding his youthful beauty. "Why, thank you, but I'm not quite as smitten." He sighs, reaching his hand out ever so quaintly. "My last name's Carmichael and I was born in Pittsburg."

Randy fist-pounds him instead. "Awesome pussy-pad, dude, I mean, cool! How'd you manage this gig?"

Dorian winks. "So, manly!"

Randy stares at the smoking-hot figure of the Asian. "Dorian, you're extremely handsome, but you're not quite my cup of tea. What's her name?"

Dorian smiles. "Fair enough! Momoko, and she's

yours if you so desire. Follow me. I'll show you to your quarters."

James eyes Tamara. "Quarters?"

She shrugs, smiling.

Two-meter squared marbled tiles with bright urban walls highlight an elegantly crafted glass chandelier. Five stories above, a fantastic array of atrium glass underlines the twinkle of the star-lit sky. The group enters one of two mirrored elevators to the right of an arched passage. Beyond, the muffled sounds of dance music and the energetic laughter of adventure invite curiosity.

"Through that portal, the party lives." Dorian resits, resting his shoulder on the back wall of the car. "Five!" He voices.

The door automatically closes, and they swiftly ascend. As the door opens, Dorian spreads his arms, flaunting amazement. "Welcome to the VIP floor." They follow him down the expanded and softly illuminated hallway. The cream carpet feels ultra-soft. Four multi-colored clover windows decorate the wall opposite wooden doors. The first five are twice the standard size with single iron handles.

Interestingly, each one has guest names posted. Dorian stops in front of the first of five doublewides. He points at the three names. "Welcome to your humble dwelling."

James looks astonished. "I didn't know about this event until a few hours ago. Even then, my decision was spontaneous."

Dorian looks inquisitively at Tamara.

Tamara winces. "I kind of assumed you'd say yes." She shrugs. "Sorry!"

James grins, knowing Tamara has a clever side.

Dorian interjects. "The ten rooms on this floor are reserved for the sisters."

James eyes Randy and whispers. "Ten rooms, ten sisters. Are you getting this?"

"Each bringing two male companions!"

"So, we're potluck?" James grins.

Randy smiles. "No, dessert! This is getting better by the minute."

James asks. "Why post the names?"

Tamara shrugs. "To help everyone get on a first-name basis. Don't forget this is the party of the year."

"So, you've done this before?" James asks.

"Sort of, but never quite so extravagantly. Mostly hotels and once on a two-hundred-foot yacht."

Randy rubs his hands together vigorously. "Nice!"

"Pricilla thought this would help with the grieving. She was close to her mom."

Dorian opens the door. "Come." He waves.

Large dark stones cover the entry, highlighted modernly with multiple rows of offset can lights. Twisted iron railings descend seven steps into a masterfully crafted sunken living room. Wall-to-wall plush white carpeting under a lofted ceiling with oversized circular white leather sectionals, love chairs, and four large leaf green plants in front of ten picture windows.

Randy whooshes down the stairs and stops in front of the bar. He eyes the bottle of Don Julie 1942 with four shot glasses. "I'm in heaven." He rejoices.

James plops down and raises his feet. "Man, oh man, this pad's amazing."

Randy asks why there are four glasses.

Dorian clears his throat. "What'm I, chopped liver?"

Randy nods approvingly and walks behind the bar. He opens the stainless door to the Sub Zero and pulls out a tray of veggies and dip. "Check this out; fully stocked!"

Tamara picks up a shot glass and walks out onto the terrace. The group joins her and checks out the expanded patio—pool—bar below. The crescent exterior of the building allows them to see inside most of the other rooms. To the right, they gaze upon the bare, sexy brunette drying her long hair with a white towel.

"Mother, son of a gun." Randy excitedly boasts while waving. "Would you look at the scenery?"

"Her name's Vicky, and yes, she's gorgeous." Tamara raises her glass. "Toast to an amazing weekend!"

Chapter 12

Randy wastes no time and disappears into the bedroom with Momoko, who recently wheeled the luggage inside. Dorian says goodbye, more or less pouting. Tamara purposefully brushes James on the way back inside. She stops a few feet past the sofa, unclips her yellow bikini top, and gently drops it to the floor.

"I don't know about you, but I'm ready for the hot tub." She turns slightly, giving James a side view, and winks.

A robust fever pulsates as James watches her gait through the living room. Her thrown-back shoulders and sway conveys confidence and sex appeal. She stops in front of the hallway leading to the bedrooms and turns. James picks up her top and gapes as she removes her skin-tight shorts. By the second, his man part thickens as he fixates on the triangle tan line on her perfect ass.

His inhibitory senses take over. James imagines cradling Tamara in his arms. Softly, he deposits her on the mattress. While his hands explore her silky body, he kisses her neck. Tamara responds masterfully by removing his clothes, and they make passionate love.

James snaps back to reality as sweat rolls down his forehead. Tamara has disappeared into the bedroom. Undeniably, he feels sexually aroused. The proof is the bulge in his jeans! Even though he pushed Amanda from his thoughts and Tamara openly made the first move, he felt nervous. James has never gone all the way before. Whenever he tried to lose his virginity—insidious guilt, what he rationalized as deserved punishment sparked regret.

James met a group of friends on his fifteenth birthday at a secluded spot by the lake. They all decided to swim in their underwear. She was beautiful and willing and confessed she had a crush on him for years but was embarrassed to admit it. She cornered James, and before she was about to guide him inside, James envisioned Amanda. Petrified, he slipped free, leaving her stranded.

The second occurrence took place during his first year of college. Not that James didn't have multiple prospects, but this episode changed his life. She was Chelsea Hummer, a petite blue-eyed platinum blonde cheerleader—a natural beauty with persuasion and glamor nearly impossible to escape. A frat party turned ugly, and he found himself alone with her. After heavy foreplay, they removed their clothing, and again, at the point of entry, he ran away with his tail between his legs. Making matters worse, she ridiculed James, claiming he was a homo.

James draws a breath to soothe his thumping shaft. Deep down, he knows he will lose this battle, especially with the muffled groans coming from Randy and Momoko. Tamara walks out wearing a skimpy black Brazilian two-piece bathing suit. Instantly, he re-thickens.

Barefooted, she saunters over. Her steady gaze reflects passion. James feels his perspiration building as Tamara seductively smiles while staring at his bulge. He quivers as she wraps her arms around his torso and delicately kisses his lips.

"You're so handsome!" She presses her lips a second time.

Her warmth ignites an explosion of butterflies. As the aggressor, Tamara lifts her leg between his thighs and grabs his package. Not prepared for this sensation, James closes his eyes. His body tightens as she skillfully unbuttons his fly and works her fingers inside. A heat wave flushes as she frees his shaft, and before he can stop her, she devours him.

"Oh, my God!" James quivers.

Being his first bona fide blowjob, James stiffens. Not because he wants her to stop or he wants to grab her hair and shove his manhood down her throat. Being on display in front of the picture window with God knows how many secret admirers watching intimidates him. The problem is that he finds himself frozen because of her inviting technique. James clasps his hands behind his head, arches his back, and, with a boisterous orgasmic cry, trumpets.

After a warm kiss, she saunters to the bar, cleans up, and pours two shots. Still quivering, James drops to his knees. He has never experienced such sensual satisfaction as he repacks his throbbing shaft.

"That was a record!"

James frowns. "Are you making fun of me?"

James frowns. "Are you making fun of me?"

"Of course not. Your cock—I mean—it's huge! Was my technique really that good?"

James buttons his fly. His legs are weak as he staggers over. Even the shot glass feels heavy. From behind, a familiar voice interrupts.

"I'm proud of you, buddy boy." Randy adjusts the white towel wrapped loosely around his protruding waistline. He walks over to the bar and slaps his back. He grins at Tamara.

"He's skilled at masturbation, but don't let him fool you. I think you might've opened up Pandora's box."

Tamara giggles. "Really?"

"He didn't tell you?"

"Shut the fuck up!" James growls. "What, were you watching?"

"Mmm, hmmm," a soft, very sexy voice appeals from behind.

Randy turns and blows Momoko a kiss. "You look so sexy naked."

Momoko chuckles and installs her top.

"Would you like a drink?"

"Water, please. I have to get back to work."

"You've gotta love this place. It's our first night, and I'm already in the 'V' column, and you, my lucky friend, have been upgraded to the 'H.' And no, we weren't watching. But, was that orgasmic shriek Tarzan or Indiana Jones?"

James grunts. "Neither!" He grabs a beer and marches into the bedroom. After a quick clean-up and some serious attitude adjustment—a few minutes trying to convince himself in the mirror blowjobs are nothing but meaningless foreplay, not bona fide intercourse— James puts on two pairs of whitey-tighties under his board shorts. He does this to keep his cock in check. Could Randy be right? Did Tamara open up Pandora's box?

James finds Tamara perched Indian style on top of the bar next to a sweating bottle of Champaign and two filled flutes.

"Where's Randy?"

"He walked Momoko downstairs. She wants him to meet her twin sister."

"Twins? Really!"

"Yeah, sounds fun." Tamara drops her feet over the side and spreads her legs. With her finger, she signals. "You're my first."

James shyly approaches. He keeps his eyes trained on hers instead of at her honey pot peeking through the thin fabric of her bathing suit. He purposefully stops out of reach. "First, what?"

"You know, virgin!"

"Was it that obvious?"

"Yes, and I loved it."

"So, I was your guinea pig." His eyes dart down to her bounding timber and then at her finger, which employs him to approach.

"No, you weren't." She bites her bottom lip, trying desperately to keep from sliding off the bar and jumping his bones.

"You mean Mr. Tattletale didn't rat me out!"

"Months ago, he hinted something of the sort, but I couldn't decipher if he was pulling my leg or being serious. You never know with him, especially when he's drinking."

"Tell me about it."

Tamara breaks eye contact and shifts her attention to the music box. She grins, highlighting her dimpled cheeks. James finds her coyness stimulating. Adding to the intrigue, she lifts one leg and plants her bare foot on the top of the bar. James stares at the natural beauty of her hourglass figure. She stretches her arm, pushes a button, and turns the volume to a techno Café Del Mar blend. Her foot begins tapping while she runs her finger around the outside edge of her lips. James does not understand her finer intricacies yet grasps her seduction. She hands him a flute.

"I would like to make a toast to deflowering the most handsome and truest man I've ever met!"

What amazes James is that he does not feel threatened. He is not perspiring, no more than usual, and his thoughts are clear. "Technically, I'm still a virgin." They toast.

"What's your story? You're handsome, have a great body, and pack some serious firepower."

James refills his glass. "Love!"

"Seriously! Listen, bucko, it's overrated."

"Tell me about it." He crunches his lips. "Childhood sweetheart!"

"Really? What're you, twenty-seven?"

"Eight–ish, but who's counting."

Tamara laughs. She sips some wine. "I outgrew mine once puberty kicked in."

James takes a step away from the bar. A vivid image of an adolescent Amanda fills his thoughts. He lets out a throaty sigh and pounds the remaining bubbly.

Tamara relaxes her legs. She grabs the neck of the bottle and refills his glass.

His mind spins while focusing on a few strands of hair nestled within her cleavage. His truth is that he has never felt so sexually attracted to a woman. James looks down at her crotch and notices a wet spot. A slight grunt breaks his stare. He feels embarrassed. Without question, this stunningly beautiful creature wants him. Could she be able to break his chains and set him free?

"Look, I'm sorry. I didn't mean to embarrass you. The truth is, it turns me on that you look at me like you do." She widens her legs.

James approaches and touches his finger to her bottom lip. "You're sexy as hell." He says, discarding Amanda within his mind. He raises his flute. "The weekend's young! Only forward thinking and no reminiscing. Deal?"

"Deal. One question, though. How the hell did you survive college?"

James chuckles. "Honestly, I don't know. I'd always clam up when it came down to the nitty-gritty." He shakes his head. "For a while, I thought I was asexual."

Tamara giggles. Her eyes travel down to his crotch. "Honey, that's so far from the truth!"

The thought of her staring stimulates James. His cheeks tingle as his man-part, which he so cunningly buried, thickens. He tries to draw on negative inspirations, but it backfires as Tamara captures his torso with her legs. Combined with the warmth of her bare skin, scent, and allure of her come fuck me eyes, James can barely keep his libido in check.

Tamara wraps her hands around his neck, inhales deeply, and blows softly over his face. A shiver runs through his body.

His mind churns. Twenty-eight years of life, and he has never experienced the love pocket of a woman. His male friends ridicule him while bragging about their sexual conquests, some divulging more than secrets. Finally, besides Amanda, he finds a woman sexually desirable.

Her kisses are gentle, a blend of texture, care, and passion as her tongue probes deeper. Ecstasy grips

James. She spreads her thighs, and he presses his aching unit like a madman in heat. Suddenly, her kiss turns aggressive. Naturally, his hands find her firm breasts. Her nipples are hard. James follows the crease of her back until he cradles her cheeks. He quickly lifts her from the bar. She moans and begins grinding.

Their breath becomes one, and even though all he wants to do is find heaven, Tamara stops. James stares into her passionate eyes. What he finds enduring causes tears to begin rolling down her cheeks. James realizes she loves him. He sets her on the bar and marches outside.

Chapter 13

His heart feels like a jackhammer trying to break through his chest. James shifts his warrior king to a comfortable position, grips the rail, and stares at the night sky. He shakes his head, realizing Tamara, not Amanda, turned out to be his angel. A cool breeze tainted with a hint of chlorine wafts past. James inspects the expanded deck below. Under the rows of multicolored lights, the green palms, and the thumping music, he notices two naked blondes swimming within the turquoise backdrop of the heart-shaped pool. From his perch, the ripples appear distorted.

From behind, James felt the soft touch of gentle fingers on his shoulders. He turns and smiles. Tamara stands with one foot in front of the other, toes pointed and knees touching, holding two champagne flutes. In the calm radiance of the illumination, her eyes almost glow, and her barely clothed body appears bronze.

"Drink this." She insists.

A million thoughts zoom, yet he cannot think of a single word. James grips the flute.

Tamara smiles and bites her bottom lip. "Friends," she toasts, and they clang glasses.

To his amazement, Tamara downs it, wipes her mouth, and throws the flute into the night sky. A rush of surprise kindles as the crystal, sparkling with each downward rotation, shatters on a soft patch of grass below. As James looks closer, multiple shards litter the lawn.

"Well," Tamara shrugs.

"Really! You want me to, umm?" James prods his head.

Tamara grins, steps up onto her tippy toes, and plants a soft kiss. "Come on, rookie. Kick it up a notch. Live a little!"

"Wow, umm, OKAY. You've done this before, I see." A

few seconds later, the lawn has a new layer.

Tamara grabs his hand and leads James inside. The beat of the music flows. There are two Gatorade bottles and two towels resting on the bar. James feels incredibly playful. Tossing the fluke sparked an adrenaline rush— his libido pulses.

Tamara has a gleam in her eye as she packs the pool bag. James finds the booming music enticing as the elevator door on the ground floor slides open. Tamara leads him through the arched passage, and they enter the flowering greenery of a botanical garden. The warm atmosphere combined with the colors, the vines, and even his skin jumps out. Strangely, his throat feels unusually parched. Under the thick canopy of sprawling shrubs, they pass an erotic threesome sprawled on a round bed. Their arms and legs are entwined and moving in rhythm. Upon closer examination, he identifies Randy, Momoko, and, he thinks, her twin sister.

Tamara grins.

They enter the expanded pool area through a

secondary curtain made from multicolored beads.

Dorian greets them. "Tamara and James, you look so perfect together." He grasps their shoulders. "How about a drink?"

A flood of energy pulses, and his foot begins tapping to the beat as two buck-naked women sprint from the hot tub and dive into the turquoise pool. As if a doorway in his mind opened, he stares at the spreading ripples. James spins, escaping the caressing hand of Dorian, touching his ass, and stares at Tamara. She looks gorgeous.

"Two beers would be perfect." She eyes James. "What'd you say we go for a swim?"

The chill exhilarates him as James surfaces from the running cannonball. Tamara emerges a few feet to his left. She shakes her head like a dog shedding water. A playful splashing session commences. After chasing each other around, Tamara swims between his legs. Face to face, her wet lips find his. Naturally, his hands explore her curves, finding her hips seductively sensuous. James discovers three triangle-shaped moles on her back. From behind, they hear Randy's familiar hoot. Tamara escapes his grip and swims underwater to the edge. She pulls herself up with incredible agility and strides to the hot tub.

James gasps as a giant wave swamps him. Randy surfaces and lets out a cowboy hoot. "Eeeyaa! Dude, I think I died and went to heaven."

James wipes his eyes and playfully spits a mouthful of chlorination. In a battle of wits, a splashing frenzy flares. It ends not in exhaustion but amazement. Tamara has shed her slinky swimsuit and gracefully enters the heated water. James and Randy drop their mouths as she turns and exposes her Goodyears. She slowly dips down until only her alluring eyes stare.

Randy props his elbows on the edge. "My God! She's such a fucking babe. I'm so jealous."

James scoffs. "Quit complaining, twins!"

"Can you believe it? Dude, they're identical. I mean I-DEN-TI-CAL!"

"Nice! I know how much you love the Asian persuasion."

"They're spending the night."

They knuckle bump.

Randy stares. "You took one, didn't you?"

James shakes his head. "Took what? If you're talking about did I finally bang her, or as you would say, pork, shag, or mashed her, no. It happened again. All I had to do was push it in, but this time she stopped me. She probably thinks I'm a loser."

"Yeah, you are. Honestly, I think you're gay."

James rolls his eyes.

"Dude! I'm fucking with you. I think she loves you."

"What?"

"Let me explain. Because Tamara didn't take your dick, that shows respect."

"You're delusional! She knew I couldn't."

"Sorry, but your inexperience shows."

"What?"

"You're fucking dumb. A hottie as incredible as Tamara knows what's up. If she didn't dig you, she would've ridden your pole like a rock star and ditched you before the morning."

James finds his words more real than ever.

"So, did you?"

"Did what?"

"Take the sex pill! They're handing them out like candy. Momoko and I both popped one. She calls it seventh heaven or something close."

"Really?"

"Yeah, and let me tell you, it works. I'm ready for round three."

"Why'd you ask if I took one?"

"Your pupils are dilated."

"Maybe that's why I feel so horny." James glares at Randy. "Yours are, too!"

"Cause I did some, bonehead. Either you did or you didn't. Maybe it's the alcohol?"

"Could be, but I didn't pop any pills."

"Who cares? Maybe she slipped you one after you gave her the freaky frigid. I would've destroyed you five times. Here's what I think. It's a build-up from years of celibacy and masturbation. Dude, think about it; you've never dipped your wick."

James shows grief. "But—"

Randy raises his finger. "Cut the crap, Ramsey. You're not talking your way out of this one. Now, get your butt over to the hot tub and make me proud. By far, you've landed the hottest peach here."

"She is, isn't she?"

"Fuckin aye clay! She's a babe on steroids." Randy narrows his eyes and prods his chest. "I'm warning you. If you go Siberian again, I'll tell Dorian you want him."

James shudders at the thought.

Randy points. "Timings perfect. The two dudes split. Now get!"

The thump of the music energizes his stride. James stops at the edge. "How about some company?"

Her luring eyes probe. "Of course. Oh, shorts are optional."

James enters clothed. The warmth exhilarates him as he stares at her sizable twins floating beneath the rippled surface. Like Randy, her pupils appear dilated. "Seventh Heaven?"

Her hand finds his thigh. "I see your best friend can't

help himself."

"Twenty-four-seven, but how and when?"

"The champagne, but I only gave you half. You were so upset, and I thought it might ease things. She must be charming?"

"She?" James narrows his eyes.

Tamara frowns. "Or is it you don't find me attractive?"

James shudders at the thought. "No, no, you're stunning."

"Good recovery!"

Tamara aggressively dips her hand below his shorts. James tries to tell her to stop, but instead, he gasps. Fortunately, she finds trouble.

Tamara grins slyly. "Smart. How many layers?"

James removes her hand, and they interlock fingers. "Two!"

"Why?"

"I've already embarrassed myself once today." James glances at Randy, chatting with the two topless blondes. Their heads turn in unison.

James tightens his chest. Did Randy reveal his secret? Sensing vulnerability, Tamara stands and steps over his legs. The water dripping from her hair and breasts and parading between her exposed legs only intensifies the moment. James swallows. A Goddess of perfect proportion, without reservation or modesty and with eyes of seduction, has cornered him. James tries to speak, but her index finger finds his lips. She mounts him. Her seductive stare declares her intentions. She pulls a few strands of wet hair from her face and presses her two man-killers against his chest. She closes her eyes and softly plants her lips. James openly accepts while naturally gripping her backside. She pulls back.

"James, I think I love you. You're so pure, so virtuous. Take me. I want to be your first."

His world shrinks around her words. The way her eyes sparkled reminds James of his youth. Amanda turned ten three days before moving. He presents a gift in his tree fort, which his neighbor Joe helped build—a small rectangular shack held together with a few two-by-fours, nailed plywood, and some scrap pieces of carpet. A ten-sentence poem took ten days to compose, and a single Red rose with the tenth thorn trimmed. After reading it, Amanda vowed she loved him. She gave him ten soft kisses and demanded he stay faithful until death.

James refocuses. "Tamara, I love you as well."

Tamara smiles.

James cups her breasts, and they indulge in a kiss so heated and untamed, combined with the dry humping, swells form on the surface. Tamara tries to remove his shorts but fails miserably.

James boldly pushes her away, not escaping the majority of his manhood protruding far above the waistline of his shorts. He quickly adjusts. "Not here, not like this; I mean, not on display." James glances at Randy. Dorian has joined. He smiles and displays an OK sign.

Tamara steps out of the water and dresses. She grabs her pool bag and hands it to James. "Here, cover yourself. Let's go!"

The door barely closes before their bathing attire falls. The thumping music only adds to the passion. They stumble down the stairs, taking only tiny breaths between kisses. James notices the ambiance of the room has changed. Dimmed lights and the curtains are closed. Multicolored candles line the bar. Incense sticks, a Patchouli, and musk envelop the room.

She grips his chubby and leads him over to the sectional. There are no words as she plants two sensuous kisses to each of his swelling nipples. She drops to her knees, cradles his tower, and devours him. James groans. He remembers how good it felt to be touched by someone who truly loved him. And even though he wants her to continue, he steps back. Tamara glares. Her eyes are glazed and full of desire. Her head nods slightly, wondering why he stopped her.

For the first time in his life, James Rawlings feels in control. Without a word, he rips open a condom, which he grabbed from a bowl conveniently positioned on the end table. His eyes tell her his desire as their fingers entwine. Tamara stands and spreads a silk sheet. He lays her down ever so gently. His senses are on overload as she grips his cock. She spreads her legs, begins touching herself, and waves him to come close. With his hands around her narrow waist, he carefully maneuvers until her moist warmth sends a spasm throughout his body. Her moans lead his direction. James pushes ahead. The tip naturally enters, and as if he had done this act a thousand times before, he penetrates deeper into an unknown universe.

Tamara groans.

James stops. "Am I hurting you?" He asks.

Tamara sighs and wraps her legs tight. She raises her head and kisses him. How she absorbs every inch of his manhood stimulates him. Together, they grind to the music, which only intensifies their passion.

"I love you, Tamara!" James groans.

Tamara finds his ear. "I love you too, James Rawlings."

PART 3

Chapter 14

The most influential moment in his adult life, without question, occurred. Fittingly, the trance version of Rod Stewart's 'Tonight's the Night' remix plays. James grins at the irony of the lyrics. Spread your wings and let me come inside, intermittently repeated between the progressive drum upbeats, yet he embraces his triumph. James feels alive, especially his jackhammer. Truly, he has entered 'Seventh Heaven.'

Tamara has her petite head tucked neatly into his chest. James kisses her forehead, knowing he is blessed to be validated by such a woman of substance. Her sultry eyes glow as she squeezes her arms around his waist. A shiver radiates outward from her skin. James covers her with the sheet, and together, they close their eyes to the comfort and warmth of love.

The sound of the door opening arouses James. He interprets it as part of his dream.

They are on his yacht anchored in a tropical lagoon, making love on the bow flowing to the gentle swell of the ocean.

The distinct voice of Randy wakes James. He sees Momoko and her sister sitting at the bar. By definition, they look identical in height, hair color, and even how their legs are crossed from left to right. James glances at the bowl of condoms, hoping he appropriately discarded the used one. Looking back, the twins stare at his well-defined unit below the sheet. Self-conscious, he fluffs it.

The clock reads two-forty-seven. James yawns and gently removes his arm from under her head. Tamara fidgets. He gently runs his fingers through her hair and, with a soft kiss on her forehead, steps into his shorts.

Randy introduces Sayuri.

"Nice to meet you." James gestures while grabbing a bottle of water.

"What'd I tell you, I-den-ti-cal!" Randy boasts.

"I can see that." James mocks. "How'd you tell them apart?"

"Momoko swallows." Randy jokes.

The twins giggle.

James tosses the cap at Randy. "Keep it down, bucko. She's sleeping."

Randy quickly catches it. "Touchy, are we? I figured you'd be jumping for joy or digging in for seconds, especially with a prize like her."

"She!" James presses his finger to his lips.

"Geez! Relax, the night's young."

"Go to bed. You're way past curfew."

Randy scoffs, sits on the bar, and cracks a beer. His voice is barely a whisper, yet his hands express amazement. "Oh, my God! Would you look at this place? The unbridled love-shack. Candles, incense, condoms, silk sheets?"

James pats his back. "Thanks. But how'd you know."

"You're welcome, but it wasn't me."

Randy eyes Momoko.

She raises her hands. "I'm the luggage bitch."

A soft voice interjects from across the room. "It was Dorian." Tamara wraps the sheet around her. "Hi, guys."

The girls wave. Randy blows a kiss.

James ponders. How did Tamara know? Could it be the sisters preordained this weekend down to the last detail? Tamara did say they participated in this type of amusement before. Or could this be a coincidence? His eyes drift to the bowl of condoms. This time, James notices they are all magnum-sized. He raises his hands. "How? I mean, the condoms?"

"Sweetheart! Don't worry about the little things. Cherish the moment."

"Believe me, I am. It's too coincidental."

"Please humor us," Randy inquires.

Tamara walks around the bar, grabbing his arm and a water bottle. "Please open!"

Randy moves next to Momoko and takes a swig of beer. "What's the big deal? He's smart like that."

"Like what? Clairvoyant?"

Tamara takes a sip. "Kind of!"

James glares. "He can read minds!"

Tamara places her hand on his chest. "What're you so worried about? I'm right here. Trust me. I'm not going anywhere."

"So, does everyone know?"

Tamara grins and plants a soft kiss. "Only Dorian and, of course, us. I promise. Besides, you're mine, and I don't share!"

Randy claps his hands. "What'd you call a fresh fucked virgin?"

James shrugs at his dry humor.

"Coming of Age!"

The twins giggle.

A knock on the door startles everyone.

Randy gives everyone his famous shit-eating grin. "Honey, I'm coming," he barks, dashing up the stairs.

The two blondes from the pool, this time wearing similar pajamas, stride inside. What stuns everyone? Five more girls wearing identical attire follow. Tamara quickly disappears into the bedroom. A few moments later, she exits wearing matching pink and white bunny rabbit-footed pajamas. They sit in the living room. Tamara waves James over while Randy and the twins serve drinks.

"Ladies, I'd like to introduce the love of my life, James Rawlings." Tamara raises her long-stem crystal fluke.

The group enthusiastically joins. "James, Hear, Hear!"

What happens next reminds him of a scene from a drama movie. The women guzzle the golden liquid, stand, and, in single file, follow Tamara over to the fireplace. One by one, they throw them inside and break them.

Randy grins. His expression is more shocked than curious.

Tamara wraps her hands around James and places her head on his back. She inhales deeply. "You know what I like most about you?"

"My innocence!" James jokes.

"Funny," she says. "Even though your body's delicious, there's an intellectual harmony about you. I can see myself in you."

James shakes his head. "Trust me. It's empty in there. Take a look!" He presses one eye tight to hers.

In the backdrop, they hear whispered words. "Oh, my God! He's amazing."

While the twins deliver drinks, Randy and James perch themselves snug to the bar and listen to their wild stories.

"James Rawlings," the redhead asks rather brashly. "Are you the same James Rawlings who saved countless people from certain death when a gunman entered the post office in Nashville and opened fire? If I remember correctly, you sprayed him with mace, tackled him to the ground, and subdued him?"

James shakes his head. "Umm, no, I'm sorry. You must have mistaken me for someone else."

"You look so familiar. I swear you're the guy."

Tamara raises her hand. "Jasmine, you know the rules. Only yes or no questions. Besides, if he were that man, he'd be a hero."

Jasmine apologizes.

Randy whispers. "Did you save all those people?"

"Shut the fuck up. I said no!"

What happens next dispels any sense of normality. The front door springs open, and Dorian enters wearing a Superman costume—blue tights, red shorts, knee-high red boots, and a red cape. Except on his chest is the letter D. Dorian saunters down the stairs, waving. On cue, the ladies stand as two more women wearing similar pajamas to the others stride in. Systematically, they clear two spots. A quiet calm ensues as the Queen Bee, a blue-eyed Barbie Doll type with flattened platinum blonde hair, defined boobs, and an ultra-thin waist, sits in the chair. Her PJs look tailored. Her facial skin is golden bronze, compared to Dorian's pale complexion. With a wave of his hand, the twins serve drinks. The taller protégée, her dark painted wide-set eyes below bobbed bangs and jet-black wig, takes the couch. Her upright posture, defined jaw-line, and full red lips below a petite, upturned nose highlight her voluptuous hourglass body. What differentiates her, besides the wig, are her bright pink gloves.

James whispers. "Slumber sleepover or an early Halloween pre-function?"

"Neither! Sorority chapter meeting!" Randy answers.

"How'd you know?"

"Momoko! Dorian hired her as a bartender in a club he managed in Manhattan. One thing led to another, and a few after-hour parties later, she landed this gig. She's been working full-time ever since. From what I can guess, the weekend is ready to be put into high gear."

"Is the Pulp Fiction bimbo with the florescent gloves the naked bird we saw drying her hair in front of the window?"

"I'm not sure. But man, oh man, she's smoking hot."

"Is that all you ever think about?"

"What else is there?"

In all, the nine women are the most stunningly beautiful creatures James Rawlings has ever laid eyes on. What strikes him odd is that Tamara suddenly seems distant. "The Barbie, is she?

Randy nods. "Yup!"

James slips through the sliding door onto the deck to test the waters. Not surprisingly, the women stare, except for Tamara and Barbie. They're busy chatting. Reading her lips, James thinks Tamara said *she's late again.*

Over the thump of the Riviera Disco music echoing up from the pool below, James draws his attention to a distinct tapping noise. Two men are standing in front of the picture window where the Pulp Fiction Bimbo was drying her hair earlier, wearing cloth diapers with oversized silver pins. Tapping the window with a half-empty tumbler, the taller one openly embraces and tongue kisses the other. James turns disgustingly.

Lost in thought, he looks skyward. The stars are out in full force. As he locates the big dipper from behind, Tamara clutches his waist.

"How's the view?" She asks.

"Much better now."

She smiles. "Come on. Let's go to bed. I'm exhausted."

James quickly glances at the window. The two men are gone. "The meetings over?"

"If you'd call it that. I'd say it was more of a weekend commencement ceremony." She grabs his hand. "I'll introduce you to the ladies tomorrow. Let's go snuggle."

James turns down the lights. They can hear giggles from the other bedroom.

"The twins?"

Tamara grins. "Lucky boy!"

Chapter 15

James wakes to the rising sun. The way Tamara has her head snugged to his chest and how a wheezy snore vents invigorates him. He has never slept with a woman through the night before, and he wants to cherish the very moment. The problem is that his five-alarm boner below the sheet proves different.

His heart pounds as Tamara grips his shaft. "Morning, lover!"

James gazes into her golden browns. They glisten. Her lips are slightly curved, and her hardened nipples protrude through the sheet. James stands and covers his telephone pole. Tamara smiles.

"Morning, umm, I gotta pee. I'll be right back."

"Hurry up." She spreads her legs. "Water, please!"

It takes longer than usual for James to relieve his

bladder, and bending his stick far enough down to aim hurts. James cleans up, grabs two water bottles, and returns to bed.

Without words, they throw their empties. James pushes the sheet down with his feet and mounts her. Her warmth invigorates him. He pecks her lips and stares. James feels connected in love. Their kiss turns steamy. Their breathing becomes one, and he sighs at how effortlessly he glides inside. Tamara absorbs him with only gentle movements. She aggressively rolls him and begins gyrating. Not up and down, but forward and back. James cups her breasts, and within moments, they climax.

James feels giddy, washing her from head to toe. He has fallen head over heels. As the morning sun brightens the window, he steps out on the balcony while Tamara puts on her face. The glass facade of the building mirrors the tree line and the lake. James places his back on the rail, looks up, and watches a passing cloud form into the shape of a heart. A moment later, it dissipates.

From below, the music begins to thump. Servants begin preparing for the day. Naturally, he taps his foot. On the lake, he watches a speed boat pulling two water skiers whiz past. James draws up as they hit a wake.

Fortunately, after performing a few discombobulated circus maneuvers, they avert crashing. James grins, knowing he would have taken a nosedive.

Randy steps out onto the living room deck. He raises a coffee mug and rubs his protruding belly.

"Morning sunshine, or should I call you *Mr. New Man*."

James grins, reeling in the meaning of his words. "Actuality, I'm fresh fucked and loving life. You, however, look haggard."

"Roasted's more the term!" He sips his coffee.

"The twins?"

"Eyes glued shut. What about yours?"

"Putting on her face."

"How's your pecker?"

James laughs. "Probably better than yours."

Randy stretches his boxers and takes a long look. He crunches his lips and nods. He's ready for another round.

"Give it a rest, Romeo. Put your pants on. It's breakfast time."

Randy nods. "I'll meet you at the front door in five."

"Flip-flops, an oversized turquoise T-shirt, board shorts, and a pair of Ray-Ban sunglasses. I thought we were going to breakfast, not surfing?" James jokes.

Randy slides down the staircase rail. The floor thuds as he lands. He inspects his outward aspect in the hallway mirror. "After breakfast."

James and Randy turn. Tamara is posing next to one of the green leafy plants. Black lace-up stiletto pumps extenuate her red toenails and well-defined calves. A white mesh sun skirt reveals perfectly toned thighs. White cat eye sunglasses and twin braided ponytails highlight her minuscule black two-piece bathing suit.

She lowers her sunglasses. "Do you approve?"

James drops his jaw. "You're stunning!"

"I agree!" Randy hoots. "Let's go. I'm so hungry." Randy opens the front door and waves.

Beyond the atrium and instep to the upbeat drum parlay, the group struts through a collection of feminine and male beauties already seated throughout the maze of tables encompassing the swimming pool. Tamara leads them up a raised staircase onto a heart-shaped platform built directly over the pool. An illuminated handrail encircles the periphery, and a similar sunshade covers an oversized circular wooden table.

Dorian greets them. This morning, his risqué attire demands a second look: skin-tight pink shorts, no shirt, and a bright pink shoulder-length wig, complete with bangs.

"You look ravishing this morning." Dorian kisses her cheek. "My goodness, James!" He places his hand on his shoulder and glances at his package. "Is it me, or are you glowing?"

James blushes. They appear to be the last ones to arrive. Tamara immediately walks over to Pricilla and kisses her cheek. She makes her rounds until she sits opposite her. She gestures for James to pose to her right and Randy to the left.

In all, there are nine women and eighteen men at the table. Each dressed in similar attire and sporting braided pigtails under bright faces. The two men James saw standing in the window in diapers yesterday smile. James notices three empty chairs directly opposite. Pricilla signals Dorian, and with a wave of his hand, an army of servants begins depositing an array of delicacies. Over the next hour, a controlled order to everything the women do, from who eats first, who makes the first toast, and who introduces their men. Not surprisingly, Tamara stands.

"Ladies, she has arrived!" Dorian announces.

All eyes turn and watch the modestly tall and

beautiful brunette stride confidently up the stairs. The sheer white sundress with ten embroidered black stars accentuates ten silver rings adorning each finger. Her full lips are bright purple, and like the other felines, she sports pigtails and a pair of white cat-eyed sunglasses. Her two boy toys, each tall, dark, and handsome and wearing matching white Calvin Kline slim-fit boxer briefs, stop behind her, fold their arms, and pose.

Her belated voice appeals to everyone. "Sisters, my humble apology. My delay started in Amsterdam. Some terrorist plot in the making. I do hope everyone can forgive me!"

James stares at the woman. A nervous excitement fills his heart. Behind her costume, he sees a striking familiarity.

"Of course. Imagine the horror." Pricilla says. With a smooth gait, she approaches. "Amanda, we're so glad your journey ended safely." She kisses and hugs her.

Amanda acknowledges her appropriately. Dorian gracefully assists in seating the trio, bathing over the two hunks. He acknowledges Pricilla. "Shall I start the festivities?"

His heart cannot beat faster as James processes her name. Below the table, he entwines his hands in a death grip.

Pricilla raises her glass. "Ladies, Salve!"

The women raise their glasses as if rehearsed a thousand times. "You'll never see me again, even if I pray for you," they chant.

The men look more confused than clear as they process what sounds like lyrics from a popular techno song. James lowers his sunglasses. They undoubtedly have high regard for each other. His dilemma was: Could this woman indeed be his angel, Amanda?

His answer comes directly. Looking overly jealous, Tamara forces the issue. "Ladies, let's begin." She stands and squeezes Randy's shoulder. "I'd like to introduce my men." She weaves her fingers through his mane. "This jersey-eyed lanky hunk, second mate to no one, is Randy, my big man."

Randy smiles, grateful for the soft applause. Amanda removes her sunglasses as Tamara steps behind James and grips his shoulders. James sinks into his seat.

"This beautiful man, however, is my triumph." Her voice expressed enthusiasm and praise. "Ladies, I would like to introduce the man who exceeds all my expectations—gifted with a profound sense of humility, unstained guilt, and handsomely attractive. And believe me, there's more to this pretty face! James Rawlings!" Tamara caresses his smooth cheeks.

Obviously, one of the three Barbie types is a woman of substance. Her two specimens, clearly twins, with deep brown eyes and chiseled jaws defined under trimmed stubble and similar in look to the other unicorns, stare at Randy and James as if they were misfits. She clears her throat. "Once again, Tamara, you've misinterpreted the meaning of our agenda." She directs her attention towards Amanda. "As our elected speaker, please inform Tootsie that her men don't fit the profile. Look at them, a couple of Laurel and Hardie's. The odd couple redefined."

"Excuse me!" Tamara boldly interrupts. "The provisions clearly state a bona fide virgin trumps all. And we all know how hard they are to find."

James feels his cheeks flush while he swallows a dry lump.

"And who's mad truth will vouch for this claim? His sidekick?" The blonde folds her arms over her inflated twins and scoffs. "He's already indulging in the hired help!"

Amanda stares. Her eyes fixed on James as if a ghost from her past suddenly beckoned her guilt. She breaks her glare and deposits a scoop of mixed fruit into her bowl. She counts out ten napkins and places them under her silverware. Her eyes quickly roam from Randy back to Tamara and then to James. A whispered word emerges.

"James!"

Chapter 16

Tamara proudly sits as the table explodes in chatter.

Amanda stands wide-eyed, fixed on the man who blended inconspicuously only moments ago. "James! James Rawlings! It is you!" Her brows furrow to the point that clear wrinkles form. "What're you doing here? Are you with her?"

James feels apprehensive. Deep down, behind the makeup, the frosted hair, and the costume, he knows this woman. And so what? Amanda left him high and dry without a care in the world.

James straightens his posture. "Yes, I'm with her. Wow, what a coincidence to see you here."

Her face shows the delicacy of the situation. The

same cold stare Amanda has shown James on multiple occasions. "Yes, quite! Small world, isn't it."

"Crazy, huh."

"So, how'd you meet?" Amanda stares at Tamara.

Sneers vent from every corner of the table.

Even though all ears await and perspiration builds, James finds himself calm and confident. He folds his hands on the table and looks at Amanda squarely. "We met at a bar if you can believe that." James smiles at Tamara.

"Really! How fitting!" Amanda gloats.

"She's one of the bartenders and a good-looking one."

"I'll second that." Randy boasts.

James nods approvingly but tightens his face. "Why the fifty questions? Does it matter how we met or why I'm here? You're not my girl anymore. Tamara is. Besides, if I remember correctly, after our last chance encounter, even after promises, you ditched me high and dry."

A slight growl exits. "You little bitch. I confided in

you; in return, you exploited my trust." Amanda pounds her fist on the table.

All the while, Tamara remains poised. Her non-blinking eyes glare, exhibiting resentment. Unknown to James, she loathes Amanda. Finally, after years of planning, she has delivered a devastating blow. Tamara does something unique. She leans over and plants a deep, wet kiss on his lips.

Amanda lets out a deeply seeded "GRRRR," which shatters any illusion of a peaceful solution. "You bitch! Now you mock me!" Her anger hits critical mass, so she picks up the fruit bowl and flings the sugary contents, missing Tamara and James and dousing half of everyone else.

Though Pricilla has a high opinion of these women, she looks outraged. She witnessed this type of behavior throughout her life. Mainly through cunning deceit driven by greed and power. A motivation that ultimately led to her mother's premature death. For these reasons, she swore never to allow this to happen within the ranks of the sisters. She stands and claps her hands authoritatively.

"Everyone except for Amanda, Tamara, Dorian, and you, James—leave this table—now!"

After a short interlude consisting of sighs, sneers, and directed profanity, eventually, only five people remain. Dorian is the odd man out. The entire time, James remained unmoving. His focus is on Tamara, specifically the symmetry of her beautiful face and how her index finger moves softly to the beat of the music while she caresses his hand. For what it was worth, Randy whispered not to worry.

Pricilla clears her throat. She takes a long look at Dorian. He nods. "Sisters, you disappoint me. It's hard enough trying to keep my wits, especially since mother passed, but your consistent jockeying, your competitive edge to outshine or outwit the other has put me in an awkward position."

Amanda speaks. "And I'm truly sorry. I am." She shakes her head mournfully. "But she has taken my trust way beyond the context of friendship."

"What trust?" Tamara asks.

James can tell the thought of Tamara fucking him angers Amanda. He was hers. She owned him.

Her welling eyes lock on her once close friend. "So, I suppose the reason you two are holding hands so delicately is—" Amanda sighs heavily, glancing at James. "You two—" She exhales a heavy breath. Tears roll down her cheeks. "Fucked?"

James stares at Amanda. The essence of the word pierces his heart.

Tamara laughs aloud. "Amendable and much better than your previous performances, but those Broadway tears don't fool me. They mean nothing." Her voice increases variably in tone.

Amanda wipes her eyes. "James, how could you?" Her stare turns gloomy. "You promised, you promised!"

Dorian stands. "Promised what?"

Amanda glances into his curious eyes. "James is my first and only true love. We made a pact as kids to wait for each other. That made our love eternal."

"You mean blind affection from adolescence?"

A lingering pause only increases tensions.

"Pacts like this have lasting effects. As I said, our love is eternal. Ask him. Ask James if he still loves me. Let him answer."

"So, this truffle is about guilt?" Dorian glares at Amanda and then at James. His subdued posture tells his story. "Well, sir James. What'd you have to say?"

James realizes before an emotional crisis destroys their friendship, he must convey honesty. "Yes, Amanda! I still love you, but not like before. And yes, our fates are intertwined, but I cannot cling to a childhood dream that has only caused me agony. The not knowing if you were alive, dead, or married tore at my soul. Besides, it was you who didn't keep your promise."

Amanda springs up. Her pinkish cheeks show bruised humility. "James, I'm so sorry. I never wanted to hurt you, but—" Her face droops, followed by a deep exhalation.

Tamara interrupts. "You're a fucking hypocrite. You're not sorry. You've been stringing him along all these years like a puppet, watching him from a distance while you pursued your eccentric and sensual lifestyle.

Look at yourself. You're incapable of love. You know what your problem is; you can't see it."

James straightens his posture and raises his hand. "Wait a second. You've been watching me?"

Tamara scoffs. "I'd like to see you get out of this one!"

Amanda sits down and places her elbows on the table. Delicately, she folds her hands and nods, implying no.

"You can't do it, can you?" Tamara insists. "Or is it? You won't." She crunches her shoulders.

Her anger builds. Amanda will not yield to these self-incriminating style questions. She has been in worse jams before and always found admirable solutions. The challenge is that the outcome could be devastating if she reveals the truth. "No, James, I haven't." Amanda appeals using body gestures. "Please believe me, it was pure coincidence running into you at the park."

Tamara scoffs, this time with a heavy throat. "Really! You make me sick. I will not allow your selfish ambitions to affect James anymore."

Amanda grins. She knows she has complete and unquestionable superiority over Tamara. Never before has Tamara won a verbal, no less a physical confrontation. The last time she tried, she humiliated herself. "Impressive poise. You must've considered your actions for a great deal of time. What concerns me is that it seems you've shifted your allegiance. Have you forgotten your oath, your fidelity to the sisterhood?"

James stands. This cruel behavior, especially her aggressive desire to manipulate with such aversion, disgusts him. "Who are you? The Amanda I fell in love with was sweet and innocent. I see a cold and evil woman in front of me now." Tamara squeezes his hand, and he kisses it. James eyes Pricilla. "Understand this. Tamara's not on trial, nor has she shifted allegiance. She's my savior. In my eyes, she rescued me from spending an eternity alone. Whatever pact the sisters made in college and the game you're playing now, it's over. I will not allow either of you to hurt her."

Dorian stands and claps. "Well, said James, well

said."

Pricilla rises. "We're done here. Amanda, I want you to make peace with Tamara. The weekend is upon us, and I don't want it ruined because of self-suspicion or jealousy. James Rawlings, I only wish it were I who rescued you. You fascinate me. Your charm is worth fighting for. I look forward to future conversations. Tamara, it seems you have your hands full, but heed my warning. Make amends and move forward. I'm sure I can entrust the both of you?"

Chapter 17

Amanda waits until Pricilla, shadowed by Dorian, makes their way through the crowd of barely clothed guests. She shifts her attention. In her mind, she plays variations of how to deal with Tamara.

"You little bitch! To hold me hostage in this fashion appeals to the worst side of me." Her voice petitions aggression.

Disgusted with her hostility, James stands and points. Tamara immediately lowers his hand. "Sweetheart, please don't!" Tamara shakes her head, appealing to his better nature, and stands. "You have no idea what she's capable of. She's not who you remember."

A passing cloud smothers the sun.

"Amanda, you'll find me much more aggressive this time." Tamara delivers her voice firmly yet soft enough to attract attention.

James draws a breath. In the backdrop, the music has inched up a few decibels.

"I've outgrown your riotous, excuse me, overpowering and toxic resentment with life. I will no longer bow to your manipulation of James. Your hunger sickens me."

Amanda taps the table. Her continuous blinking, combined with her slouched posture, exhibits tension. Amazingly, her voice sounds composed. "James, this must seem impossible, but I assure you I'm not the evil, ugly person she portrays." Her eyes focus on Tamara. "This is not the time nor the place. It was wrong calling you a bitch. Can you forgive me?"

Tamara regards Amanda contemptuously.

"Nothing to say?" Amanda asks rather impatiently.

Tamara looks at James.

He nods approvingly.

"You're right." Tamara reaches into the depths of her mega purse and rummages. She extends an empty hand. "Whoops, nothing in there!" She begins massaging his shoulders. "Yes, I'll forgive you this time. But understand. James is no longer subservient to your will. We're in love, and there's nothing you can say or do to change that."

James can tell the thought panics Amanda. Her eyes drift. She nervously folds the edge of the tablecloth. Combined with her silent stare, she unexpectedly finds herself speechless. Deep down, James knows Amanda will never release him.

Amanda grins modestly. "In love? I seriously doubt that. I'd say infatuation or lust rather than true tender affection. James, you do know the difference?"

In his mind, James hears his mother. Her voice was bright and clear, reiterating the importance of feeling love. Get to know the person on the surface and from the inside. He looks at Tamara. She squeezes his shoulder and smiles. Amanda has a point. He only knows Tamara intimately. He does not know her character flaws, quirks, or pet peeves. Yet, her spirit stood out from the moment they met, similar to his mother. Could this mean her heart has purity? Besides, his instincts have never let him down before.

James glares at Amanda. Her outward beauty shines. She looks stunning, yet within her gaze, he senses insecurity. He clears his throat. "There's no virtue greater than the human heart. And yes, what I feel for Tamara might be infatuation, yet somehow I find her pleasant. She's an angel of romance, and you, you're nothing but a grave thorn in my side."

Her face turns blank. Amanda nervously interlocks her fingers and squeezes until her knuckles turn red. "Perhaps this thorn you refer to could be my absence in your life. For that, I'm truly sorry. James, I didn't want to move. Nothing changed, no matter how hard I cried or threatened to run away. What did was New York City! I became hard, like my father. James, she's right. I'm no longer the innocent naïve girl you remember."

James perks up. Deep within, his heart flutters. He still cares for Amanda.

"James, I've never stopped thinking about you, especially our first kiss. The words we recited are embedded. I needed time, time to think. That's why I didn't get back to you after our encounter in the park. I needed to sort things out. The airplane falling out of the sky scared me. It made me think about who I was—how insignificant and small we are. James, I promise I'm not the snob she portrays."

Tamara scoffs.

"More to the point, what I'm getting at is if I were you, I'd be more concerned with her sudden appreciation. Real or imaginary, doesn't it strike you odd she knows so much about you?"

"What'd you mean?"

"How do you suppose she knew you were a virgin?"

"Use to be!" Tamara utters rather boldly. "Come, James, the atmosphere's getting thick. Didn't you say something about waterskiing?"

James stands. "She was innocent of the fact until I told her. She had no idea."

"That's so far from the truth! James, she's playing you like a poker hand."

"You're jealous. Amanda, this is no game. We love each other."

Amanda scoffs and shakes her head. "Look around. This weekend, the sisters, all of this is part of the challenge. Tamara, well, she has another check mark on the list."

Confusion fills James.

"Ask her about us, more specifically, the sisters. Our code requires direct answers without bending the truth. If she lies, she'll forfeit the game."

"Game? Disqualified?" James shakes his head.

"Seven of the other sisters have already been declared unfit, so they're bitter toward you. She's topped everyone, including me."

James falls silent.

"Amanda! That will be quite enough." Tamara pulls her phone from her purse and holds it up.

Amanda frowns.

"I've been recording everything. Do you understand my meaning?" Tamara says smartly. "James, she was the second of the seven disqualified. That's why Amanda was questioning you. She's truly jealous of us. Come on. Let's get out of here. The party has moved down to the lake?"

"James, weren't you a bit surprised when you found out your name was on the list, or are you really that naïve?"

James shakes his head. How could Amanda know this? He suddenly feels restless.

Tamara scoffs. She steps behind James and places her hands on his shoulders. "James, she's playing us. Yes, I put your name on the list before asking. So, what? I gambled. I knew you were special the moment I laid eyes on you. Besides, nobody forced you. You came on your own free will. And here we are. I'm so happy."

"Pitiful!" Amanda scoffs. "Like me, ice cubes run through her veins. James, she's using you to get back at me for stealing her last boyfriend, which wasn't worth the effort. The man was egotistical, self-centered, and had a small penis."

"This has nothing to do with him!" Tamara scoffs. "You're treading on thin ice with your indirect questioning. Pricilla will hear about this." She grabs his hand, and they leave.

"It wasn't by chance you two met." Amanda snarls. "It was premeditated down to her getting the job at the bar. Did you know her uncle's friend owns the Swing Door? Ask her, James. Ask her! The only reason she accepted was to sink her claws into you. She's a Primadonna. She hasn't worked a day in her life."

PART 4

Chapter 18

THE MANCHESTER LEGEND

Eight mid-size portraits of family members who earned the right to enter this room lined the walls. Specifically, the life-size one at the head of the table was Donald, the great, great, great grandfather. He was the grand master of the family fortune, hence the reason the Manchester heritage enjoyed such opulent lifestyles.

Coincidentally, two of the younger siblings resembled Randolph and Amanda.

DONALD MANCHESTER

Nannies raised Donald Manchester. At thirteen, his narcissistic parents sent him on a five-year sailing adventure, claiming his oppressive appetite needed cultivation. Donald protested fiercely, knowing it was only to rid him.

His fourth year abroad proved harrowing. Donald contracted a deathly fever while sailing deep into the Amazon. Cared for by an indigenous tribe, which Donald held in the highest regard, he survived. Unfortunately, he suffered from bouts of panic, anxiety, and delusion for the rest of his life. Returning home, Donald found his parents increasingly demeaning. They marginalized the tribe that saved his life and shipped him off to college. Donald soon came to terms with the painful truth. Their love was superficial. A few months later, Donald concocted the first untraceable and deadly mixture of rare roots and plants—what he labeled Dispatch, a knowledge attained while living with the natives in South America. Soon after, an inner peace settled. His parents mysteriously died while on a cruise to the Mediterranean. Donald inherited their wealth and started his quest for power.

Donald had the looks of a movie star, the tongue of a socialite, and the charisma of a politician. Donald married at twenty-six into old money and had two kids —Randolph and Amanda. Three years later, his wife passed from a supposed heart attack. Donald would marry into wealth ten more times. Like his first wife, they crossed the great divide from natural causes. Donald was never convicted, yet they found controversy at every crossroads. The social circles claimed he was a modern-day serial killer. When Donald finally passed from a heart attack at the age of fifty-six, his acquired wealth was in the tens of millions.

Amanda found Donald's life fascinating. More so, her father, Randolph, was the first male named after Donald's firstborn, but they were also spitting images. The portraits exhibited this. What solidified the ritual was that his father helped cover up an accidental murder. Randolph shot his ex-girlfriend in his New York loft. Randolph showed her the ledgers containing the learned knowledge. The deadly formula he labeled Dispatch. A mixture of plants and roots so lethal and untraceable a small dose taken internally would stop a human heart. What scared Amanda was when Randolph referred to the incantation—a generational curse brought together by the church and the families representing Donald's deceased wives.

RANDOLPH

Throughout the generations, untimely deaths, alcoholism, drugs, and depression haunted the Manchesters. Randolph's parents believed the family fortune came from blood money. To break the curse, they donated most of their wealth to charity. They assured Randolph he would live comfortably for the rest of his life—millions in cash, bonds, and real estate.

Randolph thought otherwise and persuaded them to wait until after he finished college. The burden alone would dramatically hinder his ability to study and earn his degree. A few months before graduation, Randolph concocted the secret potion and injected it into their malaria medication. His parents mysteriously passed on their trip to Africa from natural causes.

Amanda had no idea his deceit ran so deep— especially his desire for ritual child sacrifice and the drinking of their blood. Randolph maintained his DNA was similar to Donald's.

BEATRICE

Randolph met Beatrice on a cruise to the Mediterranean. She was twenty-six and recently widowed. Her husband of ten months, Peter, a wealthy Manhattan-based tycoon, died one month earlier. Peter was ninety-four. After a long and drawn-out court battle with his two living siblings, Beatrice settled for a cool twenty million and two properties—one in Florida and the other in Italy on the South shores. That was the reason for the voyage. She wanted to sell the property and set up a home base in Florida.

When Beatrice found out she was pregnant, she approached Randolph with a business proposition. Because their life stories were similar, combined with their social skills, cutthroat instincts, and energetic tongues, her 'Murder for Money' scheme made sense. Her plan was simple. She would lure wealthy men into her bed and marry them. Once they added her to the will, Randolph would put them to rest using Dispatch— his untraceable potion.

First and foremost, Beatrice would keep her child. A widowed mother showed legitimacy. She also insisted Randolph never tell the child he was the father. She wanted her to remain pure, not tainted like them. Long story short, Beatrice married ten times over the next twenty-plus years. They amassed billions.

Amanda was intrigued, yet at the same time, disturbed. Suddenly, finding out she had a step-sister yet was forbidden to expose the truth unsettled her. As troublesome, she became her number one nemesis, the Queen of her sorority.

Randolph continued.

Beatrice named her daughter Pricilla after her great, great, grandmother. Ironically, they looked similar— curly golden blonde hair, wide, deep-set blue eyes, soft white skin, and a delightful smile. Beatrice was a genius. Even though she never admitted it, her mood swings proved it. At times, she could be extraordinarily vulgar and, five minutes later, loving. Randolph accepted this as usual. He never judged and remained on the sidelines at her weddings, funerals, and multiple murder charges. Similar to Donald, she was always acquitted. They never found foul play, attributing the deaths to lousy luck or pre-existing medical conditions.

The time came when their acquired wealth far exceeded their wildest imaginations. What worried Randolph was that a team of detectives hired by the oldest sibling from her last husband was awful close to discovering their dark truth. For this reason, Randolph dissolved their partnership. Beatrice agreed, yet her obsessive compulsiveness and fondness for the hunt consumed her virtue. Twice within the first year, she approached Randolph with new prospects, which he unequivocally shut down. One year later, she threatened to expose Randolph if he did not poison her latest mark, Brian—a very dear and close friend to Randolph. His money would double their worth. This impasse presented only one solution. It was time to sever their relationship.

Amanda understood why the press labeled Beatrice North America's most ruthless Black Widow. Randolph contended that some people needed constant conflict to feel alive. Randolph made Amanda look at herself in the mirror. She, too, was cut from the same cloth. For this reason, she needed to look deep and hard into her soul; otherwise, one day, she would not be able to walk away. Randolph expressed that this was the reason for openly conveying his life story. If Amanda had not learned to control her anger, manage her emotions, and cover her tracks, she would have ended up like Beatrice. Amanda asked if he had killed her. Randolph asserted that Beatrice killed herself. Amanda asked if he believed the family curse was real. Randolph insisted that people like them must live by a code. Not unethical like the common thief, but organized, with character and structure. Killing was never fashionable. It was a necessity. One had to know their limitations. Randolph insisted this was a life lesson. Amanda was now in control of her destiny. Like Donald and directly him, she would one day change the family's trajectory.

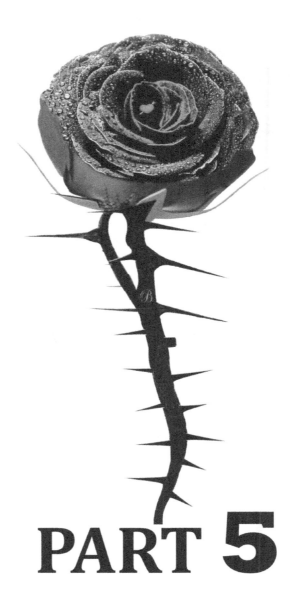

PART 5

Chapter 19

PRESENT DAY - JULY FORTH - WEEKEND BASH

"**D**o you even grasp the definition of best friends?" Amanda yells over the jabbering crowd and upbeat dance music.

Tamara frowns. "Don't pay attention to her."

James regards Tamara yet glances back at Amanda. She has both hands on the rail at the top of the staircase. Her stare looks downright furious. She has shown him the same cold, blank eyes many times before. James turns and follows Tamara down a Bluestone walkway to the lake.

By name, a well-defined man in white shorts, a t-shirt and flip flops, a sailor cap, and dark Ray-Bans greets Tamara. He opens the rope lining the perimeter of a manicured rectangular lawn in front of a white sandy beach—an exclusive tanning area reserved for the sisters and their boy toys. The sand feels thick but soft, and the water, contrasting with the blue sky, looks three shades darker. The circumference of the lake covers well over three miles. To the right, a dock extends out a few hundred feet. Multiple ski boats, a handful of wave runners, and paddle boarders are buzzing about. On the far side, two people get lofted airborne by a bright pink parasail with the word CAT in black. To the left, three sand volleyball courts parallel two giant stacks of black speakers.

A female attendant covers three adjustable sun chairs with white towels. She places water and spray bottles on the squared tables. Tamara orders beers while James takes in the surroundings. Some of the female sunbathers look bronzed, while others are gravely white. Some are topless, others completely nude, even the males. Yet, all of them have their chairs facing the sun.

Tamara peels off her white mesh sun skirt and steps out of her black lace-up stiletto pumps. She lowers her white cat eye sunglasses to the tip of her upturned petite nose. "So, are you going to peel off that shirt and stay awhile, or are you only going to gawk?"

James feels tense now that Amanda has entered the picture. The sun never felt so good. In a way, it revitalizes him. James takes his time applying sunscreen to Tamara. She slightly moans, mainly while he works her shoulders down to her slim waist. James loves that her mini bathing suit bottoms barely cover her perfect ass. Her smooth skin and curves feel amazing. James holds back his growing desire; well, at least he tries. Tamara takes her time applying his lotion. Strategically digging her fingers below the elastic band of his board shorts and playfully reaching up through the leg hollows.

James manages to soften enough to sit up without too much embarrassment. He raises his legs to disguise his bulge while taking the cold beer from the waitress.

Tamara toasts. "To the first day of many!"

The grog soothes his parched throat. James glances at his watch. The big hand is a quarter down, and the little one barely exceeds the number ten. He grins. "Vacation, right?"

Tamara winks and takes a gulp. "God, I love Mexican beer. Especially on a hot summer day with the love of my life by my side."

James blushes.

By noon, eight of the VIP chairs are full. Randy has the attendant bring a cold one for Momoko. She managed to squeeze a few hours off. Twice, Pricilla stopped by and chatted with Tamara. Every chance she got, her baby blues would connect with James. All the sisters stared, their eyes devouring his body as if waiting for their turn. By the time Amanda arrives, the champagne is flowing. James sticks to beer. For Randy, it didn't matter. He consumed anything put in front of him.

Amanda looks stunning in her Brazilian black two-piece, especially straddling her two boy toys. James finds it hard not to stare. They are wearing black socks with ten embroidered red hearts around their packages. What makes the situation even more uncomfortable is that Amanda insists the other women make room for her between Pricilla and Tamara.

Pricilla installs her bikini top and stands. "Ladies! Gather round." She waves. On cue, the women assemble. Some are topless. With their arms wrapped in a circular huddle, they chant. "We're naughty and nice with honor and price, from coast to coast, our hearts tucked tight, through thick and thin, always sisters—the grandest of things." They all grab a flute from the tray and gulp down the golden fluid.

James finds himself puzzled. Amanda's proximity poses a challenge. The way he feels about Tamara, nothing could tear them apart. James truly loves her—at least, his throbbing unit does. Somehow, James feels Amanda will hamper things. The way her cold eyes stared when she arrived spelled trouble.

"Felines on the prowl," Randy boasts.

James hears Randy loud and clear, but his stare

remains frozen. Ten beautiful vixens, arms entwined, and legs and feet moving in rhythm to the upbeat music. "Felines?" He finally replies.

Randy sits on the edge of his chair. "That's what they call themselves."

James narrows his eyes. "Cats?"

"I don't know for sure. Scuttlebutt talk says it's some secret union they've named after the domesticated four-legged mouser. But don't quote me. Look at them. They have ulterior motives. And what's up with the chant? It's right out of the doll diaries." Randy turns his attention to Amanda's two boy toys devouring overstuffed burritos. They appear oblivious to what the women are conversing about.

"They do seem unusually connected. Sorority sisters?" James asks.

"Not even close. Pricilla, Amanda, and Tamara are a given. The rest, I have no idea. They all live by a higher standard than you and I."

"That's obvious! Look at this place. We're way out of their league."

"What I'd give to be on the permanent 'A' list."

James finds Randy's humor dry. "Be careful what you wish for."

"The word on the street, they took a sacred oath. A ritual, like joining the Marines—once a Marine, always a Marine. Hoorah!" Randy pumps his fist.

James grins.

They both turn to the whine of a fleet of approaching wave runners. In unison, the drivers beach them and run back towards the dock. The women separate and join their men.

"Okay, boys, it's time to have some fun." Tamara points towards the water. "You see those two orange buoys next to the dock? Start there and follow the course around the lake. Make sure you pass through each set of smaller buoys. Miss one, and you're automatically eliminated. The fastest time wins first place—one hundred points. Second, seventy-five, third, fifty, and fourth, you get it."

"A race?" James queries.

Randy vigorously rubs his hands together. "Man, oh

man, this is going to be fun. One at a time or all together?"

Tamara giggles. "One at a time, speed racer. We don't want anyone getting hurt. Besides, we know how elevated testosterone levels control those brains of yours."

"What are the points all about?"

Tamara straddles James and digs her toes under his legs. "Come Monday, the team with the most gets first prize."

Randy pounds his fist. "First class tickets to Tahiti for two."

Tamara grins. "Don't you wish, but way better? Think of it like a balancing act. The more points we rack up, the more donations we receive." She prods her head. "All those guests on the other lawn. Every one of them wants to be on this side. Why? Because they envy us. It's the Joker and the Ace of Spades together!"

James knows he comes from the same mold. Not underprivileged, not living large, not in the least, yet here he sits. The theme of the music changes. A hard rock classic, the Ace of Spades by the band Motorhead. The crowd screams. A chill circulates from hoots and hollers and yells of approval. James looks about. Everyone, especially on the opposite lawn and the dock, even the volleyball players, stopped as if anticipating this very tune. The sisters have their arms flailing in the air.

A familiar voice catches his attention. James turns and watches Dorian standing on a scissor lift ascend high above the pool. His white shorts and green spiked hair stand out below the blue sky. His Frank Sinatra voice through the microphone sounds fantastic. Like everyone else, he's dancing. The volume spikes again. Following suit, the sisters step onto the sturdy wooden serving tables and begin singing and dancing as if rehearsing this song multiple times. Everyone participates except Randy and James.

Randy slaps James on his back and begins dancing with Momoko. Tamara jumps down, takes a sip of champagne, and wraps her arms around James. She plants a kiss and pushes some liquid into his mouth.

Naturally, James accepts and begins dancing.

The song ends, the volume decreases, and Golden Years from David Bowie plays. The crowd settles. Tamara hugs James and wipes some sweat from his forehead.

"God, I love you. And you dance divinely."

The games begin. James places third in the wave runner drill. Randy is second, missing first by a minute. He nearly planted the nose of his craft twice, cutting the corners so sharply. The beers were flowing, and he was hooting and hollering like a kid in a candy store. The sand volleyball games were next. The sisters won the first match against the guests—ten-on-ten—by two. Tamara turned out to be the star, spiking and digging like a seasoned athlete. Amanda did not fare so well. She looked out of place, similar to Pricilla and three others.

Both team games with the men turned ugly. Twice, fights broke out. Randy and James played with Amanda's boy toys. Happily, they put on shorts and were surprisingly athletic. James was the tallest and the best spiker. James played indoors in high school and college.

Randy was designated the sandman. By the end, he was covered from head to toe.

The Ace of Spades played again before lunch, sparking a frenzy. This time, two sexy girls were strutting their stuff on the scissor lift. Lunch on the sand included lobster, shrimp, and salad. The guests helped themselves from three buffet-style carts near the pool. Drinks flowed from three separate thatched Tahitian-style bars.

Amazingly, Tamara and Amanda behaved. Twice, they walked down to the water's edge to chat. Pricilla joined them once as they cooled their sexy bodies. At one point, Amanda leaned over and whispered to Tamara. As Amanda turned and returned to the chair, her face looked puzzled.

Over the next thirty minutes or so, Tamara remained subdued. Finally, when Dorian introduced the waterskiing competition, she confronted James.

"Baby, how'd you feel?" Her question seemed to sit on the edge of his tongue.

"Alive! Amazingly alive! It's been forever since I've

felt this good or had this much fun. Please, don't let it stop."

Tamara smiles, showing off her dimples. "You're an extraordinary person, James Rawlings. Remember that."

James stares. "Thanks. So are you. Why the suddenness? Are you worried?"

Tamara glances at Amanda, her glare showing impatience. "I, umm, hey, listen. Bear with me, please." She clears her throat. "Don't look at her. That's what she wants."

James shakes his head. "Did she threaten you?"

"No! No! She wants me to ask you something."

James considers her words while wiping his perspiring hands on the towel. "Okay. What?"

Tamara glances at Amanda without moving her head. Her eyes have welled. "Two things! She wants you to know she still loves you. She never stopped."

James corrects her. "No, you're mistaken. She's never loved me. It was all a lie. I was too young and dumb to realize it." He grabs her hands. "Listen. I love you. I know in my heart this to be true." James scraps her fingernails over the palm of his hand. "This simple yet tender touch sends a shiver through my body."

Tamara scratches his palm again. Tears drip down her cheeks. She sniffles. "Mine too. I've never experienced anything like you before. I can barely breathe right now."

James smiles. "What else?"

"She wants to talk?"

"With me!"

"Yeah, she promised to be kind and gentle. You should go. It might help with closure."

James shakes his head slightly. "You sure?"

Tamara nods. "Let's clear the air." Tamara inhales deeply and wipes her nose and eyes with the towel. She glances toward Amanda and nods.

Amanda nods back and immediately walks to the water with one of her boy toys. He pushes a wave runner out. Amanda climbs aboard, starts the engine, and aggressively speeds away.

James looks stunned. "Out there?"

"Yep, I'll wait here." Tamara leans over and kisses

James softly. She whispers. "I love you, James Rawlings."
She abruptly stands. "I have to use the restroom.
Amanda is very impatient." Tamara winks and walks
away.

Chapter 20

James guns the throttle and sends a water spray high into the air.

Randy yells. "Hey! Wait for me."

James catches a glimpse but disregards him and follows Amanda's wake. He easily closes. She stops twenty or so meters from the timbered shoreline. Her stare sends a shiver through his bones as he feathers the boat in reverse and glides to the side of hers.

"Bit far for simple conversation," James says aggressively.

Amanda grins. She removes her sunglasses and stares.

Her hesitation disturbs James.

"You ride that crotch rocket pretty good." She finally expresses.

James smiles and straightens his glasses. "Thanks.

You're not so bad yourself."

"You're sweet!" Amanda looks towards the property. She can hear the slight thump of the music over the purr of the idling vessels. "Beautiful house. Did you know Pricilla owns half of the lake?"

James glares. "No, I didn't. Amanda, you didn't bring me out here to bore me with small talk. What'd you want?"

"Relax, James. I've never seen you so defensive! You must be mad at me. I'm so sorry for how I treated you at the park. My father sent me on a wild goose chase to Australia. I signed documents for a new start-up business."

James scoffs, knowing the truth. "He hasn't heard of the internet?"

Amanda laughs. "Funny! Sweetheart, I said I'm sorry. I tend to absorb myself completely when I travel. I admit, sometimes I can be a bitch."

James sighs. "Sometimes!"

Amanda frowns. She straightens her posture, purposefully protruding her cleavage.

Of course, James looks. Amanda is stunning, especially in her micro Brazilian. James considers removing his sunglasses but finds talking easier with his eyes blocked. His hands are sweating, yet he feels confident. "Amanda, not so long ago, my world revolved around two people—you and my mom. I was a love-sick fool."

Amanda shakes her head. "I'm so sorry about your mom."

"I know, and thanks. But recently, things have changed."

Amanda narrows her eyes. She nervously grabs the handlebars. "I noticed."

James raises his hands. "Like you, time has changed me. It just took longer. Listen, I still love you, but not as my soul mate anymore."

"That bitch."

Frustration fills James. He removes his glasses. "You don't get it. My feelings for you changed long before I met her. She had nothing to do with my decision. You did this all on your own. What triggered it was the way you left me hanging at the park. Amanda, I'm done crying for you and done waiting for you. I finally see you for who you are. My friend and I cherish that."

Amanda tightens her face. "Did she tell you that?"

James rubs his chin, confused. "You didn't hear a word I said, did you?"

Amanda looks towards the property. "I don't believe

you."

"Well, it's true."

"Really."

"Yeah!" He installs his sunglasses.

"It sounded rehearsed. Tell me something. How'd you end up at this party? Think about it. You don't belong here. You and your friend Randy, come on. Look at all the other guys. You two don't fit."

"What'd you mean?"

Amanda scoffs. "Tamara knew the rules. She was supposed to bring two bisexual men. You do know what that means."

"You have sex with them?"

Amanda frowns. "James, you can't be that naïve?"

James looks stunned. "Why'd you bring me out here?"

"Because I love you. James, I've never stopped. You're mine. We made a pact—our ten kisses. You promised to wait, no matter what. You do remember those words, don't you?"

"Of course. I held our pact true to my heart until I finally understood."

"What'd you mean by that?" Amanda shows longing.

"You use people, Amanda. You've used me from day

one. I can't let you do that anymore."

"She told you that, didn't she?"

A suppressed anger courses. James understands her interrogation-style questions can only mean she is searching for answers. "First of all, she's innocent! I'll repeat it. Tamara had nothing to do with my decision to release you. You did that all by yourself. The years of dreaming and holding onto a distant memory of what I thought was true love, especially after my mom died, surfaced. Amanda, up to a few months ago, you were my angel."

Her eyes soften. "I still am, James. I'm still your angel. Just all grown up."

"You sure have a diluted way of showing it."

"We all have our faults. Mine, well, they're more pronounced." Amanda answers sadly.

James shakes his head. "No, you're cut from a different mold. You're cold, like your father. Damaged."

"How would you know? You don't even know him."

"That's right; he made sure of that."

Amanda looks surprised.

"You don't remember, do you? It was our first day of Kindergarten. I presented you with a flower and poem."

"Sure, I do. I think about that day all the time."

"Really! What kind of flower was it?"

Amanda wrinkles her nose and looks down. "A rose! James, you always gave me a red rose."

James smirks. "Nice try. It was a yellow dandelion. I can still recite the poem. Over the years, those remembered words kept my love for you alive. Can you?"

"That's not fair; it was a long time ago." Amanda glares. "Geez, I'm sorry. What does the poem have to do with my dad?"

"After I recited it, he walked up and rubbed my hair. He told me my chivalry was gratifying. He started talking to my mom. He invited her over for cocktails and dinner but never followed through. I mean, I asked her to come over. Did you find it odd that I never received an invite to one of your birthday parties? At the time, it didn't matter. My love for you was unconditional. But now, it proves my point."

Amanda apologizes, claiming she always put him on the list, but her father removed him, maintaining his family was too poor to bring a proper gift. She cleverly changes the subject. "Look at this place. It was no coincidence. More, a deliberate act of selfishness. Planned out to the finest details."

"I know this might be hard for you to absorb, but Tamara and I—"James shakes his head. "We only met recently."

"Yeah, I know. At the Swing Door!"

"We told you at breakfast." James grins.

"What's it been, a month?"

"Just under! She started bartending three weeks ago. But I, I mean, we never."

"Went out on a date. Kissed! Fucked! Doesn't it seem odd? She asks two total strangers to be her guests at one of the year's most talked about private parties. I mean, come on?"

"It didn't happen so premeditated. Tamara invited us casually, on a whim, as friends. It was spontaneous."

Amanda looks away. She blinks multiple times while rubbing her bottom lip with her finger. "James! She's playing you. I told you her uncle owns the bar."

"So what! She's a pretty damn good bartender and attractive to boot. If I were the owner, I'd hire her!"

Amanda grins. She pauses. "I told her about you."

"Told who about what?" James demands.

"Tamara! Did you know that we're sorority sisters?"

"Yeah, So what! I have fraternity bros as well."

"I told her everything, from the moment we met in the park at the monkey bars to your mom, how she got sick, and the rose bushes. James, she knows every detail of what happened in the tree fort: our pledge, our first ten kisses, and even how we bonded when the plane fell out of the sky —everything down to the last detail."

James opens his mouth, but no words emerge.

"James, I'm sorry I was the one to tell you this. You have to believe me. She's using you to get back at me."

"For what?"

Amanda looks around nervously. "She's jealous."

"Of you?"

"Yes, of me! It has something to do with her last boyfriend. He left her, and, well, we ended up dating. She's done it to me so many times. Long story short. She uses people to get what she wants. The notches on her wall go deep. Pretty impressive."

James sighs. "You know what; I don't care if she's jealous or angry, or how many notches or whatever. Amanda, this is about you and me. We need to close this chapter and move on. Look at yourself. I don't think you know who you are anymore."

"That's cruel, James! Downright cruel! The way you've

been looking at me all morning. You must hate me?"

James shakes his head. "On the contrary! I could never hate you. You have a special place in my heart. It's!" James looks down at the console—precisely at the RPM gauge. He feels amazingly confident and removes his glasses. "Amanda, you and I are done. I finally found the courage to accept you for what you are." He looks towards the house. "Look, I've gotta get back."

"And what's that?"

"This might sound twisted, but you're an interrogator."

"A what?"

"A person who steals or drains energy from people. Like my father."

"Quite the imagination! James, I never met your father."

"I know. I was comparing." James installs his glasses. "Look, I'm not good at conveying emotions or feelings." He sighs. "I know you love me; I get that, but not as a soul mate. Until a few months ago, I thought you would complete me harmoniously and spiritually. I loved you unconditionally. In my eyes, you were my angel, my missing piece. After the last time you ditched me, I came to terms with reality. I finally understood there was no balance between us. Our relationship was one-sided. I was in love with an adolescent idea. Blind to the fact I was the fool and you, well, you were the queen. Amanda, what became clear is that I don't think you can love anyone."

"That's cold!" Amanda frowns.

James looks sorrowful. "I'm sorry. I didn't mean to go there."

"She told you that, didn't she?"

James raises his hands. "You never stop, do you? Whatever game you're playing, stop. She told me you wanted to talk about closure."

"She didn't waste any time, did she?"

James looks dispelled. "You're kidding, right?"

"On the contrary, James, you're too naÃ¯ve to see it."

A deep sigh follows.

Amanda grins, this time showing her teeth.

"Amanda, I don't wanna fight. There will always be a special place in my heart for you. I'll always care, but I've moved on. I'm sorry."

With a gentle push, he separates the vessels and accelerates away. In his wake, he feels relieved—a huge weight lifted from his shoulders. On the flip side, he might have opened Pandora's box.

Chapter 21

James finger locks hands with Tamara. She squeezes. "You ready?"

Tamara stands, sticks two fingers in her mouth, and whistles piercingly. "I was born ready. Let's win this."

James looks left and nods at Randy and Momoko. They both have bright green bandanas wrapped around their foreheads, a layer of bright yellow sunscreen on their lips, and a florescent pink scarf securing his left ankle to her right. They have inscribed their team name —Ninja Rebels, on their foreheads with red lipstick. Randy grunts and gives James the thumbs-down signal.

"In your dreams," James roars proudly. James looks past Pricilla at the other teams and then at Amanda. Her stare has remained unyielding since returning. Amanda grins and blows him a kiss.

Tamara gently turns his head. "Baby, don't concern yourself about her right now. After this silly contest, I promise we'll go to the room and talk. Besides, we both could use some downtime."

Her wonderful face consumes James. "You called me baby. My mom always did."

Tamara shows sadness. "I'm sorry. I didn't mean to go there."

James softly kisses her lips. "No! No, no, she! Trust me. It's a good thing." James inhales. "First, we win this race, okay."

Her eyes begin too well. Tamara sniffles while nodding left. "See the blonde over there with Mr. Tarzan. They'll be our biggest challenge. She's ultra-competitive, and he looks, well—"

James wipes a tear. "Don't worry about them. Out of the gate, let them take the lead. Our strategy will be to stay close. The rest will come naturally. When the time's right, I'll give you a signal. Trust me."

"Okay. But remember Randy with team Ninja on his

forehead. I have a feeling he's pretty good at this."

James softly traces the red letters T&R on Tamara's forehead. "Team, Tamara, and Rawlings. It sounds so perfect." He inhales lightly. "Don't worry about Randy. He can't win."

"How'd you know?"

They watch Randy down another shot.

"You get it?" James grins.

"Yeah, he's drunk as a skunk."

"Exactly! Just follow my lead."

The ten teams line up, and the starting gun booms. An unbridled roar from the guests erupts. Dorian calls the race, standing high above on the scissor lift. In the background, the classic song Tequila from the band The Champs plays.

"And they're off!" Dorian announces. "Team Tarzan takes the early lead, followed closely by T&R, then Ninja, and in a close fourth, the Queenies, followed by the Strikers."

Cheers rise above the booming music.

Dorian continues. "They're closing on the first turn.

Oh no! Team Sexy, the Pornos, and Team Amanda have collided. They're all disqualified for spilling their shots."

The crowd cheers as a handful of servants untie their legs. They all stand and down a fresh shot that a very sexy brunette wearing an oversized Sombrero pours. They turn their attention to the race.

"Team Tarzan and Team T&A now have a commanding lead. Oh, my God! They're now stride for stride down the final stretch." Dorian announces.

James glances at team Tarzan. Claire's sidekick, a very tall steroid-type muscle man, towers over her head by at least a foot and a half. James knows he will ultimately be their downfall. At full speed, his stride will surely burden hers. James squeezes his arm tight around Tamara.

"You ready to win this." He shouts

"Let's do it!" Tamara acknowledges while concentrating on balancing the shot glass.

Together, James and Tamara inch ahead. In a frantic attempt to keep pace, Claire misses a step, and they tumble to the ground. Tamara and James cross the finish line five steps before Randy and the others.

After their victory shot and staying clear of Amanda, Tamara, and James work their way to the room. The way Amanda continually eyeballs them can only mean she must be planning her revenge. Tamara has experienced her wrath far too many times to ignore it.

The air-conditioned ambiance refreshes their clammy bodies. Tamara and James barely descend the stairs before their bathing attire drops to the floor. In a fierce passion, they purge their desires.

Exhausted, they fall on the bed. James laughs, thinking about how many places they have violated throughout the apartment. Tamara runs her fingers down his spine. She stops at his Venus dimples and circles them. She traces his eyebrows, follows his nose down, and kisses him, first on the neck, then his cheek, and then his lips. Her tongue sends a shiver through his spine. Tamara sits up and positions two pillows behind her back. She pats the mattress, prompting James to join her.

"Baby, what happened out there on the lake?

Honestly, she's scaring the shit out of me. I've never seen Amanda so crazed."

James shrugs and clears his throat. "Where do I start?"

"From the beginning!"

James describes the finer details and pauses with a sigh. "She said she confided in you about me."

"Really?" Her eyes widen. "How'd you mean?"

"Everything."

"I'm sorry you had to experience her lies—none of the sisters like Amanda. We put up with her radical behavior because of our oath. Pricilla especially! She's the reason we're such a close-knit band. Her faith in our unification keeps us together." Tamara climbs on top and straddles James. "Baby, there's so much you don't know, so much I want to tell you." She inhales deeply. "I don't know where to start."

James grasps her waist. "God, you feel so amazing." He kisses her stomach. "I never thought I'd experience the touch and the taste of such a sensual sweet woman." James takes in her femininity.

Tamara furrows her brows. "Wow! You continue to amaze me." She grinds her torso gently to his growing hardness. "Seriously! Again!"

Her words only increase his desires. "I hope, I mean —shoot." Self-conscious, James reaches between her legs, grabs his shaft, and straightens it behind her backside. He then purposefully pushes her body back a few inches. "I hope you don't think I'm a sex maniac. I can't help myself. I'm so hard right now—" He breathes deeply, staring at her chest.

Tamara leans forward and kisses James. She has never felt so intimate before. A cozy feeling rushes. She grips what she considers the best love tool she has ever fondled. Her breathing matches his. Again, as their kiss becomes one, she carefully maneuvers him inside, and in a frenzy of unbridled passion, they both explode. It ends in utter exhaustion.

Tamara inhales through her nose. "Oh, my God! Your fucking amazing!" She adjusts the pillow behind her head.

James climbs out of bed, cleans up, and returns with

a few water bottles and a moist towel. He dives headfirst under the sheet and playfully squiggles his way up past her legs. He pops his head out and sits up. "I feel amazing like I'm floating on cloud nine. Don't let it stop. Kiss me, now."

Tamara leans over. "Thanks, baby. I love how thoughtful you are." She sighs. "I never knew I could feel so together, alive, and in love."

James vents ever so slightly. "What were we talking about?"

"Amanda spilled the beans."

James gestures. "Not the entire can."

Tamara grins. "You're funny!"

"I love the fact you recognize that. I'm finding you more and more interesting by the minute."

"Why, thank you! I'm unsure if you know this, but Amanda has a dark side."

"She's a vampire!" James claws the air.

Tamara raises her hands and pretends to bite his neck. A playful bliss follows. "I'd call it her shadow. It follows her everywhere."

"Psych 101. We all have dark sides."

"Sure, but with her, it runs extra deep."

"How so?"

"She's sociopathic, a sadist in simpler terms. It doesn't matter. Women, men, old, young, it's all about power and control. Amanda gets pleasure from inflicting pain. Be it emotionally, financially, or even psychologically. She bakes in her glory. If you get on her bad side, she won't back down until she has her revenge."

"That's scary shit."

"Tell me about it. Trust me; Amanda is hardwired and never loses. Do you want to know why?"

James fluffs the sheet. "Sure, but I think I know. Her father, right."

"How'd you know?"

"Even though I only met him once, his love for her is inseparable. Am I right?"

"Spot on. Over the six years I've known Amanda, she's had seven assault charges. One captured on video. She smashed a guy in the face with a wooden lamp at a mid-semester party. Supposedly, he denied her sex. She broke his nose. The campus police detained her, but within an hour, they released her. The poor schmuck dropped the charges. The Manchester family never loses, especially in court."

"That explains everything."

Tamara pauses. "The way Amanda was glaring earlier." Her facial expression concerns me. "I've seen that cold stare before. The first time was the day I moved into the sorority house. She returned from a weekend getaway with her father. The sisters said it was sudden, like a death in the family or something. Amanda cornered me in my room and warned me never to cross her. Being I was the new girl, I accepted, but it was how she glared with those big dark eyes that scared me."

"Do you think she's plotting to harm us right here in front of everyone?"

Tamara nods. "Absolutely! Baby, she's plum crazy. Especially when she drinks, I'll bet she's already called her father."

James stares out the window. "She's been sucking

them down pretty much all day."

Tamara chooses her following words carefully. "I think she's capable of murder."

James sits up. "Really! Do you think she already has?"

Tamara leans over and softly kisses James. "Yes, but I can't prove it, at least not yet."

His conviction builds. "How'd you come to this conclusion?"

"When she drinks, multiple personalities come out. Sometimes violent, but mostly her animalistic sexual jealous side. It took three years for her even to consider me a friend. Another two for her to open up. And believe me, it was like pulling teeth, especially for her to give up the info on you."

"Really!" James shakes his head. "Her demons must run deep."

"They've consumed her soul."

"How so?"

"It has to do with her father—some ritualistic covenant connecting with Pricilla."

"Sounds diabolical."

"It is."

"Given her agenda, why do you suppose Amanda told you about me?"

"I don't know. I'm wondering myself."

"Do you suppose it was pre-meditated?"

"It could be. I swear she has bipolar disorder. Her mood swings range from depressive to downright crazy mean. Two years ago, she had a nervous breakdown. Her father collected her. Amanda returned three weeks later. What I found concerning was that she was relaxed for the first few months—almost a different person. That's when she started confiding in me."

"She must be frantic, upside down right now."

They both look out the window as the slight thump of the music from below increases.

"She's trying to grasp why I dumped her," James asks.

"Exactly! It's freaking her out. No one has ever dumped her before."

"How much time do you think we have."

"I don't know."

"I'm curious about something."

"You want more sex?"

"Funny! Let's save the fun stuff for later tonight. I know you like me, maybe even love me, but answer me something. Why'd you take the job at the Swing Door? I'm sure it wasn't about the money. You're a trust fund babe, right?"

"Thanks for noticing."

They chuckle.

"I took it for personal reasons. Since graduating, I've become complacent. I needed something else—the human aspect. Stimulation, which I couldn't duplicate traveling or hanging with friends."

"It's better than going to church."

"Tell me about it. I never knew how much fun it was."

"You said reasons."

"Truthfully, I wanted to meet you in person. Who was the real James Rawlings? The mystery man I heard so much about. I knew you visited the establishment;

this was a neutral place for an introduction. I'm not as forward as Amanda."

James looks perplexed. "How'd you know the Swing Door was my hangout?"

"Amanda? But please believe me, not once did I spy or stalk you. There's so much I need to tell you about her, but first, I need to talk about someone else."

James shrugs. "Okay. Who?"

Tamara clears her throat— "Me!"

Chapter 22

Tamara finger locks her hand with James and squeezes.

James captures her intensity. "You sure you want to talk about this right now? It can wait until after the weekend."

Tamara nods favorably. "It's important."

James gives her his attention. "All right, but first, answer me something."

Tamara perks up.

"I'm curious. When was the first time you saw me in person?"

Her face turns to puzzlement. "Before the bar?"

"Yes, was it a few months, a year, longer?"

Tamara ponders. "It was more like five, and it was

random. At least, I think so."

"Years?"

She tightens her lips and slowly nods.

"You're not sure?"

"At the time, it seemed purely coincidental. It was my sophomore year. We were returning from a weekend trip to Mexico. Amanda and I flew back through New York City. She wanted me to meet her father. He arranged lunch at the Waldorf Astoria. We both exited the taxi, and Amanda saw you pushing through the crowded sidewalk. She stared. I mean, downright serious. She was so intrigued we tailed you to the Double Tree Hotel on Fifty-First Street."

James perks up. "You're not going to believe this, but I remember that day vividly. Let's see, two of the most stunning women, a brunette wearing a concise pink summer dress and black pumps extenuating her long slender legs." James observes Tamara. "The other one was a drop-dead gorgeous blonde. Behind pink lips and wonderfully alluring eyes was the face of an angel. Both could turn the heads of even the pickiest of men."

"My blonde phase."

James strokes her hair. "That was you!"

"Yep."

"Both colors suit you."

"Thanks."

"I looked twice, didn't I?"

Tamara thinks. "Three times. I looked as well. You were very handsome."

James blushes. "I had no idea it was Amanda. I hadn't seen her since she was ten." He shrugs. "You followed me?"

"No, she did. I was the tag-along. Besides, you were too busy talking on your phone."

"Business."

"Likely story!" Tamara playfully punches his shoulder.

"I'm flattered."

"About six months later, she started opening up. I earned her trust by not telling anyone about you. Come to find out, she kept tabs on you for years."

"Seriously! Like stalking?"

"Kinda, but I'd call it more observing. Nothing creepy or out of the ordinary."

"Sounds obsessive."

"At first, I thought so too. I confronted Amanda. She insisted she loved you. She showed me two pictures. One, you were ten, and the other one looked like you do now. Because you lost your mom at such a young age, one day, she would rescue you."

"From what?"

"Yourself."

James scoffs. "She's the one needing rescue. No, let me rephrase, a straight-jacket."

"I agree. I found a scrapbook. Most pictures were of you at your house, driving in your car, going to work, or entering and exiting the swing door. That's how I knew about the bar. She has no idea I saw it."

"Now I'm concerned. How did Amanda acquire them? The internet?"

"I don't know. A private detective! I overheard her talking to her dad on the phone. Something about renewing his expense account."

"Didn't you think it bordered on creepy stalker weird or maybe serial killer ridiculous? There has to be some delusional motivation. Think about it. Why would someone cling to a childhood relationship they found downright offensive? If love were part of the equation, she would have approached me, right?"

"Yes, and yes, and yes," Tamara sighs. "I don't know. I'm sorry I was the one to tell you. I feel awful."

"Does Pricilla know?"

Tamara shakes her head. "No! Not that I'm aware of. It bothered me horribly, but it wasn't my place to cause friction. I couldn't." She looks with sad puppy dog eyes. "I'm not who you think I am."

His stare widens. "You mean, you're not a woman!"

Pillow foreplay commences. Tamara takes a hit to the side of the head, which stops the action. After a short cool down, they reposition the pillows, settle upright, and fluff the sheet.

"You okay?"

"Yeah, my head is pretty thick," he chuckles. "James!" A deepened sigh vents. "Please, don't judge me immoral for what I'm about to reveal. You don't know this, but I was born and raised in Texas."

"Hee-haw. I had no idea. What happened to your charming Southern twang?"

"I was forced to shed it, homogenize myself with the culture and expression of the North East."

"So, you've turned into a Yankee brat."

"Your humor invigorates me."

"Listen, pumpkin. I don't care if you were born on the moon. What matters is who you are inside." James points to her heart. "You're a keeper."

Tamara grins. "That's sweet, but how'd you know?"

James shrugs. "That you have a heart of gold?"

"No, but thanks. My dad calls me pumpkins."

"Dumb luck, I guess. It flowed. You bring out the best in me."

Her eyes widen and well.

James leans over, wipes a tear, and kisses her cheek.

Tamara sniffles. "You're so sweet. Okay, here goes." She clears her throat. "With the help of my father, mid-semester during my freshman year at Texas A&M, which was the school of my dreams, I canceled my tennis scholarship and transferred to Brown."

James looks dumbfounded.

Tamara presses her finger to his lips. "Shhh—it's your turn to listen."

James nods and exhales.

"I know this might sound unbelievable, but I'm at the top of my tennis game. Life was amazing. I beat a top seed, and my rank soared to number two. My grades were stellar. My sweetheart of a boyfriend and my family supported me at any crossroads. Suddenly, in a Texas heartbeat, my life changed. I learned my sister, Samantha, who moved to the East Coast to attend Brown, disappeared. The note she left said she quit school and was off to discover the world with her boyfriend. She apologized for the suddenness and promised to keep in touch."

"I had no idea."

"Baby, my sis would have never run away. She was motivated by college, her career, her family, and her kids. That's all she ever wanted in that order. At any rate, the police determined, they both quit school to chase love. A week later, they closed the case. I became obsessed. My dad hired a private detective. Long story short, after weeks of investigation, the detective believed Amanda had something to do with their disappearance. The problem was the leads went cold."

James looks flabbergasted. "So, your motivation revolves around discovering what happened to your sister."

Tamara tightens her lips. "We were inseparable."

James wraps his arms around her. "I'm so sorry for your loss. I had no idea." He kisses her head.

"I believe you."

"You think Amanda had something to do with her disappearance?"

Tamara sniffles. "I'm positive."

"You said the detective found no leads."

"Correct. One trait my father taught me was how to detect when someone was lying."

"Sure, you study their facial and eye expressions. But it takes years of practice."

"Believe me, I've had tons. My dad drilled Samantha and I for years. He insisted, especially since we were female and came from wealth, that this would help distinguish, or as he would say, weed out the bad guys, the users, and the gold diggers. Without giving away, I was her sister; the first time I confronted Amanda about Samantha and her boyfriend, I knew she was hiding something. Yet, six years later, I'm no further from finding the truth than the private detective. I still can't prove a thing."

"What about your mom?"

"She has no clue. She believes God will summon Samantha when the time's right; she'll realize she misses her family and come home."

"What'd you think?"

"Like my dad, I'm a realist. He lets my mom keep hope. We both know the truth."

James stares with nervous eyes. "What's that?"

"She's dead. Her boyfriend, too! The day she went missing, we both experienced a fleeting touch."

"That's terrible! I felt something similar when my

mom passed. It was the saddest day of my life. My throat closed up, and I couldn't talk for weeks."

"Baby, I'm sorry. I'm so sorry. I wish I could have been there for you."

"Thanks. There's comfort knowing your sympathy comes from the heart." James gestures with a delicate nod. "What kept me going was that my mom promised to watch over me until my true love found me."

"Awe, baby!" They embrace, finding incredible passion in the act. Tamara sighs. "Where did you learn to kiss so perfectly?"

"With you, it comes naturally."

"Good answer, but I think you've had practice."

For the next few minutes, they stare unwaveringly. The muffled thump of the dance music eddying from outside excites them.

"There's a natural purity about you."

Tamara pecks James. "I'm blushing. You know who I am, don't you?"

A tender numbness pours outwards, and his senses are on overload. "Like you know me."

Tamara breaks out in laughter. "Look at us. Lovesick fools. We're playing out the last scene from Romeo and Juliet." Her hands flail. "Your lips are the doorway of my breath. Seal my deal with death with a righteous kiss forever." She pecks James. "Taketh the poison. It is bitter and unsavory. Let us crash this sea-weary ship into the rocks!"

"Your Shakespeare's impressive! You must have played the part."

"Performing arts junior year of high school. Baby, you're my Romeo."

"And you're my Juliet, but let's leave the poison part out."

They chuckle.

Her phone chimes. Tamara leans over, scrolls her finger, and moves her lips while reading. Her thought pattern changes. "Oh, my God!"

James perks up. "Is everything okay?"

Tamara looks puzzled. "About a month ago, the private investigator working the case found traces of dried blood on the inside corner of a bedpost. The results came back. They match my sister's DNA."

This time, James looks concerned. "Who's house?"

"Amanda's!"

"I thought she lived at the sorority house with you?"

"She did, but her dad bought a luxury condominium in downtown Rhode Island, which she used on weekends. Her retreat. A quiet place to study, but we all knew different."

James looks puzzled. "For sex?"

"You sure you want to hear this?"

"Absolutely! Nothing surprises me about her anymore."

"A few of the sisters nick-named it the stabbin' cabin, a private retreat to satisfy her innermost cravings."

His mind churns. James had no idea who Amanda was or what she had become. Indeed, she was not the girl he used to know. "Sorry for being so coy, but did you? I mean, since you knew about this apartment, you must have—you know?"

"Sure, I joined in and participated. Baby, one thing I learned a long time ago was to live forward, never backward. It can only lead to disaster."

"I agree. I promise not to judge you."

"I appreciate that, but no. I've done stupid things I'm not proud of, but I always drew the line when principled morals were concerned. As I said, Amanda has no scruples."

James swallows heavily. Tamara's a cool cat anyway, which way you slice her. "How'd you find the traces of blood?"

Tamara straightens her posture. "The detective used a special light."

"How? I mean common. What, Amanda opened the door and let him search for clues?"

"Of course not, he broke in. Amanda would have never."

James ponders.

"Hey! Don't think too deep. To catch cunning takes cunning. Amanda and her father are downright notorious. Even though this evidence is inadmissible in court, at least we know the truth. It's now my job to expose them."

Her phone chimes again. Tamara reads the text and rolls out of bed. She walks over to the window and stares at the glut of bodies drowning in sun and alcohol. Her eyes wander towards the lake. A partial reflection of the house gleams off the rippled surface. She turns, folds her arms over her chest, and leans her shoulder to the wall. She stares at James unblinking. "In my mind, a feeling of togetherness, security, and wisdom flushes. You remind me so much of my father. Especially how you stare; it's as if you can see right into my soul, which bewilders me. Listen, I know your heart is pure, untarnished, and unscathed from the wickedness of society. In my youth, there was a time of innocence, a time of family where there were no lies or hidden agendas. It was a time when my sister and I, especially on the hottest of summer days, would escape down to the lake. We would sprint down the wooden dock and see who could jump the highest and furthest into the brisk water. We would splash and play and then sit on the edge with our feet dangling and swaying gently above the surface. How we would converse for hours on end about how we would make it in the world outside the comfort and safety of our father. Samantha, the oldest, would leave first. She longed for the day, wishing it would come sooner than later. Her desire to discover the unknown enthralled her."

His warm fingers swath Tamara. She embraces him. Her body feels so good, so safe. James can feel her tremble. She presses her cheek snugly to his smooth chest. For a fleeting moment, he feels secure.

"More bad news?" James caresses her with his bulky hands.

Tamara stares. "My mom misses me. She wants me to come home." She grins. "Baby, you feel so damn good." She tightens her grip.

James sweeps her off her feet, walks over to the bed, and gently sets her down. Even though he feels relaxed around her, being naked, especially standing in front of windows, embarrasses him. He repositions the pillows and pats the mattress with his hand. Tamara snuggles.

"I think I finally understand."

"What'd you mean?" Tamara asks.

"You're different, I mean, than the others."

"You figured that out all on your own?"

"Funny! For one, you're not selfish, snobby, or self-centered. You may pretend to be or try to be, but clearly, that's not your MO."

"And you're the expert?"

James raises his hands in defense.

"So, you think I'm an open book."

"Maybe a bit, but the opposite! You're not the stereotypical left-winged, opinionated rich brat used to getting everything handed on a silver platter."

"Hey, bucko, I come from old wealth."

"That's what I'm talking about. You have a creative side. I see it, yet you keep it hidden. Am I right?"

"You have quite the imagination."

"Prove me wrong."

"I believe the word you're looking for is Poseur. And yes, the sisters believe they possess a refinement of entitlement."

His interest grows. "You have a keen imagination, or you are love-struck."

Tamara leans over and kisses James. "My father told me a long time ago being patient within reflects the virtue of the heart."

"Smart man. He sounds amazing. You must be very close?"

"He means everything to me."

"You're lucky. How about your mom?"

"Same, same! She's amazing. You'd love her. She'd love you. You two would get along fine."

"You sure about that?"

Tamara scoffs. "Truth is, I'm afraid to introduce you. She'll try to steal you away with her down-home Texas hospitality."

"I'll bet she's a peach. My mom was the same."

Tamara puckers her lips. She sniffles. "I'm so sorry for your loss. Baby, I don't know what I would do without my parents. You've endured what I can only imagine."

Chapter 23

A distinct sound startles Tamara. She stares at the door for a moment and then at James. This time, James hears it. Like two kids on edge, they jump out of bed, dress, and stride into the living room.

James nonchalantly plops down at the bar and stares at Randy, standing belly first before the opened double-wide refrigerator. "That's one way of cooling down."

"Oh, my God! It feels so damn good."

Tamara chuckles and glares at the puddle of water dripping from his board shorts. She throws a dish towel on the floor. "The swimming pool seems to have followed you. Grab me a water, please."

Randy grins. "Whoops!" He wipes the floor with his foot and pushes the damp cloth to the corner. "Sorry for the interruption, but a few minutes after you two lovebirds went MIA, the shit hit the fan, if you know what I mean." Randy grabs two bottles of water and closes the fridge. He tosses one to James and sets the other on the counter.

"How so?" James asks, cracking the bottle.

"She's a doozy. Pretty as a princess, but crazy loco in the head." Randy pounds two fingers to the side of his noggin. "You're not going to believe this. About thirty or so after you two disappeared, Amanda had her two boy toys walk through the crowd, even around the pool. When they returned empty-handed, she flipped out, slapping them like the Queen of her own country. Of course, as far as I could tell, they prostrated, and she wouldn't accept their apology. Now get this. She asked Dorian to rally the girls, and she stirred up a beehive full of controversy. Pricilla sent me up here to collect you. She said a 'challenge' has been requested."

Tamara props her head. "Really!"

"Her exact words."

James stands. "What does that mean?"

"Are you two going to duke it out, octagon style?" Randy asks while punching the air.

"Our code requires resolving disputes internally. We have two options—a dual or mediation."

Randy slaps his thigh. "Seriously! A sixteenth-century ten paces, turn and shoot your opponent in the heart dual?"

Tamara scoffs. "Randy, sometimes—" She shakes her head. "We don't use real guns. We don't want to kill each other. We use paint guns. And yes, we count out ten paces, turn and shoot. The winner gets to choose how to resolve the dispute. They can quash it completely, ban it from being discussed again, or sit down with Pricilla as the mediator. Nevertheless, after her ruling, the outcome must be observed as law. If violated, the sisters vote to oust you from the club."

A warm wind funnels through the open deck. Everyone turns as the front door abruptly swings open. A hushed silence follows as if waiting for Amanda to walk in and unleash her wrath.

Randy shrugs. "My bad," he says, striding up the

stairs. He peeks out into the hallway, looks both ways, and closes the door. "I didn't shut it all the way. It must have been the wind."

"Whew!" Tamara vents. "I thought for sure it was her."

Randy looks curiously. "What the hell's going on? Did you two play a trick on her without me? What happened out on the lake?"

Tamara walks towards the bedroom. She turns. "Not everything revolves around deceit and mischief. She's pissed James dumped her." Tamara disappears into the bedroom. A few minutes later, she walks out dressed in baggy blue jeans and a white long-sleeve shirt with her hair tucked under a black western-style cowboy hat.

James stands and gawks.

"Body armor!" She poses.

Randy whistles while reaching slothfully for the bowl of peanuts. Of course, he misses and knocks it away. "Have you done this before?" He grabs a handful and fills his mouth.

"No! Of course not. I'm a regular girly girl, but I've

participated in three paintball tournaments."

Confusion fills James. "Are you seriously going to do this!"

Tamara walks up and softly blows over his face. "I must. Once challenged, I have no choice. Besides, do you think Amanda will choose mediation?"

"I guess you're right." James shakes his head. "My mother always stressed, never become your own enemy. Otherwise, you become vulnerable, a robot. Indefensible and lost in deception."

"She was a wise woman," Tamara says.

Randy claps his hands loudly. "Holy Moly! I'm so excited I can barely think straight, but being a robot might have advantages. Lighting fast reflexes, laser aiming sights, computer-guided bullets. Are you catching my drift?"

James and Tamara glare.

"It was an expression, dorks!" Randy slaps his thigh.

James grips her hand, and they stride out the door.

An energetic chill flushes as they step out from the atrium's natural coolness into the thick humidity. James lowers his Ray Bans and stares across the water. The surface reflects a stillness, a mirrored image of the sky and trees, while wave runners and boats slice flanking textures across her smooth and fluid exterior.

Randy veers. He raises his hand, two fingers spread wide, and signals the bartender.

Tamara squeezes his hand twice, prompting James to smile. Her stride slows. The music has changed to hip-hop. Mixed with the whoops, screams, and chattered laughter from the hundreds of partygoers blending alcohol and drugs—the burn of cigarettes and cigars and the distinct smell of pot and chlorine—the atmosphere suddenly has a distinctive taste of adrenaline. Or could it be fear?

The security team opened the belt stanchion, and they entered the cordoned arena. Tamara stops next to a white table. She lowers her cat eye sunglasses to the brim of her nose and blinks repeatedly. James watches as her upper lashes, heavy with blue mascara, intertwine with the glittered black and much shorter bottom ones. She slowly scans the deck. Through the crowds of bare skin, a mixture of color, sweat, muscle, and curves, an oversized white cowboy hat emerges, seemingly floating above their heads—the crowd parts yielding to Dorian, followed by a cameraman. Dorian walks to the center of the lawn and raises his hands. James thinks his costume looks downright ridiculous. Brown lace-up leather chaps reveal his white speedo style skin-tight bathing suit rather outrageously. White cowboy boots, a Montana-sized silver Rodeo style belt buckle holding a hip-high double gun holster with two pearl-handled single action revolvers. Topping it off, a white-brimmed ten-gallon hat.

Dorian points at the two paintball pistols, each in single leather holsters on the table. "The blue one's yours," he winks at Tamara and draws his guns. The crowd cheers as he aims them skyward and pulls each trigger four times. Eight distinct popping sounds boom over the thumping music. The crowd cheers again as streams of confetti and fragments of glitter parade down in a cloud of excitement.

James looks at Tamara. "It feels like we never left the

Swing Door. I'm sitting at the bar watching you walk out of the back office for the first time. You're wearing the white cowgirl outfit with a white wig. I remember how you looked at me twice. Once as you walked past and the other ten minutes later when I was refilling my mug. You remember?"

"Funny, my mind was in a similar place." Tamara smiles.

Randy walks up and presses a cold beer to James's bare shoulder. "I figured you might need this."

James greedily guzzles half and belches. "Man, oh man, that was good. I feel this burning sensation deep inside my gut. Like a part of me is about to head into battle."

Tamara hugs James. "Baby, everything's going to be fine. My dad taught me how to shoot from the hip as a child. Trust me, this pea shooter is no different. I'll take Amanda out before she knows what hit her."

"I hope so. Her behavior proves unpredictable. She must have something up her sleeve."

Randy buts in! "She insisted she still loves you."

James looks at him, confused. "She confided in you?"

"Dude! She's incapable. I overheard her talking to Pricilla. Momoko says she lacks imagination. She has a shortage of humility, and, most importantly, without bending the truth, she's pitting you two against each other."

Tamara tightens her eyes. "You might be right."

James feels a nervous excitement.

The music abruptly stops, and a hush comforts the crowd. Dorian claps his hands. He climbs aboard the scissor lift with the cameraman and swiftly rises above the deck. Dorian raises the microphone and taps it four times.

"Ladies and Gentlemen, may I have your attention." A booming stereo-type church bell echoes through the speakers. The crowd roars. A cinematic landscape resembling the American Southwest fades on the media screens throughout the property. Two rugged western gunfighters, wearing traditional sooty cowboy hats and chaps, with leathered sun-baked skin standing back to back, begin walking away from each other. They stop at ten paces, turn, and face each other. The camera zooms in on their eyes while tense spaghetti western music plays.

"The stage is set!" Dorian announces. "For your entertainment, we're about to witness a duel on the lawn at the pool's far end."

The staff struggles to keep the energetic crowd from pushing past the stanchions. They pass out temporary eye protection to everyone without sunglasses.

James helps Tamara strap her holster. He removes the pistol and examines it. "It looks like a real gun. I mean the weight and the size."

Tamara grabs it and examines the single blue paintball round through the ammo window. She inspects the CO_2 cartridge and turns off the safety. To his amazement, she skillfully twirls it around her finger a few times and inserts it back into the holster. The spectators jeer at her performance.

James grins. "You continue to surprise me."

Tamara smiles and turns.

The crowd yields as Amanda approaches. A howl in

the distance, "Amanda, you suck," animates the group further. Contrasting cheers spill over the music. The cameraman zooms in. The monitors reflect a stern face under a black Stetson Cowboy hat. To either side, her two boy toys, dressed in skin-tight black underwear and matching black cowboy hats, keep pace. Security opens the barrier, and they enter.

Amanda glares at Tamara while striding up to the table. Her attire—blue jeans and a white long-sleeve shirt—matches Tamara's. She raises her hat slightly and addresses James.

"I know you don't believe me, but I'm doing this for us. We have an unsettled destiny, which I will fight tooth and nail for." She blows James a soft kiss and again glares at Tamara. "You knew I wouldn't settle this without a fight!" She fluffs her hair, sighs, and picks up her holstered weapon.

On the far side, the sisters, followed by their men, enter. The music softens, and the video monitors come alive. The men hoot at the scrupulously attired women in their Brazilian two-piece suits. White Western pleasure show hats and white gradient Cat Eye sunglasses flaunting their voluptuous and tanned bodies. Single file, they follow their Queen, sporting white knee-high cowboy boots and flaunting a ridiculous but eloquent diamond ring, which dwarfs her petite hand but sparkles brilliantly under the bright sun. They step onto an elevated platform, and their men sit behind them. Servants immediately set up sun umbrellas and attend to their every need.

James glances at the monitor. The split screen shows Tamara and Amanda. Every corner of the arena has filled. Heads are jumping up and down as the stragglers desperately try to get a better view.

The mood tenses as Amanda straps and adjusts her weapon. She turns and purposefully grazes Tamara.

"What're you waiting for, or are you afraid?" Amanda voices haughtily.

Tamara shrugs. "Let's be frank. I'm here because it's time to expose you."

Amanda scoffs. "For what, my unconditional love for James?"

James feels a heavy sinking sensation.

Tamara smiles wickedly. "You have no idea who I am, do you?"

Amanda glances at James and quickly back. Her mind churns. "What'd you mean by that?"

The crowd abruptly roars as they watch the two cowboys fire. One man falls. A cloud of dust billows. The camera captures his wide eyes staring into the sky. They slowly close, and the music fades.

Dorian hails into the microphone. "Ladies and gentlemen! An affair of honor has come to question." An energetic drum roll stimulates the crowd.

Three men dressed in black tuxedoes, gloves, and matching top hats, followed by two servants shouldering a roll of red carpet, enter the arena. While the servants unroll the rug, the others approach the group. Two quaintly extend their hands and escort Amanda and Tamara to the center. Meanwhile, another chaperon seats James, Randy, and Amanda's boy toys on either side of the ladies. Pricilla acknowledges James with a wink and a slight nod.

Randy nudges James. "Why the red carpet?"

"Hell, if I know. But it sure sets the stage, doesn't it?"

"Shit, howdy. I'm so excited my hands are sweating."

The music changes. On the monitors, the dueling banjo clip from the 1972 thriller 'Deliverance' by John Bormann begins. The crowd cheers.

Dorian intervenes. "This event, an affair of courage and honor, will settle the dispute between Amanda Manchester and Tamara Hudson over an extraordinary and dedicated man. Mr. James Rawlings, please stand."

Embarrassed, James rises, waves, and sits.

Amanda and Tamara curtsy toward James. Pricilla stands, raises a microphone, and signals Dorian. The music fades.

"Ladies, the field has been set!" Pricilla exclaims. "The Code of Honor as it existed in the nineteenth century will preside. The gentlemen will start you back to back with your pistols holstered. Once the music commences, you will both take exactly ten paces, turn, and face each other. Once the music stops, draw your weapons and fire. The winner will be the one who hits their mark closest to the heart. A rematch will occur if you both miss, or your marksmanship results in a tie. I will enforce disqualification should any individual deviate from the rules. The winner will quash the disagreement entirely. The loser shall abstain from ever re-opening the subject. Ladies, do you agree to the rules of the duel?"

Amanda raises her hands over her head and waves to the crowd. "Yes, I agree."

Tamara nods at James and raises her pistol. "I agree."

Whistles and claps and a volley of voices erupt.

Pricilla sits down and raises her drink. The men in the tuxedos place the ladies back to back center stage. They install their protective eyewear and give a nod of readiness. The men exit the arena, and Dorian starts the dueling banjo music. The crowd falls silent. Both women modishly take ten paces and turn. A suspenseful interlude follows. Sooner than anyone expected, the music stops. Due to the amplified muzzles attached to their weapons, two realistic pistols firing explode.

A quiet static follows. Both women are still standing,

yet different in composure. Amanda has her pistol pointing towards the ground and has one hand holding her chest. Tamara has her barrel aimed chest high and has a stunned but satisfied grin.

Chapter 24

Except for random whispers, the gallery falls silent. They have never witnessed something so bold, uninhibited, and exhilarating. A testimony to a lost art, an honorable way to settle personal or social injustices not so long ago.

On the video monitor, a slow-motion replay shows Tamara outdrawing Amanda and firing first. Dorian triumphantly announces Tamara as the victor. Thunderous roars and cheers follow. The sisters stand. Pricilla steps forward. Following her lead, they remove their hats, throw them high, and chant Tamara three times.

Tamara remains steady, staring at the gun as if it were real. She hears Dorian and the applause and watches the sisters toss their hats, which means the duel is over. Her beating heart and the roar from the gallery prevent her from hearing her name. She slowly inspects her body for pink paint, only to realize Amanda missed. She suddenly looks up, drops her weapon, tosses her hat high, and lets out an unbridled Texas-style whooping "Ye-haw!"

All the while, Amanda remains static, her mouth open in dismay, her head lowered, her eyes staring at her chest now stained blue.

James stands. His pumping heart inspires tears. Two beautiful women, in an affair of honor, dueled for him. He stares at Tamara with a romantic affection he never knew existed. Her glowing face energizes his inner desires. He gasps as Randy gives him a reckless two-handed bear-style hug, lifting his feet clean off the platform and squeezing.

"You're one lucky son of a bitch," Randy pecks James on his cheek in delight. "How? Yesterday, you were a hopeless virgin, rubbing one off every other day to maintain your sanity. Twenty-four hours later, two of the most gorgeous women in the world, holding you in the highest regard, dueled for you. I'm so jealous I want to puke. But I'm damn proud. Damn, proud!" Randy releases him.

James gasps for his very breath.

Tamara hoots as two suited men loft her onto their shoulders and carry her to the platform like a victorious God. They gently set her down in front of Pricilla.

Randy nudges James. "What are you waiting for, bozo? Get over there and congratulate your champion!"

His stroll past the sisters proves rewarding. Each one, slender and near-naked, warmly hugs and pecks him, some on the lips, while others grab his butt and whisper desires. "You are such a catch," but none more aggressively than Pricilla. She snuggles her body close, pressing her breasts tight, and while staring into his eyes, she places her hands around his muscular neck and kisses him, tongue and all! James gasped, realizing her soft, moist lips felt amazing. She pulls back and whispers with envious eyes, knowing Tamara is watching. "James, I wish it was I who challenged

Amanda. You're amazing. Now get down there and congratulate your victor. She's earned your love. I'm so happy for both of you."

With open arms, James wraps his arms around Tamara, who energetically jumps up, straddles him tight, and kisses him passionately. Another round of applause and cheers erupts.

In the backdrop, Amanda glowers with an unmistakable hatred and anger. Deep inside, rage has consumed her. This challenge was supposed to turn out differently. She was not supposed to lose. She knew she could not beat Tamara fairly and paid the merchant supplying the paint guns handsomely to remove the firing mechanism from her weapon.

The crowd quickly dispersed. Each guest went back to what they were doing before the show. Pricilla gathered the sisters, and after a brief but precise order, ensuring Amanda understood she could never again bring up or challenge Tamara on James Rawlings's concern, they rejoined the party. Amazingly, she agreed.

By mid-day, everyone has turned a shade darker.

Tamara looks even more beautiful. James knows six of the ten sisters by name, which he discovered were not all from the same sorority. His muscles, down to the smallest, especially in his back, are tender from waterskiing. His butt feels raw from riding the wave runners. He has sand in every crack from playing volleyball, and his stomach is full after gorging on a thick tuna steak sandwich with fries and a beer. Even better, he feels fulfilled and in love. James cannot stop kissing Tamara. Her breath, mouth, lips, and essence have found a place in his heart.

By eight o'clock, they are showered and dressed. Nine of the ten sisters, their hair braided in single ponytails, are seated at the candle-lit table the servants set up lakeside in the sand. Their outfits are identical. Pink summer dresses with seven black coral bracelets, rubies, sapphires, and pearls around their left wrists. What stands out are the heart-shaped diamond rings on their right forefingers, which signify their loyalty and pride to each other. To either side of them are their barefoot boy toys. Each sporting black board shorts and custom short-sleeved dark dinner jackets embroidered with their initials in gold over bare chests.

The guests who are not staying at the villa have gone home. Security had to remove a few stragglers physically. In the background, Frank Sinatra's greatest hits set the mood. The only contradiction is that Amanda is MIA.

Dressed in similar attire to the men but sporting a black low-rimmed top hat, Dorian sits opposite Pricilla at the head of the table. He clears his throat.

"The valet confirms she left an hour ago. Bags and all."

Pricilla sighs deeply. She glances at Tamara. "I thought she would be more dignified, but Amanda has chosen her fate. Ladies, we will discuss this tomorrow. Tonight, we commemorate our men and a near-perfect first day to this incredible weekend." She lifts her glass of wine. "Everyone—"

Two hours later, the table empties, and dancing poolside begins. Before long, most of the sisters and their men retire. Tamara and James naturally escape.

Everyone expresses congratulations on their new-found love. Randy and Momoko take a wave runner out onto the oily lake and romantically find pleasure in new ways.

The ambiance of the room feels inviting. Calm and relaxed compared to the truffles and humidity of the day. Tamara throws her bag down, pushes James to the side of the bar, and kisses him tenderly.

She ignites his inner desires. James comes up for air, rears back, and sighs. "Your kisses are so amazing!" He marvels at how symmetrical and beautiful her mouth is.

"So, you like me for my lips. Hmmm!"

James plants his to hers. "Yup!" He spins her around, lifts her onto the bar, and softly caresses her smooth legs. They both turn in suspense. Someone just knocked on the door.

James dashes up the stairs and peers through the peephole. "It's Dorian." James looks at her, surprised. "He's by himself. Should I?"

"Of course, ding-dong. Open the door."

Dorian apologizes for the interruption. He has

changed from his pool attire into a pair of rather unflattering polo-extended grey-length shorts with star-studded flip-flops. His gray T-shirt has a stick figure picture of a man with rabbit ears in the shape of hearts on a bicycle with oversized wheels. He marches over to the bar and hefts an aluminum case. He unsnaps the latches and opens them with a look of disgust. Dorian places his grey-black striped cap embroidered with an American flag onto the bar stool.

James and Tamara stare at the three paint guns in the protective foam. Dorian casually walks around the bar, opens the fridge, and pulls out three frosty beers. He twists the caps and distributes them.

"Tamara, honey!" He sighs, setting his bottle down. "I'm sorry I have to be the one to disclose this, but through a friend of a friend, I've learned a very nasty truth."

Tamara grabs one of the two blue paint pistols. She inspects it. "Are these the ones we used today?"

Dorian nods. "Uh-huh."

"Why did you bring them up here?" she asks

inquisitively. "And why the third gun?"

Dorian sips his beverage. Over the next few minutes, he explains the third pistol, the one with the tape around the barrel, had the firing pin removed. What made it enjoyable was that Amanda paid the merchant ten thousand dollars to remove it and keep it under his hat.

Tamara glares.

James senses her suppressed anger will soon rally her spirit.

" That bitch!" She tosses the gun into the case and gathers her beer. "Are you serious!"

Dorian exhales. "It was dumb luck I found out."

James inspects the third gun. "How do you mean?"

"I'm friends with the manager who works for the company we rented them from."

James scratches his head. "Friends or lovers?"

"Does it matter?"

Dorian sighs. "I guess not. All this—the house, the party, the people, the sex, the lies, and the deceit— seems like a suspense movie. Do you want to know what

I think? Everything's about to come to a dramatic conclusion." Dorian shakes his head.

"She has no self-worth. That's why she stoops to trickery." Tamara presses. "She doesn't know how to lose."

Dorian nods in agreement. "James, you have no idea."

James spins the gun around his finger. "So, you're friends with the owner?"

"No, the manager! He's an acquaintance."

"What's the difference?"

"Touché."

"You asked him to bring a third gun with a working firing pin?"

"Of course. Once I found out about Amanda's duplicity, I couldn't bear to watch knowing the truth."

"Don't you share the same loyalty for the both of them?"

Dorian leans on the bar, crosses his legs, and taps one foot nervously. "Yes, and no! Look, I love both of them. I'm in charge. Everything runs through me."

"Okay! Still, something doesn't add up."

Dorian fidgets. "What'd you mean?"

"Did Amanda send you up here?"

Tamara perks up. Her eyes roam.

"We all witnessed her shock in the gunfight."

Tamara interrupts. "I had the drop on her before she pulled her pistol."

"I'd hate to be on the opposite side in a real gunfight." Dorian grins.

"Quit dodging the truth!" James asks irritably.

Dorian shakes his head. "Look. Promise me you'll keep this between us. You can never tell a soul. Both of you promise with your hearts."

They both agree.

"Look. A few years ago, Amanda played a dirty trick on me—an elaborate scheme that left me embarrassed and hurt."

James looks concerned. "How so?"

"She swayed a straight bartender at a nightclub to hit on me. At the after-hours party, when it came down to the nitty-gritty, he humiliated me in front of everyone.

Amanda laughed, adding scorn to my embarrassment. That night, I swore one day I would have my revenge."

Tamara hugs Dorian. "I had no idea."

"Over the years, I've watched her hurt so many; well, it was about time for me to give her back some of her own medicine."

"Does Pricilla know about this?" James slugs some beer.

Dorian shakes his head no. He kisses Tamara on her cheek. "Sweetheart, I love you. You know that."

"Of course."

"She already has too much, especially with her mom passing. This would devastate her."

"Do you know where Amanda went?"

Dorian latches the case. With roaming eyes, he clears his throat. "I confronted her men as they loaded her luggage in the car. I've known them for years. They said she was on the phone with her father for the longest time. For the most part, hysterical. She was clamoring about how humiliated she was. The doors were closed to her bedroom, but they heard something about revenge. I left before she came down. I didn't want to confront her."

Tamara grabs his hand and caresses it. Dorian seems to absorb her softness. "I'm so sorry. She's a cruel human being. You did the right thing."

Dorian wipes his tears.

"Where'd she go?" James asks.

"They didn't know. I have a feeling, the airport. Every time she's distressed, she runs to her father."

Sparked by impulse, Tamara grabs her purse. "That's her MO," she says, digging inside. "This time, I don't think so." She pulls out her phone and browses through a string of data. "Right here. Yesterday, I received a message from her father. At first, I thought it was strange. We haven't talked for a while, but now it makes sense."

"How do you mean?" James looks inquisitively.

"In an indirect way, he asked me to be nice to her for the rest of the weekend. He didn't say why, but he insisted."

"Insisted?" Dorian asks.

"Capital letters. Take a look." She hands him the phone.

Dorian moves his lips while reading. "The good news is he's in Canada for business and won't return until Thursday next week."

"He's coming here?" James asks.

"No, he lives in New York, Manhattan. I can't stand the snootiness, but I love the nightlife."

"Amen!" Dorian hands Tamara her phone back.

"What's the bad news?" Tamara asks.

Dorian glares. His face shows certainty. "Honey, this can only mean he knows."

James shrugs. "Knows what? His daughter blew a gasket, or you switched the guns."

"All the above! Let me put it this way. For Mr. Manchester to dispatch this message can only mean he sent Thomas."

James raises his hands. "Who the hell is Thomas?"

Tamara drops her mouth. "Oh, my God! I'll bet you're right."

"Excuse me. Hello. Can someone please tell me who

this Thomas character is?"

Dorian looks wildly at Tamara. He nods, forcing her to answer.

She exhales. "James, honey! Thomas, well, he's—umm, how can I say this."

Dorian interrupts. "Sweetheart, let me help. He's Mr. Manchester's henchman."

James drops his mouth. "Seriously!"

Chapter 25

Her heart races. Amanda has never felt so lost, out of control, or angered, which surprises her. Being the antagonist, she thrives on misdirection and chaos. She glances at her face in the rearview mirror. Her smudged makeup behind bloodshot eyes highlights her true misery. With every breath, her rage draws further and further into emotional overload. Outside, the glistening lights of the city pulse. She grips the steering wheel of her Audi Sports coupe and, careless of the police cruiser waiting at the intersection, accelerates swiftly through a yellow light. In two heartbeats, her pulse rate climbs. From behind, the blaring siren and parade of swirling blue lights color the interior.

Amanda quickly conceals the snub-nose pistol on

her lap, barrel first below her short skirt. The cold metal on her bare thighs, especially the thickness of the hollow but deadly shaft, embraces her privates. She decelerates, signals, and pulls over. She places her purse on her lap, fluffs her hair, and rolls down the window.

"Good evening, Miss—license and registration, please," the tall and very robust police officer standing cautiously to the side of the window politely inquires while flashing the beam from his light onto the smooth contour of her thighs.

Amanda smiles and pushes some loose hair behind her ear. "I know why you pulled me over. I'm so sorry for speeding through the light, but I'm sure it was yellow." She opened her designer purse and removed her license. She reaches into the center glove box and retrieves the registration. "Here you go, officer." She squints at his badge eclipsed by the beam from the torch.

"Officer Talbert," he says while examining the documents. "The light was red, and your speed was well above the limit of forty-five."

"Oh! I'm sure I was under fifty." Amanda blinks repeatedly.

Officer Talbert cocks his head slightly and focuses the beam throughout the interior. He returns to her smooth legs. His eyes show a hint of approval. "Miss Manchester, please remain inside. I'll be right back."

Through the rearview, Amanda watches Officer Talbert. His movements are slow and deliberate, which she finds appealing yet frightening. She rotates her hips, adjusting the barrel below. Knowing the danger ignites a sexual craving, which further energizes her spirit. A few minutes later, Officer Talbert returns.

"Miss Manchester. Your father's Randolph Manchester?" He shines his torch onto her legs.

"Why yes! Do you know him?"

He hands back her documents. "Let's just say he's very respected at the precinct. Miss, I'm curious. You're in town for Pricilla Wellington's lakeside mansion party, correct?"

Amanda narrows her eyes. "Why yes! Do you know Pricilla?"

"Not personally, but a few fellows were bragging about how much fun they had. They can't stop talking about how two beautiful vixens dueled with paint guns for love. Lucky guy. Are you leaving town?"

Amanda looks up, surprised. Deep within, her gut feels hardened. She swallows. "Why yes! I have a pressing engagement back home."

"Home. New York?"

"Manhattan."

"Are you flying out tonight?"

"Why? Is there a problem?"

"No, ma'am! You may be aware, but the airport's in the opposite direction. Are you lost?"

"No! No! Of course not. My father has a vacation home up the road. I depart tomorrow morning."

A radio alert on his headset prompts his attention. Officer Talbert answers using precise police jargon. He looks at Amanda. "Ma'am, you're free to go, but please drive carefully. There are a lot of drunks out this weekend, especially this time of night. The drunks are out in full force." He takes a step away from the window and turns. "Are you sure you're not lost?"

Amanda grins, knowing he hit on her. "Positive! Officer Talbert." She squeezes her thighs tight. "I'll be fine. Thanks for caring."

"Yes, ma'am!" Officer Talbert nods and marches to his cruiser.

A warm gust funneling through the window relieves her tension. She removed the pistol and stared at the moisture-laden tip glistening within the reddish glow of the dash lights. She reaches between her legs and, within seconds, climaxes. A semi-truck speeds past, which rocks the suspension. She closes the window and adjusts the A/C vents towards her face. The cool air sends another rush through her body. She grabs her phone and re-activates the map program. The computer-generated Australian male voice advises her to stay on 5th street for two-point six miles. She will then take a left on Brook Hollow Drive. The destination address will be four blocks up on the left.

●●

By the second, his suspicions heighten. Could Amanda's father be a gangster, a racketeer, and Thomas, his roughneck shylock who collected on bad or outstanding debts?

Her expression turns serious. Tamara grabs Dorian by the hand and leads him over to the couch. "James, would you be a sweetheart and lock the front door."

A sudden panic confronts Dorian. His confusion builds, watching Tamara close and lock the patio door. She draws the curtains as if privacy is paramount.

Tamara has Dorian and James stand, place their hands over their hearts, and swear they will never divulge what they are about to hear to anyone. She raises her beer. Together, they toast and, with stone-face glares, gargle before swallowing. Dorian plops down, attesting that he knows what she wants to disclose.

"Maybe bits and pieces," Tamara declares. "Did you know Hudson is my real last name, not Brewer? And I'll bet you didn't know Samantha Hudson, the stunning and gifted young woman who mysteriously went missing during her second year at Brown six years past, was my loving sister."

Dorian looks blank. "I had no idea."

"You don't know the half of it."

"Are you serious? Brown?"

Her face shows sadness. "Yep!" She swallows a lump. Her voice softens. "We were different. She was dead set on an Ivy League college. I was homegrown."

"Older?"

"Fourteen months and bigger boned, but prettier by far."

James looks towards the door, thinking he heard a key engaging the lock tumblers. Dorian and Tamara express concern.

"They alleged she ran away with her lover. She even left a memo." Tamara stares at the wall. "She wrote it on a notepad, a stupid iPad. She would have never."

Dorian looks expressionless. "Alleged?"

Tamara wipes her eyes. "The police closed the case due to a lack of evidence."

"You're saying she never surfaced?"

Tamara sniffles and raises her head stoutly. Her stare remains engrossed.

Dorian recognizes her pain. "I'm so sorry."

"She vanished off the face of the earth. It didn't make sense. She would've never eloped. My dad raised us properly. We had rules, especially with boys."

"How so?" Dorian crosses his leg.

"Because we come from wealth, they must be approved."

"You mean scrutinized?"

"My dad's very protective! He runs cross-checks, or his lawyers do. Anyway, unless we have his blessing, we move on."

James fidgets. "Did your father run a background check on me?"

"You passed with flying colors." A smile highlights her tense face.

"I knew he was a keeper." Dorian winks and gently folds his hands. "What about Derik?"

"He bombed. Samantha kept him as a friend with benefits."

"Interesting."

"Nothing wrong with casual sex, especially through college, right?"

Dorian clears his throat. "I agree." He grins. "Tell me about her note. What made you challenge the authenticity?"

"She was a literary genius. The note she supposedly left was heartless, especially regarding writing romance or non-fiction. I know she didn't write it." Tamara glares at the door. "Did you hear that?"

Everyone turns. This time, James springs up the staircase and peers through the peephole. "It's clear."

Tamara looks worried. "Open it. I'm sure I heard something."

His heart soars as James clears the deadbolt and throws it open. Everyone looks shocked at the wrapped package with an envelope secured to the top. James looks both ways and picks it up.

"It's addressed to you, Dorian." James shakes it and locks the door. "It feels empty."

Everyone stares in hushed silence as Dorian rips it open.

• •

Amanda stopped two houses down from her destination address. A street light illuminates the green lawn lined with shrubs before the faded yellow single-story house. The windows have the curtains drawn, and the lights are off throughout. Amanda glances at her watch. A few minutes later, she looks again. Under her breath, she keeps repeating two words. "Come on. Come on."

Ten minutes later, a slight knock on the passenger window Startled her. She unlocks the door, and Thomas, dressed in black, enters.

"Where've you been?" Her voice stresses anger.

"It took longer than anticipated."

"Did you?"

"Yes, the package was delivered."

Amanda grins. "What were they doing?"

"Just as you thought. They were in Tamara's room. Three people. Dorian and Tamara, but I didn't recognize the other one. Tamara was doing most of the talking. Something about her sister, but I had to cut it short due to a few servants delivering room service."

"Did they see you?"

"No."

Amanda glares. "Are you positive they were talking about her sister? Tamara doesn't have one."

Thomas pulls out his electronic device. "The receiver had a tough time picking up their conversation, especially over the outside ambient noise, but you can hear bits and pieces."

Amanda listens attentively. Her eyes widened as the name Samantha rang. She prompts Thomas to play it again.

"Oh, my God! That little bitch. All this time, she's been playing me. Lying and sneaking behind my back."

Thomas looks concerned. "You mean her sister was Samantha, the one we buried with her boyfriend?"

●●

Dorian drops the stem of the black rose into the box.

"What does it mean?" James picks it up, careful not to puncture his skin on the thorns. He removes the soft paper lining and inspects the interior for a clue. "Nothing! Not a thing!"

Tamara sits on the armrest. Her expression shows concern. She sighs heavily. "I knew I heard somebody out there."

"I did, too. Multiple times." James adds. "Why a black rose?"

"Death!" Dorian answers grimly.

Tamara jumps up. "Or it could be the opposite." She points at the rose. "Listen, it's a deception. I think I know who sent it."

Dorian shakes his head. He cannot bear the thought. Dorian has never been so scared. Could this be a prank? He has no enemies, none at least he can remember. "It must be, I mean, a bluff, but who sent it and why?"

"The antagonist! That's who? She wants to instill fear. Lead you from her scent. Remember, she's the master of manipulation and deceit. We've both experienced her wrath so many times."

"Amanda?" James inquires.

"Exactly! Your long lost angel." Tamara directs her attention to Dorian. "She murdered them. I know it."

"Who?" Dorian asks.

"Common!"

Dorian opens his mouth. His eyes narrow, and his lips tremble as the certainty of what he assumed for years slaps him hard in the face.

"For years, I've been searching for a weakness in her armor, waiting for a mistake. Finally, it happened. The rose proves it."

Dorian stares blankly. Whispered words emerge. He finally nods as if the truth suddenly manifests. "I'm so naïve it makes me puke. All these years, I watched with eyes closed, knowing deep down Amanda's personality bordered on evil. I couldn't hurt a fly. I step over ants on sidewalks, trap spiders in my house, and release them safely. I trust pretty much everyone, yet here I sit again, being taken advantage of."

James stands more confused than ever. He addresses Tamara. "What significance does this flower play in connecting your sister to her?"

Tamara clears her throat. Her eyes dart from James to the flower and then to Dorian. She sighs. "I don't know where to start. Come to think of it, for years, the evidence was staring me in my face. I was just blind to the truth."

"Sweetheart, you're not making sense." Dorian rises. "Slow down. Take a deep breath. A moment ago, something of importance came to light. Start there."

Tamara picks up the rose and counts to nine. "Look, the tenth thorn from the bottom is missing."

James silently counts. He scoffs. "I don't get it. What's the significance?"

Dorian taps his finger on his forehead. "Ten, ten, ten, ten! Yeah, ten," his eyes widen. I'm following you. Ten boyfriends and ten ten-dollar bills in her wallet. Ten dresses on trips. Ten embroideries on almost everything she wears. Ten rings on her fingers. Betting on double zero ten times. Ten shots and ten-dollar tips. Let's remember the ten-napkin thing and her ten cars. Shall I go on?"

James raises his hands.

Tamara hugs him. "Baby. I figured it out."

Dorian bear hugs the both of them. "You're a regular Sherlock. James and Tamara discovered a major clue. Amanda has this thing with the number ten. We don't know why it's so significant. She's never told anyone, but she's obsessed with it."

"I'm not following."

"Baby, think about it. I know you can figure this out."

James examines the rose. Behind the dark pedals, he sees the truth. Black roses are not natural. James plucks a few inner ones, spreads the interior, and discovers the actual color. He grins. "I gave Amanda a ten-line poem and a long-stemmed red rose the day she moved. We were both ten years old. I trimmed the tenth thorn to signify our eternal love began on this day."

Tamara plants a sloppy kiss. Dorian grins jealously. "Baby, she told me the story years ago, but I never understood the significance until now. All of her quirks suddenly make total sense. Even though she abandoned you, she never forgot that day. Your eternal love has remained a thorn in her side. The number ten is the key." She grabs the flower. "Look! The tenth thorn is missing, which indicates she's come to terms. James, she's finally released you."

"That might be true, but why'd she address the package to Dorian?"

••

Amanda grips the steering wheel so tightly that blood veins form. "That little fucking slut! She's been playing me all these years." She glares at Thomas. "I think she knows I killed her sister. That's why she stole James from me."

Thomas straightens his posture and places his gloved hands on his knees. His world revolves around protecting Amanda. No matter what the outcome, this new threat will have lasting implications. "I understand. I'll deal with them later. Do you have the package?"

Amanda sighs. Her face flushes. "It's in the trunk. Are you sure there's no other way?"

"There can be no loose ends. On your drive back to the house, stop at the store and buy anything. Let people see you. Use your credit card. You need a rock-solid alibi." Thomas looks at his wristwatch. "Once done here, I'll call you on the secure phone."

"You flew on the company jet."

"Yes, but you can't be seen with me. Stick to the plan.

Book a ticket home tomorrow on a commercial flight."

Amanda frowns. She cannot stand commercial airlines. "Okay, but don't do anything rash until we talk. I mean it. Do you hear me, Thomas? Do you hear me?"

He nods. "We'll conference with your father tomorrow." Thomas exits the car, retrieves the suitcase from the trunk, and disappears into the night.

Amanda makes a sharp U-turn and speeds away.

PART 6

Chapter 26

After cumulatively wracking their brains for a rational answer, the trio migrates over to the bar.

Tamara pounds her fist. "I've got it. At least I think I do, I mean."

Dorian looks anxiously.

"She's going to do what she always does. Dorian, like me, you know her intimately—her shenanigans, slanderous pranks, and antics. Think about it. She follows a similar pattern whenever she finds herself at an impasse, especially when ridiculed. Either she runs to Daddy, locks herself in her room sometimes for days to plan her revenge, or she calls Thomas. I'll bet anything he delivered this package."

Dorian looks intrigued yet afraid. The reason is that he fears Amanda, especially Thomas. He sighs heavily. "A few years back, I witnessed Amanda beat to death a young man while practicing a version of her sadomasochism." Dorian clasps his hands. "To ensure secrecy, Thomas threatened to kill my mother if I ever told a soul. You might think this sentimental, but there's a time in a man's life when he comes to terms."

Tamara and James look dispelled.

Dorian places his hands on his cheeks and sighs. He looks up at the ceiling. "Mom, I'm so sorry, but I can no longer hold this pain inside. Please forgive me." He winks at James and directs his attention toward Tamara. "Sweetheart, you're so right." He reaches out and massages her shoulders. "Thomas delivered this package. The brown paper box is his signature. The black rose signifies that I should keep my mouth shut."

Tamara shakes her head, confused. "What're you trying to tell us?"

Dorian clasps his sweaty hands. "When I first started working for Pricilla, I introduced one of my dearest androgynous friends to Amanda. It was a good gig with good pay, and he was attracted to her. It ended badly for him. He died."

"She murdered him?" James asks.

"She claimed it was an accident, but I knew different. Thomas threatened to hurt my mom or friends if I continued digging. For all these years, I've held this inside. Tamara, I'm so sorry. I didn't witness the act, but I know she killed your sister."

Tamara slumps and stares at the floor. A few moments pass before she raises her head. "Dorian! I understand. You would've warned me if you knew I was her sister."

"Of course, without question. I love you."

"Thank you for your bravery. I know how difficult it must have been to reveal something dangerous." Tamara presses her palms together. Her expression shows remorse. "I knew Amanda killed her a long time ago. I couldn't prove it."

Dorian breaks down in tears.

Tamara comforts him. "Hey! Look at me." She lifts his head. Dorian inhales deeply. "I love you like family. You know that. I came to terms with my sister's disappearance long ago." Tamara sniffles. "Yeah, it sucked. It took years for me to pull my head up. And yes, I miss her so, very, very much, but negative thinking only leads to depression."

James hugs Tamara. "I know this all too well. After my mom died, I nearly drowned in sorrow. Your sister died horribly, but now penance is due. Tell me something. How many times has she done this? What I mean—do you think she's a serial killer?"

Dorian fills in the blanks. He does not know how many people Amanda killed, but his knowledge of her perverse behavior turned him into a confidante. He was required to attend a ritual and recite written words while Randolph plucked his eyebrows and Amanda whipped his bare back with a leather strap. For years before Beatrice died, they would take him to the basement and confide in him. Dorian became the listening boy.

"This type of shit doesn't happen in the real world, does it!" James looks perplexed.

"There's so much more I don't know. The Manchesters are a very private family full of deep, dark secrets. Their heritage goes way back; believe me, it's not good." Dorian opens his wallet and pulls out a picture. "I snapped this years ago at their country house. The one outside the city limits." Dorian hands it to Tamara.

Her eyes widen. Dorian explains the man in the portrait over the fireplace is their great-great-great-grandfather. The two children on either side were his kids.

Tamara bites her lower lip. "Holy shit!"

James grabs the photo. "You've got to be kidding. These are his siblings?"

"Remarkable! They're dead knockoffs. They even have the same names. Randolph and Amanda!"

Tamara looks dumbfounded.

"From what I could pick up over the years, Amanda and her dad were the first siblings to resemble them."

"What does it mean?" James asks.

"I have no idea. Spooky though, isn't it?"

"No, unnerving!" James hands the image back to Dorian. He tucks it away in his wallet.

"Even with the lengthily time spans between generations, the dominant gene faithfully shows up," Tamara interjects. "Yes, their resemblances are remarkable, but it's normal. Let's not look deeper into this than what it is. We should concern ourselves with Amanda and Thomas. What are they planning? Is the rose a warning, or could it mean something else altogether?"

James agrees but queries the normality. He poses a question. "Do we know anything about the siblings?

Were they upstanding citizens, psychopaths, bank robbers, murderers?"

Dorian stares suspiciously. "You and I think alike. God, I only wish you were gay or bisexual. We'd surely be best of friends." He blows James a kiss.

James blushes and interlocks fingers with Tamara. She kisses him gently.

"Relax, James. I hit on all the good-looking ones."

Tamara giggles and punches Dorian in the shoulder. "Focus, bucko. He's mine."

"Owe." Dorian rubs his shoulder. "All right already! I meant to say I had the same uncertainties, so I did a little research. Long story short, their history is nothing but controversial. The boy, Randolph number one, followed in his father's footsteps, I mean to the *T*, the *E*, and the *E*. He married ten times, and like his dad and his spouses, they all died mysteriously. The daughter, excuse me, Amanda number one, was mentally unstable —multiple personality disorders. She never married but had a trail of men and women until her untimely death on her twenty-sixth birthday. The police couldn't prove it, but they suspected foul play."

Tamara furrows her brows. "You mean the father and the son both married ten times, and every one of their spouses unexpectedly became land owners?"

Dorian chuckles. "That's a funny way of putting it, and yes, they all came from wealth. And they all signed the checks. Get this: Randolph number one doubled the fortune before he kicked the bucket."

"It seems they both climbed the golden staircase. Did it reveal how they passed?" James asks.

"Mostly heart issues, but mysteriously."

"Sounds like two shooting stars competing for the bunch."

Tamara shakes her head. "What bunch?"

"Galaxies! It's an expression."

Tamara hugs James. "I love your innuendos."

"Donald and his son were indicted for murder numerous times but were acquitted each time. Did you know they charged Randolph number two with murdering his parents? They croaked unexpectedly on a vacation."

"How old was he?" James asks, his mind rummaging through the memories of his youth.

"I'm not sure. In the early twenties! Still in college."

"Did the police discover how they died?"

"No! Like his relatives, they acquitted him. The bonus is that he inherited the lot. Excuse me, the bunch."

In our day and age, with all the forensic sciences available, they could've found traces of foul play.

Tamara scratches her head. "When Amanda talked about her family heritage, she mentioned reincarnation. I laughed, shrugging it off as make-believe. We all know her narcissistic personality. Now, it makes sense. She thinks she's the re-embodiment of the late Amanda."

"Did she or Randolph study the Samsara doctrine?" James asks.

Dorian shakes his head. "Do you mean did they practice Buddhism? I have no idea."

"Not even close. Amanda doesn't believe in God or anything spiritual, especially Hinduism." Tamara widens her eyes. "You know what? There's a correlation."

Dorian sits down. "How so?"

"It seems some of the men in the family share a dark secret. Something so guarded it's only passed down to a select few. Randolph's dad wasn't one of them. Otherwise, he would still be alive. What about his granddad?"

"Funny you ask."

Tamara and James perk up.

"In the basement, there are six full-length portraits. The picture I showed you earlier, which I'm sure you both agree has a chilling semblance, puts the others into perspective. They all depict a full-grown father and son. Get this: they all have full-length beards and are named Donald."

"Interesting? Do they take after their grandfather?" James asks.

"Not even close. They look completely different. Crazy, huh?"

James straddles the stool. "Are there any more?"

"Get ready because I'm about to throw a monkey wrench into the bucket. Two more on a separate wall, framed in gold instead of the traditional silver, and they portray Randolph and two very different young girls. The first one represents Amanda. She's in her early teens and strikingly beautiful. Two pigtails, a white knee-high dress, and that cold, deep stare." Dorian shakes his head and exhales.

"Tell me about it. When I picture her, it's the first thing I see."

"I know what you mean. It's like she can see directly into your soul." Tamara shrugs. "Ew!"

Dorian quivers. "The other one, which threw me for a loop at first, looks hauntingly familiar to someone we are close to. She too was in her early teens, wearing a white dress with pigtails, but her facial features are distinctly different."

Tamara shows confusion. "Wait a second. You mean Randolph number two has a second daughter?"

"Precisely! Let me pose a question. Doesn't it seem coincidental Beatrice followed a similar path?"

Tamara raises her hands in doubt. "I'm not following. To whom?"

"Donald and Randolph the first—who else? You did read the papers?"

"Of course. She died mysteriously. We all know that."

"What'd they call her?"

Tamara grins. "The Black Widow! I see where you're going with this. Are you sure?"

"Positive! I've kept this secret for so long it's finally worn thin on me."

"Does she know?"

James asks. "Does who know?"

Dorian sighs. "Pricilla! We're talking about Pricilla."

• •

The footprints in the grass gradually diminish, leaving only a few broken blades. Thomas stops and waits for a lone car to pass. Before making his way to the backside of the house, he remains unmoving until the tread of the tires and the tail lights fade. His movements are smooth. His body blends with the shadows. With precision, he picks up the deadbolt lock. The hinges squeal slightly but mix readily with the hum of the kitchen appliances. Thomas latches the door but keeps it unlocked for a quick exit. He makes his way through the interior, paying attention to step softly. A slight popping noise within the hallway startles him. Another one creaks, seemingly in front of him. Thomas stops and slows his breathing. A few moments later, he continues, reassuring the sounds originated from the framework. He peers inside the ajar bedroom door. The time display from the cable box within the cabinet softly illuminates the room. He identifies two bodies in the bed. A light snore, which he distinguishes, comes from the female. Thomas steps inside and places his back on the wall. He identifies his mark as a fifty-six-year-old business colleague who pushed the boundaries of partnership with Randolph. The man rolls over, lets out a restless cough, and begins snoring loudly.

Thomas activates the red laser sight and positions it squarely on his forehead. Abruptly, he lowers the pistol. To his right, the bedroom door slowly creaks open. Without turning his head, he watches a small girl dressed in white-footed pajamas with a pink bunny embroidered on her chest enter. She stops beside the bed, wipes her nose with her arm sleeve, and stares at his darkened silhouette. Thomas knows she sees him.

But how? Could the creaks have come from her?

His morality flares. Thomas does not kill women or children. Amazingly, the child remains silent, which only heightens the situation.

"Daddy, what are you doing?" Her voice softly whispers.

Before she can say another word, Thomas smothers her mouth with his hand, which inadvertently covers her nose. He hoists her into his arms, slips into the hallway, and enters her bedroom. A night light illuminates the breadth. Thomas places her on the bed and stares through the slits in his full-face mask. Her eyes are closed, and her head rolls sideways as he removes his hand. His heart rate increases, realizing he blocked her airway. Instinctively, he lifts his face mask, places his cheek next to her mouth, and listens for exhalation. Fear grips Thomas. He puts his hand under her neck, pinches her nose, and gently blows until her chest rises. Thomas repeats the procedure while scanning the doorway for movement. A slight cough followed by a heavy wheeze energizes his spirit. Thomas snugs her head to the pillow and covers her with the blanket. Thankfully, she begins to breathe on her own. She opens her eyes. They are welling. Thomas feels relieved yet finds his task all that more discomforting. With time being of the essence, he lowers his mask, exits the room, and, within seconds, purges his mark.

Thomas finds the drive home painful. Tonight, he entered an unknown world with no apparent exit. Thomas did something he vowed never to do. He killed a woman. In all his years of living on the edge, he separated his everyday life from the tragedy and violence of his profession. Thomas suddenly finds himself at an impasse. He goes over the events in chronological order. He entered the room for the second time, placed his back on the wall, and aimed the laser sight. How he emptied four silenced rounds in his marks chest and how the woman, at the last possible moment before he was about to finalize the execution, yelled out, threw her body over his, and took the round to the back of her head. He stood in shock as the child entered the room and jumped onto the bloodied bed.

Thomas pulls over and looks at his face in the rearview. He sees the frightened face of the little girl covered in blood. Thomas accelerates ahead, keeping his speed precisely the limit. Without incident, he parks inside the garage next to the black Audi. Thomas feels the warm hood, which tells him Amanda deviated from the plan. After washing, he approaches her on the couch.

"Where'd you go?"

Amanda stares impatiently. "Never mind. Is it done?"

Thomas nods. "Of course. I said where'd you go?"

This time, Amanda sighs. "It's no big deal. I went back to the party. I left something important in my room. Why do you look so distraught?"

"Never mind. Did anyone see you?"

"Would it matter?"

"Absolutely! If you wouldn't have gotten pulled over by the cop, then no. Remember you told him you were heading straight to your father's house? This could jeopardize your alibi. Amanda, keep your head. If you continue deviating from my advice, you'll become a suspect. Don't forget; I still have to handle a few loose ends."

"Nobody saw me. I'm sure of it."

"Your dad will be angry. Let me ask you something. Did you stop at the guard gate?"

"Of course. How else would I have been able to get up to my room?"

"Did you have the valet park your vehicle?"

Amanda suddenly looks worried. "I'm sorry. I fucked up again. I'm sorry, Thomas. I wasn't thinking straight. I was angry. Nobody saw me. I'm sure of it. It was late, and everyone was asleep."

"Let's hope so."

●●●

"Our prints hardly show. It's obscene. Don't you think?"

Momoko chuckles. She takes two giant strides, jumps high, and buries both feet deep into the soft sand. She steps ahead, leaving two temporary relics, turns, and, with a wide grin, displays her bare and beautiful attributes. "How about now?"

Randy inhales deeply. He had never seen such a stunning female posing sensuously in the moonlight. He softly tackles her. They both playfully roll down the embankment into the coolness of the lake. They kiss and again find warmth.

They sit silently, staring at the wonder of the shoreline. The trees, the house, and the dock are magically lit, with hundreds of lights sparkling across the oily water.

Momoko looks curiously. "I didn't tell you, but Sayuri told me she saw Amanda when I went to the room to get my stuff earlier."

"Really! I thought she split hours ago."

"She did. Sent her two boy toys away as well."

"I don't get it. Why would she come back?"

"I don't know, but she was only here for a few minutes. The valet boys said she went up to her room. Funny, though, she used the freight elevator and returned with a small box. She paid them handsomely to keep their mouths shut and peeled out like a mad woman."

"Strange."

"Tell me about it. I think she has a few screws loose."

"That's an understatement!"

"Two years ago, I worked a party similar to this one, but it was on a three-hundred-foot private yacht. It was huge."

"I love yachts."

"The theme was pirates. Each sister brought three companions. Two men and, can you believe it, a female French bulldog."

"Man, oh man, they sure know how to party. Why dogs?"

"I never figured it out. Every dog was different. Pink, blue, gold, and even bright red. I was her bitch."

"Amanda?"

"Yep! My hands were full, especially taking her dog on bathroom breaks."

"K! So, what happened?"

Momoko grins. "You catch on pretty fast for a Gaijin. On the last day, her dog died. I collected it. It was awful. I can still picture her stiff as a board. Her tongue was hanging out, and her eyes were wide open. Amanda said she thought it was a heart attack. She paid me extra to keep my mouth shut. I dumped her overboard before we docked."

"I'm sorry about the dog, but the punch line, please!"

"There was this small leather-handled box. It was gothic, but the contents caught my attention."

"The suspense is killing me!" His expression tightens.

"Small plastic jars filled with herbs. I also saw a syringe, spoon, rolling papers, pipe, and small plastic bags with twist ties. Are you following me?"

"She's a junky?"

• •

In his mind, James pictures a young Amanda. Two strangers are meeting for the first time at the park. An angel had found him. "You're not an angel," he exclaims.

"James! You OKAY?"

James shakes his head.

Tamara rubs his shoulders.

James blinks multiple times. He hears her voice but remains lost in thought. He makes eye contact. "I'm sorry, babe. What'd you say?"

"Earth to James? Hello. Are you home?"

"Umm, sorry, I was daydreaming."

"Of who?"

"Why do you say that?"

"Never mind. I know who it was. I'm not worried. I love you. We were discussing Pricilla."

"Yeah, I get it! Randolph has an illegitimate daughter."

"Crazy, huh! Who would've ever guessed? I suppose it would have come out eventually."

"I suppose."

"I believe in karma," Dorian says. "What comes around goes around. And for that reason, both of them, even Thomas, will get what they deserve."

"How so?" Tamara asks.

"In this life, one can only elude deception for so long. Their history clearly shows this. The curse of the Manchester family is real."

"Interesting analogy. Please continue." Tamara opened another beverage and placed it in front of Dorian.

Dorian nods approvingly and takes a sip. "There are so many things about Randolph not to like. During some of his drunken episodes, especially when I found myself alone with him, he would mumble on about how the kinfolks of the deceased wives placed this terrible vex on the family. For half a century, they tried to destroy the family, using the church and the law, yet in the end, they all lost. Randolph is the proof. He bragged about how he now controlled the family fortune and how he had quadrupled their net worth."

"Did he ever talk about his parents, especially how they died unexpectedly?" Tamara asks.

"One night, we were sitting on the couch before the fireplace. Randolph talked about his parents wanting to donate most of their wealth to charity. Something about cleansing the family curse frightened me: Randolph looked up at the portrait of Donald and his two kids, and as if a ghost from his past heard him, he stopped. Cold turkey! Let me tell you; it spooked the hell out of me. I hated going down there. It felt like all those eyes were watching me."

"That's creepy! What about Amanda? Did she ever go down there with you?" Tamara asks.

"At first, yes, but she started making excuses. I think something frightened her."

Tamara looks perplexed. "Does she know about Pricilla?"

Dorian gestures. "She must, but I don't know for sure. We never talked about it."

James asks. "Does Pricilla know Randolph is her father?"

Dorian shakes his head assertively. "No, I'm sure of it. We've talked about her biological father multiple times. Beatrice gave her a fabricated story. Supposedly, he died in an airplane crash in the Rocky Mountains two months before she was born. They never married. Because he was an orphan and didn't know his real parents, there were no relatives for her to contact."

James scoffs. "Let me see if I can read between the lines. Beatrice had an affair with Randolph. Bore his kid and fabricated some shanty story about a make-believe father to cover it up."

Dorian shakes his head. "Pretty much."

"Why?"

"I don't know. So Randolph could keep face with his family or her. Who knows?"

Tamara grins. "No, because she was like him."

Everyone looks at each other, perplexed.

"Of course." Dorian finally agrees.

"Think about it. The media labeled her as the modern-day Black Widow. I remember the headlines." Tamara uses her hands to help convey. "Hundreds of millions in inherited wealth, in big, bold font. The article was about how she lured men into her bed, secured their wealth in marriage without a prenup, and after a few months but no more than a few years, each of them mysteriously became worm food."

"Similar to the Manchester family!"

Tamara nods. "You're catching on, baby. Ironically, the autopsy report on Beatrice established that the cause of death was a cardiac failure—similar to all of her late husbands! I'll bet if we research this, we'll find everyone died similarly."

Chapter 27

Randolph tries to keep his temper. "Sweetheart, did you?" He glares with tight eyes.

Amanda sniffles. Her heart rate feels uncomfortable. She takes a deep breath and exhales loudly.

"No, I mean, just a little teaser. I was so upset I couldn't think straight."

"I'm disappointed, angel. You broke your promise."

"Daddy, I'm sorry."

"Thomas tells me you went back to your sister's house. That was not a good idea."

"Daddy, you know I don't like it when you call her that."

"Never mind. Right now, I need to discuss business with Thomas. Go upstairs and pack. You're coming home with him on the company jet."

Amanda whimpers and marches upstairs. Thomas adjusts the computer monitor. "Sir," he says assertively. "There was an unavoidable hiccup."

"Explain!"

"His wife, sir!"

Silence follows.

"She woke and surprised me. She didn't make it."

"Unavoidable, it seems. You OK?"

Thomas nods. Deep inside, a nagging itch tears at him. "I'll manage."

"How's our timeline?"

"On schedule."

"The documents and the ledger?"

"Recovered."

"The cash?"

"Only seven-hundred forty-thousand!"

"The product?"

"All there!"

"Chicago's not going to like this. Did you send the image?"

"Yes, sir! They were not happy."

"Why?"

"Two reasons. The money! They want the balance paid by tomorrow."

Randolph grinds his teeth. "Goddamn it! We should have fixed this last month. I knew he was skimming. What else?"

"The woman was protected. They're demanding retribution."

"I'm not following. Do they want more money?"

Thomas shakes his head.

"Oh shit! Male or female?"

Thomas sighs. "Female, sir!"

Randolph looks horrified.

"I'm sorry. This was my fault. I'll explain what happened and offer myself as retribution."

"It'll be a cold day in hell before I let any harm come to my family. That includes you. I'll handle this on my end. For now, concentrate on your next task. What did you find out at the party? Did you deliver the package?"

"Dorian's been duly warned."

"Outstanding! We can rest easy."

"I don't think so."

"Explain."

"James Rawlings collected the box."

Randolph displays a quizzical frown. "What was he doing with Dorian?"

"No, you have it all wrong. They were both in Tamara's room."

Randolph tightens his lips—his trademark trait for trouble.

"She invited him and a guy named Randy for the weekend. That's what rattled Amanda."

"Why didn't she inform me earlier?"

"I don't know."

Thomas spends the next few minutes filling in the blanks. He explains what happened with the duel. She paid the merchant supplying the paint guns to remove the firing pin, only to lose due to trickery.

Randolph shakes his head. "This's about love, which is odd. He's a simplistic-minded boy. What'd you suppose changed his heart?"

"Hard to say. I think Tamara."

"How so?"

"Duplicity, sir!"

"He's in love with her?"

"I'm sure of it. There's more. She's not who we think. Remember Samantha?"

"Is there another detective on the case?"

"No, she's her sister."

Randolph's expression turns serious. "You have proof?"

Thomas plays the recording.

Randolph shakes his head. "We must assume Dorian has lost face. Call Felix. Tell him I want answers by noon tomorrow. Go collect Amanda and get her out of town. You have business tomorrow morning."

•••

Tamara shares the corroborating evidence the private detective found in the off-campus apartment. She reveals she was born in Texas and emphasizes critical points about her youth and how she earned a tennis scholarship at Texas A&M, the school of her dreams. By thirteen, she had life planned nearly to the end: boyfriend, college, and marriage by twenty-six, with two kids by thirty. Samantha, too! She opens a folded piece of paper with a numbered column of words. Half the numbers have a line through them.

"I was dead set on making my dad proud. After graduating with honors, I'd pump out a few kids and take over his oil business. Then Samantha went missing, and my world—excuse me—our world turned upside down. I dropped out of Texas A&M, moved to Providence, Rhode Island, and enrolled in Brown. Of course, with the help of my dad."

"I knew your father was an oil barren, but I had no idea you had a sister. You have quite the poker face." Dorian jokes.

"I suck at gambling in general, but thanks. Nobody knows, well, except you two now." Tamara looks at James. "I filled in some of the blanks for James earlier."

Dorian winks. "Who do you think wrote the note,

Amanda?"

"Not even close. Her distinct writing style would have exposed her. I'll put my money on Thomas. He's probably the one who cleaned the room and buried the bodies."

"How can people live with themselves knowing they committed murder and, nonetheless, helped cover it up?"

James shakes his head. "The world's full of corruption, deceit, and lies."

Tamara inserts the memory stick Dorian gave her and opens the file containing classified information on the Manchester family. What they discover shocks them. After Donald-the-first killed his parents, he changed his last name from Eccles, which he considered familiar, to Manchester, self-proclaiming his aristocratic place in society. He aligned his business dealings with many notorious gangsters throughout England and Scotland and earned the honorary 33rd degree of Master Mason. To date, sixteen siblings carried on the Manchester code. Twelve boys, yet only eight, including Randolph the

Second, took the oath. The rest fell to the curse. Tamara opens up a series of files relating to Donald the Fifth. Similar to his great-great-grandfather, handsome with alluring blue eyes and a chiseled chin, by forty-five, he married six times. Each spouse with vast family wealth found untimely deaths. Even though he was never found guilty of murder, he was the first incarcerated for racketeering and drug crimes. He spent ten years behind bars and died shortly after his release.

Tamara opens a document released by one of the families of the deceased spouses. It is the theoretically untraceable formula: A potion made from various rare plants in some areas of the Amazon rainforest. When blended with the roots of the poppy plant at high temperatures, cooled moderately, and taken internally, it would stimulate the heart to stop.

Dorian shakes his head. "Trust me. This is not the smoking gun." He opens the link. "Do you remember the conspiracy surrounding Bill Clinton?"

Tamara looks confused. "Yeah, what about it?"

"They claimed he was a murderer!"

"The Clinton Foundation! The Rockefeller Foundation! They're all corrupt." James interjects. "They belong to the 33rd Degree Masons. Everyone knows that."

Tamara glares. "That's hearsay; how does he relate to the Manchester family?"

"Nobody could produce any solid concrete evidence." Dorian opens another link. "Read this."

James takes the lead. "It's dated September 1937."

"OK!" Tamara questions.

"Give him a chance."

James skims through the first paragraph. "Let's see. It says an anonymous man, claiming to be a cultural anthropologist, who for three years lived with an indigenous tribe deep within the Amazon jungle discovered the formula. Upon returning to Europe, after reading about the Manchester curse, specifically how so many affluent women mysteriously died shortly after marriage, he mailed it to one of the families. Long story short, they hired a team of forensic scientists and sent them to South America." James skims through the next paragraph. "Here we go. Two years later, they returned." James browses through the following passage.

Tamara displays an impatient glare. "So—?"

"Hold on, I'm reading through the lines." James finally looks up. "You're not going to like this. The formula was a hoax."

Tamara's facial expression shows discontent.

"The team employed the help from multiple indigenous tribes, one of which had no contact with the outside world."

"They still exist?" Tamara asks.

James shrugs. "I guess. Let's see. After months of searching, they failed to locate two key ingredients. They experimented on rats using a host of other comparable plants. One formula did increase the heart rate to fatal levels, yet every autopsy showed traceable toxins."

Dorian takes over at the computer, opening a spreadsheet with dates and air shipments from South America. "I found this in one of Randolph's briefcases he left open on his desk. I snapped a photo when he took a bathroom break."

Tamara scrutinizes the data. "What is it?"

Dorian grins. "There was a time when Randolph and Beatrice met secretly. She would arrive and depart from the private garage. Thomas was always the driver. Randolph built a secret passage connecting to the basement. Nobody ever saw her come or go."

Tamara looks intrigued. "They were in it together?"

Dorian nods. "Randolph is a very private person, especially regarding Beatrice. He always made me wait upstairs. I didn't care. I didn't want to know more than I already did. On this one particular day, I brought down a portable medical refrigerated cooler with a digital lock. I was supposed to knock and then leave it at the door. Thomas warned me if Randolph thought I was snooping, he would not look lightly."

James scrutinizes the data. "What does it mean?"

"Proof!" Dorian points at the screen. "Each highlighted input reflects a shipment of ingredients from South America. The production date is to the right."

"So the formula's real?"

"I'm sure of it. Randolph owns a Bio-Tech company." Dorian opens another link and minimizes both windows. He aligns them side by side. "These dates reflect when her husband's passed. If you look closely, they died no more than two days after the production of the formula."

"Beatrice?" James asks curiously.

"Yes."

"So, it's perishable." Tamara looks intrigued.

Dorian points to the last highlighted input. "This shipment was synthesized two days before Beatrice turned up dead. The pattern matches. Randolph killed her."

Tamara looks horrified. "But why?"

"I don't know."

"What about all the other entries?" James asks.

Dorian shrugs. "I'll bet if we do some research, we'll find a string of deceit." Dorian removes the flash drive and looks at his watch. "I don't know about you two, but I'm exhausted." Dorian stands and hugs Tamara. "We'll look deeper into this tomorrow. Let's get some rest."

Chapter 28

Amanda opens the zippered kit. She eyes the syringes, the two small plastic containers that contain the dope, the cotton, and the two spoons, re-zips it, and pushes it away. She flips on the television and scrolls through multiple channels. All the while, her eyes keep migrating towards the kit. She sighs heavily and pushes it even further to the edge of the mattress. She removes her four-inch ultra-skinny black pumps made from crocodile leather from her suitcase. Again, she stares at the kit. This time, Amanda brings her right leg towards her chest and carefully inspects the skin between her big toe. Two scabs are visible, and they are sore to the touch. Amanda sniffles. She has been chasing the dragon for years. She thinks back to her first time. It felt fucking amazing like everything was floating, somehow magical, as if nothing mattered. Her heart rate and breathing increase.

In a matter of seconds, it kicks in. This time, Amanda snorted a small amount of China White powder. Amanda feels warm, like she put on a wool sweater, a bit dizzy but calm. A few minutes passed, then a few more, and she felt better. Amanda knows the ropes. Too many times, she sniffed too much. Fortunately, Dorian was always there. She closes the kit, puts her shoes on, and marches out of her room. She feels energetic, almost invincible.

Thomas left a note. Amanda glances at the riddles and more riddles. Indeed, there is nothing she wants to read: diamonds, sapphires, gold, and privilege. Nothing matters. Her life came to a crossroads, and she knows it. She glances at a few words. "Amanda! Your father demands that you remain inside."

Amanda crumples the paper into a small wad and tosses it into the trash. Her mind does not register the meaning. She scoffs, raises her nose, and marches out the front door. Right now, she has to take care of personal business.

• •

Felix

In a perfect world, the heroine would sit beside you in the café or on the bus. This person would enable or exploit. This person would reward for hard work, not penalize and teach instead of command. The list would be endless. The problem is that there was no reward for hard work in his world, only punishment. Felix was always forced to comply, either with a fist to the jaw or a broom handle to the back of his head. To dispute in any form or fashion meant agony. His strength was measured by how much pain he could endure. Felix never saw the inside of a hospital or had the luxury of medication. He was required to heal his wounds and set his broken bones. Felix had to fight for his right to live.

The moonlit landscape finally gives way to the dawn of the new day. Slowly, the shadows dissipate, and the room brightens as the sun breaches the horizon. Felix stands. He straightens his black pinstripe, walks over to the dresser, and gathers a pair of jeans and a t-shirt. He walks over to the closet, collects a pair of white sneakers and a New York Mets baseball cap, and moves over to the side of the bed. Dorian has his feet hanging over the side. His heavy breathing and the slight twitching of his eyelids could be from a dream. Felix reaches down and swiftly removes the sheet.

Dorian wakes in a flurry. At first, his stare remains confused. He sees the man and even recognizes him, but his sleepy eyes and waking mind have trouble focusing. Dorian rubs his eyes and swallows heavily. He blinks continuously, fearful of this man.

"Felix! What the hell are you doing here?"

His dread escalates as Felix tosses the clothing over his naked body. He places the shoes on the edge with the hat and motions accordingly. Felix grunts, pointing at his wristwatch watch, and raises two fingers.

Dorian only wonders why Randolph would send such a vile man to collect him. He remembers the black rose. Dorian understands his orders. Felix hates speech. He has barely said two words over the past six years. Though Dorian towers over him by four inches and outweighs him by twenty-five pounds, he knows not to reckon with this man.

Dorian follows Felix down the staircase. His pace remains swift until they reach the black SUV. Felix opens the back door and nods. Dorian hesitates but finds himself at the mercy of his captor. Felix pushes him inside. They exit through the back gate on the far side of the property reserved exclusively for Randolph. Felix remains silent until opening the door at the country house. He says one word.

"Basement."

The haunting eyes glaring from the portraits convey fear as Felix walks over to the third portrait, slides his finger down the side of the frame, and opens a hinged notch. He presses a button. To the left and mid-frame, a secret access panel pops open. Dorian feels uneasy as Felix punches in a seven-digit code, and the wall slides open. He glares and waves him inside. Dorian slowly steps through the threshold and stops. The lights are off, and it smells musty. Dorian can scarcely make out the four walls. Suddenly, Dorian finds it hard to breathe—beads of sweat form. From behind, Felix pushes him. Dorian loses balance and falls. He raises his head and squints as six rows of double fluorescents brighten the white-tiled room. A circular grate in the floor is below what looks like a Smith Squatting Rack, minus the cables, the pulleys, the lifting bar, and the weights. What worries him, integrated on either side of the upper supporting crossbars, are retractable cables with handcuffs. Two more connect the lower support beams, and a stainless sink with a rolled-up garden hose snugs the corner. Dorian knows he has entered a torture chamber.

Dorian stands. Felix has already removed his jacket and installed black leather gloves. Dorian worries about how he flexes his fingers and pounds his fists into his palms.

"What's this all about?"

Felix grins, shrugs, and points at the machine. Felix waves his hand, telling Dorian to step over to it. His mind swims with fear and his eyes well.

"There's no fucking way you're going to handcuff me to that—that torture machine. Where the hell is Randolph? Why'd you bring me down here? I have a party to manage. That's what I do. Pricilla and Amanda need me. You know Randolph knows this. They can't get along without my guidance. What's the meaning of this? Answer me!"

Felix remains silent. It frightens Dorian. Felix steps towards him and, with both hands, forcefully shoves him. Dorian stumbles. He recovers and raises his hands in defense.

"I might be gay, but I won't let you bind me without a fight."

Felix chuckles. His eyes almost sparkle. Their authority was not in question. Felix retreats a small step.

A renewed courage flushes over Dorian; however, it quickly fades into utter dejection as Felix lands a devastating blow to his lower right jaw. Dorian falls heavily and looks up, stunned. His brain feels rattled, and his lower bleeding lip sends a shock wave of horror through his mind. Are they going to kill him? Dorian tries to stand, but everything goes dark.

When he regains consciousness, Dorian finds himself handcuffed to the torture machine. His arms and legs are stretched outwards like a railroad crossing sign. His wrists and ankles ache from the pressure, and to draw a breath feels laborious. His eyes regain focus. He spits out a mouthful of blood. Felix has removed his shirt and is drinking a beer in a chair.

"Welcome back." Felix tips the bottle and takes a heavy guzzle. He burps and tosses the bottle into the trash.

Dorian struggles but quickly withdraws as the discomfort from the restraints intensifies. "Why are you doing this to me?"

Felix stands and walks close. "The boss wants to know everything."

Dorian needs clarification. "About what?"

Felix clears his throat. "That peach, Tamara!"

Dorian whimpers. His mind churns in a confused paradox. Did they discover that Samantha was her sister? But how? Nobody knew, not even him, until last night. His mind fades in and out. "Tamara!"

• •

After an energetic and sexually rewarding morning, James and Tabatha find relief under the steamy water's spray. Wearing only board shorts, James ventures into the kitchen and pours two cups of coffee. Randy greets him, wearing a pair of checkered boxers.

"Morning sunshine!" His hair looks like someone vigorously rubbed tonic throughout.

James chuckles. "Good morning Medusa! Nice hairdo! Coffee?"

Randy scratches his noggin and yawns. "Does a fat lady love Twinkies?"

"You crack me up, dude. Cream, sugar?"

Randy entertains the idea. "Black. Skip the poison." He finger-combs his hair and plucks the black rose from the box. "What the hell is this? I'll take two scoops of revenge. Did someone die?" He smells it.

With mugs in hand, James and Randy migrate to the couch. James pushes the truth about the rose.

"A secret admirer! Wow. The gay guys have all the fun."

"You're not doing so bad yourself." James prods his head towards the bedroom. "Both of them, again?"

Randy grabs his package and grins. "Um hmm— double trouble." He reaches into the box and pulls out a black zip drive. "Did it come with instructions?" He holds it up.

James snatches it out of his hand. "Was that in the box?"

"No, I pulled it out of my butt. Of course, it was. What's the big deal?"

"Never mind."

A knock on the door surprises James. He springs up the stairs and heedlessly opens it, not thinking caution would be prudent, especially after last night. James stares at the attractive blue-eyed blondie holding a grey box-type clipboard. Dorian introduced her as his assistant yesterday.

"Good morning, James," she smiles. "I'm sorry to bother you, but," she shakes her head worriedly. "Have you seen Dorian? Is he here?" She looks past him.

James gazes into her troubled eyes. "No, he's not. I'm sorry."

She grips the clipboard.

"What's going on?"

"He didn't make it to the staff meeting this morning. That worries me. It's not like him."

"Did you check his room?" James folds his arms.

"Of course, he's not there. I called him as well. What's weird is that it went straight to message!"

"That is strange! If I see him, I'll tell him to contact you immediately."

She smiles. "I'm sure it's nothing. Thank you." She looks past James and waves at Randy. He waves back.

James plops back down on the couch. "That was weird."

Randy sips his coffee. "I saw Dorian late last night. He was sitting in a lawn chair by the lake. He didn't say much, but he looked tired. Maybe he's catching up on sleep."

"Maybe."

"Sweetheart, who was at the door?" Tamara has her shoulder propped to the wall. She has a white towel wrapped around her torso.

"It was Penny, Dorian's assistant. She was looking for him."

Tamara looks concerned. "What'd you mean? Is he missing?"

"I didn't say that. Dorian didn't make it to the staff meeting this morning. He's probably caring for Pricilla or one of the other sisters."

"Oh! Did you make coffee?"

James jumps up. "Whoops! Honey, I'm so sorry; I'll bring you a fresh cup."

Tamara disappears into the bedroom.

Momoko and her sister look haggard. They kiss Randy goodbye, smile, and disappear out the front door.

●●

The back gate slides open and closes before the dust from her vehicle settles. Amanda has no idea Felix kidnapped Dorian. In her state of mind, it would not matter. She passes through a secondary gate and parks in an enclosed garage beside a Land Rover. She lowers the sun shade and stares at her face in the mirror. Her pupils are extremely dilated, and the whites are bloodshot. She grabs her phone, which is on silent mode, and checks for messages. Thomas texted three times.

Amanda sighs. She puts a drop of prescription medication into each eye. The tingling sensation energizes her. She grins at how fast the redness dissipates. A heavy-throated sigh exits. She sips some water and sniffs while inspecting her nostrils. A chill passes, which she acknowledges as the first sign of a craving. This time, instead of a snort, she pops a pill. She knows this bump will keep her sharp.

A suddenness confronts her. Her phone vibrates. Randolph has called twice already. Should she answer? Amanda swallows a dry lump, knowing there will be hell to pay if she shuns him. Taking a deep breath, she activates speaker mode. "Hi, Daddy!" She stares at her face in the mirror.

"Angel, where are you?"

"At home, where else would I be." She grins, knowing her lies are as convincing as her truths.

"Thomas has been trying to reach you for the past hour. He'll be back to the house shortly. Something's come up. I don't want you alone right now."

Amanda knows this means trouble. "Daddy, now what?"

"Don't worry, you're pretty little head. Listen." He pauses. "I know you're not home."

Amanda stares in silence. She forgot to deactivate the GPS function in the car and the phone.

"Do me a favor. Stop whatever you're doing. Go home now. Angel! Do you understand what I said?"

Her mind spins in a flux of apprehension, yet she finds truth in his voice. "Yes, yes, Daddy, I understand. I'm sorry. I'll be home within the half hour."

Her mind focuses only on her newfound direction, so she reverses out of the garage and smashes into the adjacent building. Careless of the damage to the quarter panel or the deep cracking sound of the collision, she retraces her route through the property and exits out the back gate. The tires squeal as they make contact with the pavement.

●●

Her first impulse fringes on guilt. Did something happen to Dorian because of what she revealed to him last night? Tamara cannot help but worry. Through the mirror, she watches James set the steaming mug on the make-up table. She wraps her arms around his waist and squeezes.

"Thanks, baby." She sniffles.

"You okay?"

"I'm worried. Where do you suppose he is?"

James tries to lighten her burden by petting her head. He feels so content, safe, and in love. "I'm sure he's fine." He places the drive on the table. "He left this in the box."

Tamara picks it up and glances at James through the mirror. "That's why he left it. The rose was the sign. Dorian knew this would happen."

James wipes a tear from her cheek. "There must be a logical explanation, or you're not telling me something."

"Amanda gave a black rose to an ex-boyfriend after he won a substantial amount of money in what she called a frivolous lawsuit—a business deal with her father that went south. Six months later, they found him beaten to death, I mean horribly. Ankle and wrist bruises proved ghastly torture to his body. The police questioned Amanda and her father, but their alibis were rock-solid." Tamara quivers. "I swear, Amanda, had something to do with it. She showed no remorse. I overheard her talking to her lawyer, which solidified it. She said he got what he deserved."

James changes his expression. "So, Dorian knew trouble was on the horizon, yet opted not to tell us. Why?"

"I don't know. His knowledge of the Manchester family far exceeds mine."

"We should inform Pricilla. I'm worried."

James and Tamara gather Randy and proceed downstairs.

Pricilla immediately cancels the morning's events and coordinates a search. By noon, the mood lightens. Two epiphanies come to light. Penny unexpectedly receives a text from Dorian. Supposedly, he left early this morning and drove to Wisconsin for a family emergency. On a private note, Tamara receives some valuable insight about Amanda. For now, she opts not to share it with the sisters. They orally express their concerns about Dorian, the majority agreeing his downright irresponsibility is grounds for dismissal. They unanimously decided to wait until he returned. Allow him to explain. For now, Penny will assume his responsibilities. The party resumes.

Randy asks. "Okay, guys. You're acting weird. What's going on?"

Tamara locks the door to their room. "Sit down. We need your help." She explained what had happened earlier this morning with the security guard.

"Amanda tried to run her down?" Randy inquires.

"Sort of. While making her rounds, she noticed the secondary garage door was open. Upon investigation, she found Amanda in her car. It was running. She could hear her talking on the speakerphone. She sounded hysterical. Suddenly, the car recklessly backs out. At first, she thought she was trying to run her down, but soon realized after smashing into the adjacent building, which pretty much crunched her right rear quarter panel and the way Amanda peeled out and disappeared down the back-property road, she had no idea somebody was there."

Randy questions. "She's a security guard!"

"Her name is Sandra. I know her personally."

James raises his hands. "Why didn't she report it to Pricilla or her boss?"

"I asked the very same question. She opted not to because Amanda would fire her. That's why she confronted me."

"Makes sense. What's this back road all about?"

"A private entrance and a dirt road winding through the wooded section on the opposite side of the property. It's strictly for family. Sort of like an emergency exit. Randolph built it a few years ago."

"Does Sandra know about her drug habit?"

"I'm not sure, but neither did I. I mean, not about the hard stuff until yesterday."

Randy looks concerned. "Momoko confirmed she's a junky?"

Over the next few minutes, they enlighten Randy about the rose and how it was delivered to the room, omitting the secretive details about Dorian.

"You mean the black rose was some sort of warning?" Randy questions.

They both nod.

"Which you think is tied into his sudden disappearance?"

They nod again.

"Amanda and her dad are behind this?"

Tamara nods.

"Then why do you need my help? I know nothing about their family."

"We want you to cover for us. We're going to look for Dorian. We think we know where he is."

"And where's that?"

"Randy! The less you know, the safer you'll be. Tell Pricilla we'll be back later tonight. Make up something. You're good at piling on the bullshit."

Chapter 29

Amanda takes the backroads through the city. About an hour before dusk, she screeches to a stop next to a black Range Rover. Careless of the damage to her car, Amanda walks around the side of the house and enters through the servant's access. She bypasses the kitchen, avoids Thomas, and disappears into her bedroom. Her mind challenges her father's words, knowing danger looms. A few minutes after snorting another bump, she hears a knock on her door.

"Go away. I don't want to talk."

"It's important. Your dad, he told you, yes?"

She quickly slides her kit under the pillow, cleans her nose, and opens the door. "What now? Are the bad guys after us again?"

His expression turns serious. "Your father will be home soon. He'll explain." Thomas looks at his watch. "Where've you been? Your dad told you to come straight home, didn't he?"

"None of your business!" She scoffs. "It's my prerogative to change my mind. Besides, here I am. Safe and sound."

Thomas glared. He knew she had started using again. Her droopy eyes and constricted pupils betray her. "Careful, young lady. You don't have to sharpen your nails with me."

Amanda scoffs, fluffing her hair.

"What happened to your car?"

"Never mind. It's only a scratch. I'll have Leroy fix it."

Thomas takes a small step inside. "Are you aware Felix collected Dorian this morning?"

Amanda raises an eyebrow.

"He's downstairs."

Amanda looks worried. "What for? He's harmless."

"It appears his conscience was stronger than his honor."

"What'd you mean?"

"Tamara knows you shot her sister. Dorian confirmed it. What surprised me was how long he held out. It was much longer than Felix thought he would."

Amanda jumps up and runs out of the room, purposefully jolting Thomas on his shoulder. "They'll be hell to pay if he hurt him!" She races downstairs, and after fumbling three times with the seven-digit code, the panel slides open. Amanda's heart drops to her stomach. She slumps down and places her hands over her shocked face. Dorian hangs limp. His arms and legs are black and blue from the pressure of the metallic restraints. His face is bloodied and swollen. His red eyes send a shiver of terror throughout her body. Dorian looks helpless. She takes a small step towards him. To her right, she sees Felix sitting on a wooden stool. He has his back resting on the tiled wall and the sleeves of his white dress shirt rolled up beyond his elbows. He removed his tie, and the three top buttons were open. Blood splats highlight the front. One hand has a black leather glove. The other holds a cigarette. He takes a long drag and blows multiple smoke rings. Amanda looks back at Dorian and shudders. His labored breathing confirms her worst nightmare. Felix hurt him badly.

"He talked."

Amanda glares at Felix. Her lips tremble with guilt. "About what? He's one of us. He took an oath, a sacred one. Dorian, what have you done." Her words falter into whispers. "What have you done?"

Felix presses play on the recording device.

Wide-eyed, Amanda listens. Her welling eyes dripping sadness down her cheeks as she stares at his broken face. Dorion tries to move his lips, but only tired wheezes exit.

A familiar voice beckons from behind. Amanda turns. She sniffles. "It couldn't be helped, angel." Randolph extends his hand.

Amanda grits her teeth angrily. "He would have said anything to stop the pain. Why daddy, why him?" She glares at Felix. "He's a monster."

"Take him down and clean him up. He's had enough." Randolph grabs her hand and pulls her out. Thomas closes the door. Randolph sits Amanda down on the couch in front of the fireplace. She stares up at the portrait of Donald and his two siblings. Her lips tremble.

"Angel! Dorian betrayed us. He knew full well the consequences. I'm sorry. I liked him."

Amanda glares. She presses her lips tight, which traps her tears. "They're right, you know."

"What'd you mean?"

"Our family is cursed—you and me." She points to the portrait. "Our fate, like grandfather's siblings, was sealed long ago."

"No!" Randolph gestures with his head. "We alone shape our destinies." He pets her hand. "I understand your pain, but it was necessary. Some of my business associates are irrational. An accident happened, and now they want revenge. I'm sending you to the safe house in Puerto Rico. Go to your room and pack a light travel bag. Please do not bring your phone or your laptop. Thomas will collect you within the hour. Do you understand?"

Amanda stands. She straightens her shoulders.

"How long this time?"

"I don't know, angel. Not long, I promise—not long."

●●●

Tamara turns off the main highway. They pass an upside-down yellow triangle sign. The county does not maintain this road. Private residents only

The road has no other cars. There are no lane lines, and they pass through a thick forest for the first mile or so. Tamara navigates a sharp corner, and the landscape changes dramatically. For the next few miles, they pass luxurious mansions on both sides. Some are enclosed behind iron fences and artsy concrete slabs, while others use trees. Flood lights mounted to supporting columns illuminate the depth and scope of each property.

Tamara finally slows. "We're here."

Giant oak trees spaced twenty or so feet apart line a ten-foot-high concrete wall. Each one is illuminated with floodlights and trimmed to perfection. Tamara stops in front of an illuminated iron gate fitted with multiple cameras.

"Why the concrete barrier?"

"He's paranoid. When Randolph bought the place, he removed the iron fence. The neighbors complained the property looked like a compound, so he planted the trees to appease them."

"This place is sick." James studies the three-story, squared, ultra-modern, lightly illuminated structure. "It looks like a garrison."

"Funny you say that. It reminds me of a bunker. The white car belongs to Amanda, the Range Rover Thomas, and the blue Maserati, Randolph."

Tamara accelerates ahead. She turns down a narrow dirt road at the far end, paralleling the wall, and stops under the canopy of a tree. She turns off the engine and douses the lights. Darkness settles quickly.

"Why here?" James asks.

"Amanda showed me this place. It's her emergency escape route exit. Randolph cut foot notches on either side to climb over."

"You mean if Scar Face-type gangsters attack?"

"I'm not sure. Randolph keeps his business affairs very private."

"You sure you want to do this? He must have video surveillance, guard dogs, and guns. Come on!"

"Probably all the above, except for the dogs. Randolph hates them." Tamara reaches behind the seat. She drops a black full-face beanie and a pair of black gloves on his lap. "Put these on." She grabs her phone and opens a map application. A blue icon flashes. "He's here." A few minutes later, a slight tap on her window startles James. Tamara opens her door and steps out.

James looks curiously at the very tall man dressed in black. A slight sheen highlights the whites of his eyes.

"James, I'm Cameron. I work for Tamara's father."

Tamara installed the dead-pool type full-face beanie. "Cameron discovered the blood in Amanda's apartment. He's going to help."

James looks confused but relieved. He has never done anything remotely illegal. "Nice to meet you," he says, looking at Tamara. "When did you call him?"

"I didn't. He's been staking out the house for about a week now. He planted a remote camera near the front gate and rigged an electronic grid to mark all the video cameras. When Amanda went MIA, he picked up his surveillance. We've been waiting for a break. This might be it."

Cameron activates his phone. "You were right. He arrived early this morning at dawn." He enlarges a photo of a black van entering the gate. Two men are in front. "You can't see his face, but it's Dorian." Cameron presses an icon and plays a short video clip. "This is the drone footage as they exit the van." Tamara and James huddle close. "He entered the house independently without force or at gunpoint but never left. I've been monitoring the gate all day."

"That's Dorian, all right. The green hair under the hat gives him away." Tamara agrees.

"The man behind is clearly in charge. How his hand remains in his coat pocket suggests a firearm or weapon." Cameron closes the application. "Listen, kiddo. I talked to your dad. He agrees I should investigate. He forbids you to enter the property. Wait here. I'll text you when I find something."

Tamara sinks her shoulders. "Really! He knows I can take care of myself."

Cameron stares. "Not this time," he says. "Both of you stay here." Cameron hands them a secondary phone. "You can keep track of me on this." He activates the wireless connection to a miniature video cam attached to his collar. He looks up into the night sky. "I have a man operating a remote drone above the property. Press this icon to switch the view back and forth. If something happens to me, get the hell out of here. Go straight to the State Police, not the sheriff. Randolph has them in his back pocket. Give them this phone. It records everything."

James and Tamara watch Cameron climb the barrier and disappear into the shadows from inside the car. The video link remains black as he walks through the tree line. James switches to the drone view. It shows the house and most of the wooded property line. They watch the darkened silhouette of Cameron enter the outside edge. He switches back, and they eagerly watch.

Cameron quickly closes in on the structure, keeping well outside the depth of the security cameras. He stops with his back to the side of the house, next to what appears to be the garage. He stays low between the cars, swiftly moves around the back side, and peers in through a window. They see one man sitting on a couch opposite a large wooden desk. Dark paneling and books line the walls.

"That's Felix! He's very dangerous." Tamara fills in the blanks.

The video feed cuts momentarily and then resumes. Cameron must be on the move again. He stops at the inside corner of two exterior stucco walls. Like Spiderman, he shimmies over a second-story balcony.

"This guy's good, a real-live Parkour assassin."

"My dad says he's ex-Navy Seal."

Using a tool, Cameron picks the lock to the sliding glass door. Before entering, he passes an electronic device around the exterior threshold.

"What's he doing?" Tamara asks.

"I think deactivating an alarm."

In suspense, they watch Cameron enter. For the next few moments, the video goes dark.

"He must be standing behind a curtain!" James suggests.

A whispered voice comes through.

"Kids, I've activated the external audio. You can hear me, but not the other way around. If something goes down, I want everything recorded." He opens the curtain, and a bedroom comes into focus. "It's probably one of the guest rooms. It smells musty." Cameron cracks the door. "Pretty quiet. Let's check downstairs. Okay, here we go."

His voice goes silent. They watch Cameron traverse a long hallway. Not a sound of his breathing or footsteps comes through. He passes two closed doors and stops at the side of a partially open one. He peers inside.

Tamara points at the screen. "It's her." Amanda has her back turned and is rummaging through a closet. An open suitcase, clothes, dresses, and some shoes are on the bed.

Cameron descends a stairwell. He makes his way through an expanded foyer, through a secondary seating area, and stops behind an open double door. The video doesn't show the interior of the room. Cameron whispers. "Two men are sitting at the kitchen table. A bottle of whiskey and some smokes. It's the same chap in the study. Wait, someone's coming."

The screen goes dark. Cameron whispers. "I ducked into a closet. Someone's ascending the basement stairwell!"

They remain captive. A sliver of illumination highlights the screen. Through the crack in the door, they see a man walk past.

"That's Randolph!" Tamara expresses.

A light voice comes through. "I don't know if you saw, but Randolph came up from downstairs. He was carrying a bloodied cloth. He walked into the kitchen. Here's my chance—Dorian must be down there."

Cameron glides down the stairwell and walks through an expanded living area. He stops before an oversized fireplace and examines a life-size portrait above. He whispers. "This is odd. The two youngsters in the painting have a haunting resemblance to Randolph and Amanda, but the date reflects 1847."

"God, I wish we could tell Cameron who they are." Tamara expresses.

"Don't worry. He's probably already figured it out."

Cameron scans the two rooms. They are empty. He walks over to the far wall and inspects the other portraits. He looks down at the floor.

"What's he looking at?" Tamara asks.

James looks closely. "Yes, yes, I see it. The carpet—" He points to a worn area.

"What do you see? I don't get the significance?"

Cameron inspects the paneling to the side of one of the portraits. He activates a purplish light on his device and passes it along the wall several times.

"Check it out. Fingerprints." James says.

Cameron flips open a hidden compartment, presses a button, and opens an access panel to the side.

"What's that?"

"I don't know. A keypad must open a secret room.

Where'd your dad find this guy? He's good, really good."

Cameron shines the light from his phone device on the keypad, which reveals smudges. After adjusting the illumination, he presses a few icons and begins pushing the buttons on the keypad.

"Do you think he'll crack the code?" Tamara asks inquisitively.

"Look at him. His brain thinks like a computer."

A few moments later, a section of the wall glides open. Cameron quickly enters and discovers Dorian curled up in the fetal position on the floor next to a metal grate.

"It's a torture chamber." Cameron kneels. "Dorian," he whispers, "can you hear me?" Cameron gently feels for a pulse on his neck. "He's alive but badly beaten. I think they broke his ribs."

Dorian cracks his eyes. His lips move, but they cannot hear his scratchy voice.

Cameron whispers. "Hang on, buddy. I'll send help. Do you hear me? Hang on."

Tamara wipes a tear. "Oh, my GOD! Look at what

they did to him."

James wraps his arms around Tamara. He has no words.

Cameron turns and stares out the door. He stands and, without a word, marches out. He quickly closes the door, and before they can grasp the situation, he dives to the floor behind the span of the massive sofa.

Chapter 30

The screen turns dark, and a haunting silence follows. Not a whisper comes from Cameron. James switches the screen to drone view and back.

"Everything looks normal outside. Someone must have come downstairs; that's why he cannot talk. I think the screen went dark because he must be belly first tucked tight to the back of the couch."

Tamara shivers. "I wish we could talk to him."

"That's exactly why he didn't activate the two-way. Even the slightest whisper could give his position away. Don't worry; he can take care of himself. He's a pro."

Tamara sniffles.

Two arguing voices slowly come through on the audio. "I told you he'd be angry. You were only supposed to scare him, not kill him."

"Careful never works!" The man scoffs. "Besides, he's still alive."

"Barely!"

Tamara recognizes the bold accent of the second man. "That beady voice can only come from one person, Felix. God, I hate him so—especially now."

James raises his hand as if telling Tamara to hush. They stare in silence at the darkened screen, and cumbersome footsteps only heighten the suspense.

"Did you leave the frame panel open again?" One man asks.

"No, maybe Randolph!"

"Must have."

On edge, they listen. The distinct buzz of the secret panel opening can only mean the men have come to collect Dorian. A slight illumination clarifies the truth. Cameron has moved. Within his darkened recess, they watch Felix unzip a black body bag. He lays it on the floor, and together, they drag Dorian out by the arms. They carelessly drop his limp body, tuck his limbs inside, and zip it.

Tamara weeps empathetically. She has never felt so helpless, so worthless, so empty. "He's still alive; tell me he's still breathing!"

James swallows a dry lump. He feels stricken. "I don't know. He didn't move, not once." His words were on the verge of whimpering.

"Poor chap. He was harmless." Thomas expresses. "How do you know he told the truth? I've told you a hundred times people will say anything to stop the pain."

Felix replies. "His eyes."

Thomas finds his answer unnerving. "Next time, I'll do the interrogating. Come on, let's do this. You take the heavy end."

With troubled hearts, they watch Felix and Thomas carry the bag upstairs.

Cameron moves over to the edge of the stairwell. He peers around the corner. The two men have reached the top. A moment later, they disappear from view. "Kiddo, I feel your pain. I know you held this man in high regard. I'm unsure if you heard, but he told me something important before he passed. Listen, keep your head high. I promise these men will pay for this heinous offense."

Tamara breaks down. James does his best to comfort her, but she pushes him away. "I want their entire family wiped from the face of this earth if it's the last thing I do." Her angry words echo within the confines of the vehicle.

The suspense heightens. Cameron made it safely out of the house but inadvertently found trouble near the garage. A motion light activates. They watch him disappear into the side door. The screen goes dark. What causes alarm? The audio picks up what sounds like the clanking links of an iron chain.

"What's that noise?" Tamara asks.

James shakes his head. "I don't know. Maybe a chain or a tool fell to the floor. I don't know. It's too dark to see anything."

A few long seconds pass. "Kiddo," his voice finally comes through. "Listen, I've activated the two-way audio. We can now communicate. Are you reading me?"

"You scared the hell out of me. Are you okay?" She breathes a sigh of relief.

"Still here, Kiddo. Listen. I think they're on to me. I took cover in the garage. I must have tripped one of the motion cameras. James, I need your help. Switch over to drone view. Tell me what you see."

"Hold on. I got it. Okay! Felix and Thomas finished loading Dorian into the trunk of a black sedan. They're walking back to the house. Everything looks normal, no, wait." James points to the screen.

"That's Randolph," Tamara says, sniffling. "Why's he waving his hands in the air?"

"Cameron! Randolph ran out of the house. He's pointing to the garage. Oh, my God, they both have pistols. Get out of there; get out now! They're coming towards you."

They watch with concern as Cameron slips out the rear entrance. A motion light illuminates. He immediately breaks the bulb and takes off in a full sprint for the tree line. It looks relatively close on the screen, but the distance exceeds half a football field. Suddenly, a series of floodlights illuminate the grounds.

"That's not good!" Cameron voices between breaths. "Do you see anybody following?"

"Not yet, all clear. They opened all of the garage doors and entered. Randolph went back inside the main house."

For the next few moments, heavy breathing and rapid footsteps fill the audio. They watch his obscured silhouette disappear beneath the darkness of the dense canopy.

"Kiddo," he takes in a heavy breath. "How are you holding up?"

"I'm fine. Just get back here. What are you waiting for?"

"Not yet! As I said, it's time for these blokes to pay the piper. James, you copy?"

"Roger that. What'd you need?"

"The second icon on the bottom, the one resembling a half moon. Press it."

Tamara leans closer.

"Wow. What happened?"

"Thermal imaging with inferred is sort of like night vision enhanced. You can track anything producing body heat, even through the tree line. Can you see me waving?"

"Holy crap. Where did you get this equipment, NASA? It's like the aliens tracking Arnold Schwarzenegger in the movie Predator?"

"Kiddo, your father spares no expense. Listen. I'm switching the audio to the external ear jack. This way, you'll still be able to talk without giving my location away."

"Got it. What else?"

"Stay inside the car. Lock the doors and keep an eye on the monitor. Let me know the second they exit the garage."

"Wait," Tamara expresses. "What'd Dorian say before —oh, my God," she bawls heavily—"before he left us?"

"He told me where I could find Samantha."

●●●

Amanda shouts, but no one hears. She storms downstairs and enters what Randolph calls the security room. "Daddy, my bags are ready. Why didn't anyone answer me?"

Randolph raises his hand. "There's a situation. Someone infiltrated the property. It's random, but we're on it."

"Is it them?" She glares.

Randolph sighs. "I don't think so. They would have sent an army."

"Thank God." Amanda folds her arms to her chest and examines the multiple monitors. "So, where is this Houdini? I don't see anyone."

Randolph points. "Somewhere in the tree line out back. The cameras didn't pick him up, but I'm sure he breached the house. I think he knows about Dorian."

"Really!"

Randolph replays the security footage. "The cameras caught a glimpse of him running across the lawn to the tree line. Right there and there." He snaps his fingers nervously. "It's as if he knew where every lens was and their focal depth. He stayed outside their range and always with his back turned."

"Daddy, you're scaring me. Who's this man?"

"I'm not sure, but I think he's the same guy who broke into your apartment in Rhode Island a few years back. His characteristics are similar." Randolph rubs his forehead. "It's got to be him. I'm sure of it."

Through the partially open window, a small white bird flies inside. In a frantic attempt to escape, it circles Amanda. Naturally, she ducks and bats at it with her hands. Amazingly, she connects and sends it, smashing head first into the glass pain. The window cracks, and the bird falls lifeless to the floor.

Amanda stumbles. Her frantic eyes stare without blinking. She raises her hands and covers her open mouth. She begins shaking her head. "No! No, no, no, no, no, no," her distressed voice beckons. "No! No! No!"

Randolph quickly kicks the bird under the desk. A gust of wind funnels through the window, kicking up a few feathers. They float almost magically in front of Amanda. She stares, mystified, until one lands in her open hand. Frantically, she lets out a bone-chilling scream.

"Angel, it was only a bird. It's OKAY. I promise. It was attracted to the light." Randolph walks over to the window and notices the outside screen lying in the dirt below. "Hmm," he says to himself.

"It was white, wasn't it?"

Randolph wraps his arms around Amanda. He lightly squeezes and rubs her shoulders. "The bird?"

"Yes, was it white?" She sniffles.

"I think so. Don't worry. Something was probably hunting it. That's why it flew inside. It was trying to find safety."

"It's a bad sign."

AMANDA SHARES HER NIGHTMARE

It always starts with her standing on the crest of a hill. In the backdrop, she hears what sounds like the mounting strain of jet engines. She searches the horizon and identifies an extremely low-flying airliner. The nose cone, the shiny front windows, and the massive wings descend straight toward her. She drops to her knees with only seconds to react, skirting the landing gear. She gasps as hot turbulence and jet fuel suck the oxygen from her lungs. She stands and watches the smoke trail disappear behind a hill. Strangely, she waits for an explosion from its descent angle and speed. Instead, only a billowing cloud of black smoke rises. She runs over countless rolling hills until, out of breath, she stops. Oddly, the smoke has dissipated. She looked back and watched the sun set below a cloudless sky. She can see her trail through the knee-deep brownish grass. It seems like a river snaking through an endless prairie. Confusion confronts her.

Did she imagine the plane? She climbs to the top of yet another hill. There, amid a sunken valley, she sees the fuselage. From the wings forward, it appears intact. The engines and the landing gear are broken and scattered. What confuses her is that the exterior looks burnt and deteriorated, as if it had crashed years ago!

She enters. Strangely, the seats, the overhead luggage compartments, the window shades, and the carpet appear brand new. She walks up the aisle and peers in through the open cockpit door. Amongst the numerous digital displays and avionics, the pilot and navigator do everything humanly possible to keep the plane airborne. As frightening, through the windows, the ground closes rapidly. She braces for the inevitable. She closes her eyes, but instead of feeling the force of the aircraft smashing into the hardened earth or experiencing a shock wave of explosive heat, she senses the inertia of quiet peace.

She opens her eyes. Shards of broken glass cover the floor. Outside, the landscape looks parched. Fires had raged. As strange, the pilots are missing. She exits the cockpit and sees Brian, the boy who committed suicide in the tenth grade, standing in the aisle a few rows back. An aura of white surrounds his body. He walks up and takes her hand. His skin feels cold, and his eyes are empty, like when he begged her not to dump him after devouring his virginity. He hung himself one week later, leaving a note declaring his endless love. His parents blamed her cruelty for their loss. Brian points to the window. Outside, she sees hundreds of people.

Some are moving their lips as if trying to communicate—one young man, holding a red apple, waves for her to come outside. Looking back, she sees an adolescent, James Rawlings. Similar to Brain, a white glow surrounds his body. Interestingly, he has a red apple. He points to the window. Like before, the people outside stare. The difference is that they now have colored auras surrounding their bodies. What becomes clear is red means hell—blue, neutral, white, heaven. James offers the apple. Within the rind, she sees two white birds. James points at the window. Outside, they are flying towards her. They smash into the glass and fall to the ground. Looking out, they are lying motionless. Their heads cocked sideways with red auras surrounding their bodies.

The dream always ends with her trying to exit the aircraft. She never reaches the end because it always maintains a relative distance.

RANDOLPH COMFORTS AMANDA

Randolph kisses her forehead. "Angel, it was a fluke. It had nothing to do with your dream. Things like this happen. I'll have one of the groundskeepers bury him out back."

"It means death."

Randolph shakes his head. "No, I've told you, this family does not believe in superstition. I'm not going to let anything happen to you. I promise."

She walks over to the window. "Why's the screen missing?"

"I don't know. Maybe they were cleaning and forgot to put it back up." He closes the window.

"Daddy, I'm scared. The nightmare proves it."

Randolph hugs her, places his chin on top of her head, and kisses her skull. "Sweetheart! Listen. Enough with the superstition, you hear me? We control our destiny. It's not up to chance. Now, go to your room and stay there. I need to concentrate on finding the intruder. Will you please do this for me?"

"What are you going to do?"

"Felix and Thomas will flush him out. Look." He points out the window. "They're wearing night vision gear and are armed with shotguns. Now, go upstairs and lock the door. I'll come and get you when it's over."

Amanda sniffles and exits.

●●

"Cameron!" Tamara cries out. Two men exit the back door. Oh, my God!" She looks at James. What're they wearing?"

James studies the screen. "You're not going to like this. I think night vision equipment, shotguns, double barrel, and body armor."

"They must think I'm special."

"That's not funny," Tamara expresses. "Cameron, please get out of there. These guys are serious. You're outgunned. Come on, let's go home."

"Kiddo, I might not get another chance as clean as this one. Samantha and now Dorian deserve closure. James, you with me?"

"Hundred percent!" James gazes at Tamara. Her lips tremble.

"Does that mean you're going to kill them?"

"An eye for an eye! That's what the bible says."

"Sure, but shouldn't the police handle this?"

"With his money and connections, Randolph will have them out the next day. Tamara, you know of his ruthless nature."

Tamara nods in agreement. "He's right. They always seem to find a loophole, or an eyewitness emerges from the woodwork."

"Kiddo, times short. James, where are they now?"

"They entered the tree line. They haven't split up, at least so far."

"Okay, listen. Under no circumstances are you to leave the car. Keep the doors locked, and keep me posted. Talk to me. Give me their locations. How close they are, especially if they split up. Don't be shy about anything. The more details, the better. If, for any reason, something happens to me, or if you don't feel safe, or if a vehicle approaches, get the hell out of there. Don't worry about me. I can take care of myself. Remember, drive straight to the State Police. You hear me?"

Tamara releases her grip on the steering wheel, flexes her hands, and stretches her fingers. She lets out a slow breath. "Yeah, I got it." She stares at James. "This is not your fight. You don't have to be here."

James shakes his head. "You're wrong. They made it my fight by torturing Dorian and zipping him in a body bag. He didn't deserve to go out so horribly."

"Kiddo, we both knew it would come to this."

Chapter 31

Randolph surveys the tree line through high-powered binoculars. He grabs the two-way wireless headset. "Thomas, where are you?" His voice is firm and clear.

"Inside the tree line," a whispered voice comes through.

"I want him alive if possible. Do you read me?"

"We've got to find him first. He might've already vacated the property."

"I don't think so. Camera six picked up motion at the top of the hill."

Thomas signals Felix, emphasizing their new directives. Felix grunts. This only reinforces what Thomas already knew about this man. He will shoot to kill, not wound. Thomas drops to one knee and inspects the ground. What worries him so far is that the intruder has been easy to follow. Suddenly, the signs faded, identifying that he was a professional. They continue towards the hill. Every footstep, the snapping of the underbrush, the bark of a distant dog, even the roar of a high-altitude aircraft racing east directly above, and the whine of a distant siren causes alarm. Without incidence, they reach the apex. They locate the camera. The intruder destroyed the lens. Thomas knows this man is a pro. Actually, at this point, they are the prey.

Thomas informs Felix. "Stay alert. He's close."

Felix grumbles.

From behind, branches rustle. Felix turns. Thomas thinks he sees movement. Another sound comes from the opposite direction.

Could there be two intruders?

●●●

With the insight of a predator, Cameron crouches

down and rests his back on a tree. His rouse has worked. He yanks on the thin rope attached to a fallen branch ten feet to his left. The noise confuses them. They split. The one to his left has no combat skills. His clumsy approach gives him away. The other one must be Thomas. His movements are precise and careful. Twice in the past few years, he eluded his cunning. Cameron grips the chain, careful not to rattle the links. He raises it over his head. Another twig snaps from his right. Fortunately, his eyes have adjusted to the darkness. His dilated pupils catch a slight movement. The man tracking him has aimed his weapon.

The crackle of the underbrush intensifies. Another snap, this one from behind, signifies they are both within striking distance. Cameron holds his breath and listens. He can hear slight whispers. They must be communicating via radio headsets. He hunkers down. Suddenly, an immediate and piercing pain paralyzes his left shoulder. Cameron grits his teeth, knowing any sound would further give his position away. Fortunately, by squatting when he did, the blade would have found the center of his chest instead of grazing him. Careless to the clanking of the chains or the snapping underbrush, Cameron rolls forward. His instinct to keep his adversaries guessing has worked. He hears the slight whoosh from a second blade sailing past his head. Cameron realizes they want him alive by using throwing knives instead of shotguns. To even the odds, he ruptures the internal chamber of a high-intensity phosphorescent chemical stick, aggressively shakes it, and tosses it high. Instantly, the surrounding area ignites. Cameron identifies the enemy. They are standing approximately ten feet apart and wearing night vision goggles. In the few short seconds before the orb falls to the ground and before they can counter—provisionally blinded by the sudden brilliance—Cameron stands. He swirls the chain over his head and, with all his strength, crushes the skull of the closest man. Felix falls heavily to the ground. His depressed body is unmoving, with no apparent revenge. Without hesitation, he again whirls the chain, takes a step sideways, and releases it. His aim proves worthy. The crunching sound proves the headgear of his adversary shattered, suggesting he died. Strangely, he remains standing, most likely due to the overhanging branches. What Cameron did not predict was the piercing sting penetrating his right shoulder. Looking down, he stares at the blunt handle of yet another throwing knife.

James unlocks the door and exits the vehicle. He joins Tamara, who is already waiting by the barrier. James reaches up and helps Cameron climb down. He favors his right side. The slight illumination highlights a knife handle protruding from his shoulder.

"Oh, my God, you're hurt. Should I pull it out?" Tamara asks.

"No!" Cameron grimaces, entering the passenger rear door. "Both of you, get in. We've got to make tracks. Something dangerous is about to go down."

••

Randolph throws his radio headgear to the table. Five minutes have lapsed since the last contact with

Thomas. This means one of two things. Most likely, they are close to finding the intruder. It could also signify trouble. What worries him beyond the lack of communication is that he heard the distinct sound of muffled rotor blades about a minute ago.

Randolph opens the door and steps out into the warm night air. He lights a cigar and looks up. The flicker from the television illuminates the partially closed curtain from Amanda's bedroom. He kisses her, knowing her confusion, especially after the freak bird incident. He hears slight noises coming from the tree line. He takes another long drag and exhales. His mind races. Are they from Thomas and Felix? Did they flush the intruder back toward the house? Unsure, he marches inside and inspects the security monitors.

Amanda opens the bag of white powder. Her eyes blur to the slight brown tint glistening from within. She seals it and throws it to the edge of the bed. For she knows another bump would push her far beyond her cognitive boundaries. She flings her legs over the side and walks over to the vanity. The lines on her face in the mirror show uncertainty. Her superstitions scare her. Never before has she experienced such an omen. She opens the top drawer and pulls out two white ponytail hair ties. Her good luck charms, which she maintained, always helped in distress. The same ones she wore the day she met James Rawlings at the park. She stares at the embroidered flower arrangement, rainbow-colored in length. How they sparkle and align so uniformly. She parts her hair, attaches them, and admires how youthful she looks.

Randolph adjusts the focal length on security camera number three. On the edge of the tree line, he sees movement. With a few quick adjustments, he identifies two men. They are kneeling behind a shrub and looking towards the house through high-powered scopes attached to automatic rifles. To confirm his notion, he zooms in on their faces. What he sees verifies his worst fears. South American.

Amanda installs her ear pods and increases the volume. She places her phone to the side and lays on the bed. The softness of the pillow relaxes her. She closes her eyes and begins lip-sinking the song.

All the while, Randolph pans the outer perimeter. Seven more men have taken up strategic positions. He tries to contact Thomas, but only dead static. Out of time, he races upstairs.

"Amanda, get up now!" He yells.

Amanda sits up and removes the pods. "Daddy, what now—" she raises her hands.

Randolph eyes the drugs. Not waiting for approval, he physically yanks her to her feet. "We have to move now." He places a pair of tennis shoes next to her feet. "Put these on."

"Daddy!" She reaches for the bag.

"No! No more—they're here."

Her heart could not beat faster as she followed Randolph downstairs into the basement. Strangely, the walls are bare, and the portraits are gone. Randolph opens a secondary secret access panel. They enter the emergency evacuation tunnel, and the reinforced cement door closes.

"Daddy, stop. I need to catch my breath."

Randolph grumbles. He grabs Amanda by the hand and aggressively marches her down the long spherical passage, which has strategically positioned lighting on the sides to make it appear endless. At the far end, he punches another code. They stand back as a whining motor opens a bunker-style two-foot-thick concrete doorway. They enter an expanded room. Two golf carts await. Randolph quickly seals the corridor.

"Get in and keep quiet. I'll explain everything once we're safe." Randolph removes the trickle charger and accelerates down the expanded corridor.

•••

The tires screech as Tamara turns onto the paved road. She accelerates towards their destination, the private airport sixteen miles west. Cameron opts to leave his rental. A tow truck will pick it up tomorrow. James stares at the knife protruding from his shoulder. The black metallic handle has three small holes, each progressively prominent towards the bolster. His mind struggles to comprehend his agony. Cameron tears open a first aid kit. He carefully cuts his body suit and pulls the fabric down over his wounded shoulder.

What intrigues James is that he sees very little blood or bruising. He exhales loudly.

Cameron eyes him. "Take a breath, son. Everything will be all right." He motions with his head. "Move to the back. I'm going to need some assistance."

James climbs over, opens three of the larger gauze bandages and alcohol wipes, and unscrews the tube of anti-biotic ointment.

"Kiddo, how are you holding up?"

Tamara adjusts the rearview. She watches Cameron spread a thick layer of white cream around the wound. "Fine. I'm fine. You don't look so good."

"What this? It's not so bad."

Tamara cringes. "Does it hurt?"

"I've hurt worse." Cameron wipes his fingers with an alcohol wipe.

Tamara negotiates a slight turn in the road and glances back through the mirror. "Are they—I mean—

Thomas and Felix?"

Cameron eyes her. "Let's say they opted for early retirement."

Tamara swallows a dry lump. Even though they both deserved punishment, the thought of them never breathing again lies heavy. She skids to a stop at the four-way. "I feel sick to my stomach."

"Kiddo! Take a deep breath. They lived on the edge. Think about your sister and Dorian. They're vindicated."

She sighs. "It's in knots."

"It'll pass. Kiddo, I need you to focus. You may have heard their distinct signature, but two choppers operating in stealth mode arrived before I climbed over the barrier. Your dad sent a cleaning crew."

James looks dumbfounded. "You mean this was pre-planned?"

"For two long years. We've been waiting for the right opportunity. Randolph has a host of enemies. Most of them arms and drug dealers. He has no idea who's coming after him."

"He's a drug dealer?"

Cameron nods. "Worse, a modern-day gangster! Freemason!"

"Why didn't you guys fill me in?"

"Never mind. Right now, concentrate on getting us to the airport. Kiddo! Take a left. You'll see the onramp to the freeway on the right a few miles ahead."

Tamara sighs. "What about you? Shouldn't we go to the hospital? I don't know if I can handle another dead body."

"Thanks for caring. Don't worry. The armor fabric in my suit prevented the blade from doing serious damage. Now get us to the airport. Your father has a plane waiting." Cameron glances at James and nods.

By the time they reached the terminal, Cameron had removed the knife and bandaged both wounds. James helped put his arm into a sling. Admittedly, even though he attended multiple first aid courses and completed preliminary EMT ambulance training, as Cameron pulled the knife out, he almost passed out.

●●●

Randolph exits the long tunnel into a sizable underground garage and stops at the side of two black range rovers. He grips her hand. "Angel, how are you holding up?"

Her face shows stress. She nods softly. "I'm okay. I never thought we'd ever have to use the tunnel. I thought you were overly cautious and protective every time you made me practice." Amanda slowly scans the interior of the garage. Four video monitors to the right of the windowless steel roll-up door show a fierce gun battle with the remaining guards and mercenaries.

Randolph lightens her anxiety. "We're safe. Only Thomas knows about this escape route."

Amanda looks worried. "Where is he? He's supposed to be here with us. Who's going to drive the second vehicle?"

"I sent him with Felix to find the intruder. I'm sorry, but I lost communication with him approximately thirty minutes ago."

"What does that mean? Who's going to protect us!"

Randolph squeezes her hand. "Thomas will meet us at the airport. I promise. Now listen. You're going to have to drive one of the trucks. We have a schedule to keep. Are you good with this?"

Amanda sighs. "I'm scared, Daddy, scared." She stares at the video monitors. An explosion sends two of the security team airborne. A slight thud vibrates through the ground. Amanda cringes as a cloud of dust filters down.

Randolph opens the door, helps her climb in, and snugs the seat belt. He starts the engine. On the navigation screen, a blue line marks her route. An automated male voice welcomes her. "Approximate time to destination: twenty-six minutes."

Randolph kisses her cheek. "Sweetheart, you can do this. Follow the route exactly like we've practiced. Remember, do not alter. I'll meet you at the private airport. Are you ready?"

Amanda sniffles. "Make sure you're there. I can't do this alone."

Randolph squeezes her bicep. "I love you, Angel." He

shuts the door and quickly enters the second vehicle. A few seconds later, the bulletproof door rises, and the two trucks exit.

Chapter 32

James finds the sleek exterior of the Bombardier Global 8000 aircraft exhilarating. He has never flown on a private jet before and marvels at how simple the boarding process was. They did not have to pass through the metal detector, allowing Cameron to carry his duffle bag packed with specialized fighting equipment. Tamara guides him through the main cabin. She explained the function of the automatic controls on the extra plush leather seats. Showed him how to flush the toilet and took him through the fully equipped kitchen and into the cockpit. She introduces the pilot, Jeff, the co-pilot, Nick, and Jacky, the stew. They invite him to come up and chat once airborne. Tamara completes the tour in the private bedroom. She winks and asks if he wants to participate in the mile-high club. James happily accepts.

Cameron buckles up in the front row. He lowers the phone. "Kiddo, time to strap in! The cabin doors are closed. Wheels up in five."

As the agile aircraft climbs skyward, James stares at the sophisticated wings, mesmerized by how the flaps neatly tuck away and the winglets vibrate to the turbulence. Before long, they level off at cruising altitude. James glances at Tamara. Her grin, especially how the right side of her mouth slightly slants, reminds him of his mother.

"Kiddo," Cameron holds out the phone. "Your dad wants a word."

Tamara unbuckles her belt and puts the phone to her ear. Her conversation revolves around simple yes and no answers, with a few noncommittal um-hums. She hands the phone back to Cameron. "He'll call you back in thirty."

Cameron nods. "You two hungry?"

"Starved. How's your wound?"

"Took some pain pills."

After the snack, Tamara grabs James by his hand. "Come on, baby. We both could use some sleep."

They quickly find comfort under the sheets. James can barely hold back, discovering the orgasm at forty-thousand feet incredibly intense.

A knock on the door wakes James. He glances through the portal. The morning sun has breached the horizon. He opens the door.

"Morning, son," Cameron nods.

"Morning!"

"We've started our descent. Wake Tamara, and meet me in the main cabin.

Cameron increases the volume on the television. They all listen as the platinum blonde newscaster dressed in bright red reports.

"The motive's still unclear," she begins, "but the authorities are confirming a major gun battle took place within this ten-acre compound owned by Randolph Manchester, a prominent business tycoon." A picture of him flashes. "Neighbors confirmed low-flying helicopters buzzed their properties late last night. Soon after, one of the bloodiest shootouts in the great Buckeye State of Ohio occurred."

A video from a nearby neighbor shows three black helicopters hovering while men with shouldered weapons repel down. Crushing explosions soon follow.

The reporter continues. "We've learned that a handful of armed security personnel confronted the invaders head-on. They held back the brutal attack in a miraculous standoff until the swat team arrived. In a daring retreat, the helicopters landed, and the remaining men escaped."

The camera pans across the smoldering house. Body bags litter the bloodied driveway and the surrounding property. Black smoke billows from multiple burnt vehicles. "So far, the body count exceeds twenty-seven. Yet, out of the ruble, a hero emerges." The camera follows the reporter to an ambulance. Two paramedics are bandaging the head of a man wearing black body armor. His tired face has multiple bruises. His swollen right eye tries to focus as the camera zooms in. "This man is Thomas Falk. The chief security officer." She moves closer. "Mr. Falk, can you tell us what happened?"

Cameron listens as Thomas fabricates an incredible story. He insists his combat training and the devotion of his hand-picked security force helped curb the invaders. "The leader of the attacking force thought he killed me, but my knife instead found his heart." Thomas finishes with a statement that pretty much exonerates Randolph. "I don't know why they invaded the property, but I'm sure the truth will surface soon. Randolph Manchester has no idea why this happened. I believe this was a premeditated act of terror on the homeland of the United States of America."

Cameron turns off the television.

"I thought you—" Tamara inquires.

"I guess not! The man must have nine lives."

●●

Amanda pulls into the designated dirt parking area next to the private runway. There are no buildings— only a long stretch of cracked black tarmac surrounded on either side by shrubs and a wire fence. The rolling gate automatically closes. She turns off the engine and stares at her face in the rearview mirror. Her mascara has run from crying, and the inside corners of her eyes are bloodshot. She scans the area. The plane has yet to arrive. She digs through her purse for her phone. After three attempts to contact Randolph, each time prompted to voice mail, she threw it back inside. She digs deeper and pulls out the plastic bag of white powder. She does not hesitate this time. The bump energizes her spirit. She impatiently reclines the chair and stairs at the splotchy sky through the moon roof.

Her mind begins to churn. Amanda shakes her head in disgust. "Why? Why is this happening!" She sobs uncontrollably. "Daddy, where are you? Where are you!"

Amanda gradually settles. She cleared her eyes and sat up, thinking she saw his vehicle approaching. Her face shows disappointment as a black pick-up truck filled with boxes fades into the morning haze. Some clarity surfaces inspecting the navigation console. She should be able to track Randolph using GPS. She presses an icon, yet frustration again fatigues her sedated mind. The automated voice advises his tracking function is deactivated.

A fear that her father found trouble triggers confusion. The white bird was a sign—the family curse exists. She glances at the portraits in the back. Everything was pre-ordained, starting from Harold and his ruthless lifestyle. Now hers, especially when dealing with her mother. From an early age, Audrey was always on some crusade. Health foods or drugs, drinking. Then the parrots, which Amanda despised, especially the constant gawking. Her mind wanders further into an emotional relapse. Her collection of forgotten gifts from past parties, which her mother stored in the basement of their New York residence. Memories of her spoiled childhood. Audrey swore she loved Amanda but never once bought her a gift.

A slight reflection in the sky draws her attention. She focuses on an approaching aircraft. Amanda clears her eyes and watches it loop the field. It rapidly descends, lands, and stops a few meters away from her vehicle. Suspense consumes her as the cabin door springs open, and a very buff man dressed in a white suit and blue cowboy boots steps onto the tarmac. His natural brown skin combined with shoulder-length black hair frightens her.

Unsure who it is, she locks the doors. Her heart races as the man steps up to the window. He nods and gestures for Amanda to roll it down. Confusion fills her thoughts. Amanda needs to figure out what to do. Again, the man gestures. Cautiously, she cracks it.

"Who are you?" Her voice was merely a whisper over the roar of the turbo-powered engines.

"I'm Victor. I work for your father." His accented voice scares her.

She nods. "Where is he?"

He points at the plane. "Inside, come we must go. We have a tight schedule."

Amanda glares at the man. She feels something dubious about him. She senses it. "No! I want to see my father. Go get him, now!" She rolls up the window.

Victor smirks, revealing two silver front teeth. Suddenly, a new danger confronts her. He opens his jacket.

Amanda covers her face with her hands. He pounds again forcefully, yet the window doesn't shatter. She swallows a dry lump. Suddenly, she remembers the protocol. If, for any reason, they changed the evacuation plan, they would either call, text or activate the emergency transponders. Amanda quickly looks at the blinking icon on the right-hand corner of the navigation monitor. Her heart raced, realizing Randolph had already activated his. For whatever reason, her sedated mind overlooked it. The truth suddenly becomes clear. This man is going to kill her. Her eyes widen. She quickly strategizes.

First and foremost, she needs to start the engine. But that in itself would be her death sentence. He would cap her before she could engage the drive and accelerate to safety. She must use surprise and cunning to escape.

Amanda takes a deep breath. She lowers her hands and glances at the man.

Victor looks impatient. This time, he aims the gun. "You have three seconds to open the God Damn door," he roars. "Or I will shoot you in the face."

Amanda grabs the bag of white powder from her lap and holds it up. She deposits it inside her purse and places it on her lap. Victor grins and lowers the gun. His silver teeth sparkle. Amanda points to the lock mechanism on the door. He nods approvingly. She presses it. The sound of them disengaging sends a shiver through her spine. Victor immediately reaches for the handle; however, before he can open it, Amanda starts the engine, engages the drive, and slams the gas pedal to the floorboard. Her adrenaline flowing, she turned the wheel hard right and clipped Victor. Through the mirror, Amanda watches him sail to the ground. She fishtails around the plane and clips the wingtip with the side mirror, which sends shattered fiberglass fragments across the windshield. Disregarding the damage, she accelerates aggressively and smashes through the closed gate. In the rearview, she watches the fence bounce across the pavement. For a quick second, a surge of relief comforts her. Her bliss fades, and a new panic emerges.

Victor runs out into the road. A moment later, the popping of gunfire followed by two distinct cracking noises pushes her reflexes. She ducks only to remember Thomas installed bulletproof glass months ago. She grins, knowing that, for the time being, Victor cannot hurt her. She swerves to the opposite lane as another volley ricochets. Amanda tightens her grip on the wheel, straightens the front, and luckily avoids the ditch. Her hands were shaking, but she managed to navigate the slight curve in the road. Glancing in the rearview, Victor has disappeared. She decelerates to a safer speed and swallows heavily. She knows she was lucky to escape. Unfortunately, the damage to the aircraft was not sufficient to ground it. To her left, she watches the white fuselage go airborne.

•••

Cameron understands the slight innuendo. By winking, Thomas signaled this battle would not end until one of them was dead. Cameron secures his equipment and exits the plane. Tamara has already found comfort in her father's waiting arms.

"Oh, my God! It's so good to be home." She buries her head into his thick torso. "Daddy, I missed you so much." Tamara releases him and introduces James.

He extends his thick paw. "Son, call me Frank, you hear. It's sure good to finally put a face to your name." Frank grips his hand tightly and shakes it with purpose.

James grits, absorbing the pressure of the Texas handshake. "Yes, sir, it's good to meet you as well. Tamara has told me so much about you."

From behind, Cameron's familiar voice lightens the mood. He pats James on his shoulder. "He's a good man. Solid to the core!"

James caresses his throbbing hand. Frank is more significant than he imagined—a six-foot-ten hunk of a man with a gallon-sized cowboy hat, which makes him look even taller.

James remains passive during the twenty-minute drive to the house—a mansion between two hills and a winding lake. The driver, who everyone called Frog, told numerous jokes, the funniest about a hillbilly and a donkey. Everyone laughed. Tamara grips James by the hand as they enter the house. A very youthful-looking

Latino woman, well-rounded and light-skinned, greets them. Tamara runs up and hugs her for a long minute. Her mom recites a special prayer in Spanish, thanking God for returning her little angel safely. She says hello to Cameron, repeats something in Spanish, and steps up to James. "And who's this handsome young buck?"

"Mama, I'd like to introduce you to my boyfriend, James Rawlings." Tamara pecks James on the cheek. "Mama, I told you you'd approve."

She takes his hand and softly examines the lines in his palms. She looks into his eyes and studies his face. "It's nice to meet you, James. And yes, I approve." She gives him a firm welcome hug with a few pats on the back. "I noticed you've endured much hardship early in life. I also see why Tamara likes you. There's goodness pouring from your soul. Welcome to our home."

James feels his eyes well. He has not felt this much family love since his mother passed. He wipes a tear. "Thank you so much for the warm welcome." He sniffles. "Your daughter, she's amazing. And yes, I'm crazy about her." James sniffles again. "Oh, my God! Look at me." He lowers his eyes, embarrassed. "A sniveling fool, I'm sorry."

Her mom puts a finger to his mouth. "Hush now. Real men show emotion."

"Ah, bobby crap," Frank expresses. "We have so much to talk about." He inserts two fingers into his mouth and lets out a piercing whistle. A moment later, a balding elderly Asian man with long white eyebrows, sagging ear lobes, and a thin mustache wearing baggy white shorts and a t-shirt walks through a swinging door. "Namnuk, iced tea, and some sandwiches on the porch. And bring the bourbon."

"Yes, boss man. You want the good stuff?"

"Of course, you nincompoop." Frank voices strongly. Frank paws James on his shoulder. "It's so hard to find good help anymore. Come on, son. Let's eat—I'm starving."

After lunch, Cameron and Frank disappear into the study. James follows Tamara upstairs to her room. She opens the curtains. "Come here," she motions.

James steps up and caresses her shoulders. Her skin feels smooth.

She looks at James with swollen eyes. "I almost broke down at lunch. I can't get Dorian in the body bag out of my mind." She tucks her head to his shoulder. "I feel so horrible. I should have seen it coming. The black rose was the warning. I should have been there." She bawls. "I couldn't even help my sister. What's wrong with me?"

James hugs and kisses the top of her head. "I'm sorry, I'm so, so sorry. Baby, don't blame yourself, ever. That's the first rule. Besides, there was nothing either of us could've done. Think about it. Without Cameron, we'd probably be zipped in one of those bags too." He focuses on the pictures lining the fireplace mantle. James points. "Your sister?"

"Yeah," Tamara sniffles. "God, I miss her. It makes me sick to my stomach that witch of woman still breathes, and she's not."

"I know. I'm truly sorry. Amanda will get what's coming. Keep your head high. You're an amazing woman."

"What about you? I mean your mom. You were so young. How'd you endure?"

James lowers his head. "At first, nothing helped. I blamed everybody, even God."

"Do you believe, I mean now?"

James scratches his head. "That's a different topic!"

"I understand."

They hug. A few minutes pass. Tamara wipes her eyes and points out the window. "See the oak tree on the top of the second hill."

"Yeah, it's huge."

"My dad planted it when I was born. He said it was the same size as me. On the other side, it slopes down to this amazingly lush valley. A small creek flowing down from the South feeds a lake."

"It sounds amazing."

"It is. That's where I will build my house; excuse me, our house."

James swallows. "Umm, OKAY!" He grinds his jaw.

Her eyes sparkle.

"You're so beautiful." James pecks her forehead. "Your family, this house, and you, wow! I don't know if I fit in. I might be too poor for your father. I mean, he has a private jet."

"Four!" she smiles.

James holds up four fingers. They giggle. For the time being, James plays along. The stresses of the last few days have weighed heavy on his conscience. James grabs the cigar Frank put in his side pocket, removes the paper label, and drops to one knee. He takes her hand

and looks at her directly. "Tamara," James carefully places the band on her ring finger. "Will you marry me?"

● ●

Powerful emotions surge as Amanda watches the plane bank hard right. Twice, it circles. She can hear the bite of the propellers cutting through the thick atmosphere. She accelerates aggressively. What worries Amanda is that the road straightens for the next few miles. Farms on either side spot the flattened landscape. Amanda can only wonder what their intentions are. A moment later, her plight comes full circle. The plane has descended and initiated a head-on assault.

"Is that all you've got!" Amanda screams, flipping the bird as if the pilot can see her. She tightens her grip on the wheel and grits her teeth. At this point, she has nothing to lose. The adrenaline combined with the drugs kicks in. Amanda looks at her speed, ninety-two miles per hour, and climbing. The suspension buckles over a slight hump, and the tires chirp as they regain traction. That little hiccup does not alter her mindset. Her speed has reached one hundred and five. She ducks down and closes her eyes as the fuselage zooms overhead. The sound vibrates through her bones, and she swears the landing gear clipped the roof. Amanda swerves releases her heavy foot, and manages to regain control.

The next mile passes quickly. Amanda enters the wooded area and screeches to a stop. She looks up through the towering trees at the plane circling above. She feels safe for the time being. Her concern is how long she has before they send a cleaning crew.

Her heart jumps at the high-pitched chime. Amanda recognizes the ringtone. Her hands shake as she answers. "Thomas, is this you?" Her voice verging on hysterical.

"Yes, it's me. Calm down."

"Why weren't you there?"

"Listen. A group of mercenaries attacked the house. Look, I'm sorry I wasn't there for you. But I'm close now."

Amanda pans the road ahead and then behind. "Where! I don't see you."

"I'm close. I need you to stay focused." His voice calms her. "Remember what I taught you, your training. Take a deep breath. Listen to my voice. Look at the navigation monitor. My blip should be flashing green. I've already passed the airport. Do you see me?"

"That fucker shot at me and tried to run me off the road with his plane." Amanda begins to bawl. "They said they had him. Is he okay?"

"Amanda, listen to my voice. Concentrate on the green flashing blip?"

She sniffles. "Okay. I'm looking at it." Amanda turns and stares through the spider-cracked rear window. "I still can't see you."

"I noticed the airport gate busted out and heavy tire tracks. Was that you?"

"Yeah," Amanda breathes heavily. "I smashed right through it."

"You put the move on them, didn't you?"

"Like in the movies."

"Good girl! Tell me what happened."

"When I arrived, nobody was there. Not too long after, a plane landed, and this buster with thick black hair and dark skin exited. I immediately locked the doors and rolled up the windows. He told me Daddy was inside. I didn't believe him, and he pulled a gun because I wouldn't unlock the door. I don't know how I did it, but

I tricked him. How did he know about the airport? I thought it was our secret place."

"I don't know, but I promise to make them pay. Amanda, listen to my voice. Keep the windows up and the doors locked. The bulletproof glass will protect you. Can you see the plane?"

Amanda looks up. Her voice turns hysterical. "Yes, it's circling. What does it mean?"

"Nothing, focus on my voice. I see it now. You did well hiding under the canopy. I'm proud of you. Okay, I'm less than three out. Keep talking. It'll help keep your head clear."

"Why are they doing this?"

"You know why. Your father will set this straight. I'm almost there. Keep talking."

Amanda sniffles. "Hurry up. I'm scared. I can't do this alone. Oh my God! Thomas, I see a car. What should I do!"

●●●

"Why there?" James asks. "Is that plot of land special?"

Tamara glances at her temporary ring. A heartfelt emotion surges. "Very much so! My daddy promised it to me on my twelfth birthday. He told me he'd build my dream house when I found the right man." Tamara opens the top dresser drawer and pulls out a tablet. "I drew this when I was fourteen."

James studies the sketch of an incredible house. "It's amazing. You have many talents."

By nightfall, he feels at home. The dinner conversation flows. Frank was impressed with the cigar ring. Before the desert, Cameron interrupts.

"There's a phone call. I suggest you take it in the study."

Frank excuses himself. Everyone remains subdued, wondering what could be so urgent. A few minutes later, Frank rushes into the dining room. "Everyone downstairs, now! Cameron, you know what to do."

Chapter 33

An unknown fear confronts Amanda. The vehicle, a squared older style four-door sedan with a vinyl roof, stopped a hundred feet behind. The windows are heavily tinted, and dark smoke escapes from the tailpipes. What worries her? Why did they stop so far away and keep the engine running?

"Amanda, how are you holding up?" Thomas asks.

She clears her throat. "I've never been so scared. The car stopped on the side of the road. It's just sitting there."

"Can you see inside?"

"No! The windows are tinted. Thomas, what should I do?"

"I'm here. I see the car."

Amanda searches the road. "Where? I don't see you."

"Never mind. I see you."

Amanda hears some rustling through the speaker. A moment later, his voice returns. "Amanda, I count four in the car, and they're not friendlies. They know your vehicle has bulletproof glass. That's what deterred them. Here's what I want you to do. You see the big tree with the yellow sign a hundred or so feet in front of you?"

"Yes."

"On the other side, there's a turnout. When I give you the signal, punch it! Once you're behind the tree, stop, put the transmission in park, and duck below the dash. Can you do this?"

Amanda sniffles and prepares the vehicle. "Okay, I'm ready."

It happens faster than expected. All four doors open, and four men yielding weapons jump out. One man places a rocket launcher on his shoulder.

"Now Amanda! Punch it!"

The tires squeal, and a dust cloud fills the air as the super-charged black Range Rover accelerates. Not prepared for her sudden maneuver, the men scramble. Amanda brakes heavily, turns the wheel, and guides the vehicle onto the narrow dirt road. Thomas aims and drops the man with a single shot, preparing to fire the missile. In retaliation, the other men engage. Thomas quickly takes two more out before they can acquire his position. Outflanked, the driver dives behind the car. He climbs in and accelerates wildly after Amanda. Thomas steps out from the bush and aims. With a single shot, he blows out the rear passenger tire. The car skids out of control and slams head-on into the tree with the sign. Thomas quickly adjusts the scope. He places the crosshair on the bloodied head of the injured man but decides not to fire. Instead, he runs up, opens the door, and rifle butts him.

Russel, the pilot, welcomes Amanda at the alternate airport.

"I'm holding you to your promise." Amanda insists.

"I guarantee your father and I will join you tomorrow evening in Puerto Rico." Thomas hugs her. He finalizes a few orders with Russel and exits the plane. What happens next sends Amanda into a hysterical screaming frenzy. Before Russel can close the hatch, a small white bird flies inside. In a frantic attempt to escape, it swoops head-first into one of the portals and drops dead on her lap. Russel immediately scoops and deposits it outside. Amanda believes fate followed her. She insists on doom. With the help of a powerful sleeping pill, Thomas takes another thirty minutes to calm her. He wipes a heavy bead of sweat from his brow and sighs as the jet rockets skyward.

An inevitable realization confronts Thomas. Even though he does not believe in superstition, he cannot overlook the cold, hard facts. In forty-eight hours, two small white birds, which Amanda firmly believes were omens, killed themselves before her. Adding fuel to the fire, a handful of well-trained mercenaries, most likely one of Randolph's many enemies, have declared war on his family. They have already skillfully captured him, slaughtered half of the men at the compound, and scared Amanda half to death. Could Amanda be right? Could the Manchester family be living on borrowed time? Are they jinxed? He shakes his head.

The interrogation of the driver went better than Thomas had expected. He tells him everything before dropping into unconsciousness. Thomas discovers they're holding Randolph captive inside the plane at one of the local municipal airports.

●●

Tamara finger locks her hand with James and swings

her arm. She nods. "Come on, baby. Follow me."

"What's going on?" James asks, running down the extra wide wooden staircase. What bothers him? She doesn't answer.

Halfway down, Tamara stops, turns, and winks. "Something special! Don't worry. I think you'll appreciate this."

They pass through an expanded gaming area. Pool tables, a four-lane bowling alley, foosball and air hockey, a mini-kitchen, and, centered in the midst, a circular sit-down bar. A spinning reddish neon disco ball with the words *Hudson Saloon* hangs from the ceiling. On the far wall, large block letters highlight the upper threshold of the entrance to the in-house theater. Tamara leads James through double gothic-style doors and enters a chapel.

She stops short of the pews. James releases her hand and glowers at the life-size depiction of Jesus nailed to a cross positioned above a golden white laced alter. He fixates on the words inscribed on the wooden emblem.

I forgive your sins

Tamara takes his hand. "You all right?" She asks.

"My goodness, I've never seen such a beautiful church before. The attention to detail is remarkable. I had no idea your family was so religious."

"Roman Catholic, born and raised."

"You're a pew baby!"

Tamara tells him to shush. "I bend the rules, actually quite a bit." She leads him over to a large table filled with colored candles. She reaches into a slot and pulls out two long wooden matches. Tamara gives James one. "Light it here." She scratches the tip across the rough surface, igniting a yellowish flame. "Say a short prayer directed to anyone or anything, and pick a candle." She douses the match.

James whispers some words and completes the ritual. Tamara leads him over to the back-row pew, and they sit. She places her hand on his leg.

"My mom built this after Samantha went missing. She came down every day, sometimes twice, to light a candle and pray for her return. We're all here now because the phone call was from the forensic guy Cameron hired. He found the skeletal remains of Samantha and Derik."

"So Dorian came through."

Tamara nods. Her eyes immediately tear. "I miss him already."

"I do, too! How do you know the bones are hers?"

"He found her necklace. A present my dad gave her the day she left for college engraved with her name."

His heart feels heavy. James looks at Tamara's mom, crying on Frank's shoulder. She has a white Rosary wrapped around her hand.

"We all now have closure. After the police complete forensics, we'll bury Samantha on the property." Tamara kneels on the cushioned hassock, blesses herself, and says a silent prayer. She takes James by the hand. "Come on. I wanna show you something."

They exit through the back door and climb aboard a replica Hummer golf cart-type electric vehicle. Tamara turns on the row of lights strung across the roof and accelerates down a gravel road. About a quarter mile ahead, she stops in front of a boat house. Behind the rise of the four-story mansion, the constellation-rich Texas skyline greets them.

"Come on."

James follows Tamara around the structure and down a long-drawn-out wooden dock. Lights above each pile, shaped like sitting birds, illuminate the shanty planks. They creak to the weight of their steps. Halfway down, she stops. A warm breeze wafts her hair. Her eyes are glazed. Tamara steps up, kisses James, and quickly undresses. With a naughty grin, she takes off in a full sprint, jumps high into the night air, and athletically summersaults before piercing the choppy surface.

For the longest time, she remains submerged until she finally breaches. With splashing hands, she yells. "Come on, chicken butt. What're you waiting for!"

●●

Thomas surveys the repair crew completing the installation of the new winglet on the twin-engine plane. He zooms in on the open aft cargo hatch. There are no signs of movement. Two other aircraft, idling, await departure in front of the private terminal. Thomas can tell the men who kidnapped Randolph differ from those who raided the compound.

An hour passes. The repair crew departs, and the tarmac in front of the terminal empties. Simon watches two clean-shaven, well-dressed Caucasian men exit the building, most likely the pilot and co-pilot. They walk casually toward the plane. The taller one strolls around the exterior, obviously making a physical inspection of the new winglet, while the other enters the fuselage. Towards the rear, one of the blinds from a closed portal quickly opens and shuts two times. A few seconds later, it happens again. Thomas studies the interior schematic of the aircraft and determines Randolph must have signaled from the lavatory portal. About a minute later, two men exit through the cabin hatch. Both are South American. One wears blue cowboy boots.

"Are you ready?" Thomas asks Simon through the secure communication link.

"Ready and waiting."

"The others?"

"They acquired the luggage truck. You were right—it was a shipment of guns. Derik and Tim will be coming around the terminal at two o'clock. Their ears are on."

Thomas understands these men are the gun runners from South America whose daughter he accidentally shot. He activates the video link on the electronic device. He re-acquires the two soldiers through the scope. Derick and Tim pull up to the aft cargo compartment.

The man with the blue boots walks up. His accented voice shows impatience. "Load everything except the briefcases."

While Derik climbs inside the cargo hold, Tim begins

hefting the bags. Blue Boots watches for a bit and orders his subordinate to carry the briefcases inside the cabin. He talks to the pilot, inspects the wing, and disappears into the terminal.

"Simon, I want Blue Boots alive."

"Copy that. I'm on it."

"Derik, you copy?"

"Loud and clear."

"You in position?"

"Affirmative."

"Have you planted the device?"

"Affirmative."

"Green light in ten seconds."

"Copy that."

Derik cracks open the interior cargo hatch and slips inside. Two men are playing cards on a fold-down table. They have no idea of his presence. A pile of cocaine and beer bottles line the top. Derik readies his silenced pistol and cleans the interior with two precise shots. He quickly unlocks the aft head door and liberates Randolph from his handcuffs. No words are said. Randolph quickly steps into a pair of work coveralls, and they both exit the cargo hold. Randolph hides inside an empty luggage container, and

Derik drives away. Inside the terminal, Simon has moved into striking range. Blue Boots entered the restroom. Simon places a closed-for-service cone next to the door. He wheels the cleaning cart inside and locks the door. Simon drops to the floor and inspects the other stalls. Blue Boots has entered the far booth. Favorably, the others are empty. Remaining low, he readies the tranquilizer pistol with a fast-acting knockout drug. Patiently, he waits. What he was not ready for, after Blue Boots flushed, he kicked open the door, yielding a pistol. How Blue Boots knew danger loomed only pushes the situation. Being a professional, Simon doesn't hesitate. The first dart hits his mark squarely in the chest, and the second his shoulder before Blue Boots can aim. Simon quickly cleans the room and exits.

Two hours later, Thomas injects the serum and wakes Blue Boots. At first, he struggles but settles after realizing his wrists and ankles are bound. Blue Boots squints to the blinding light. He notices, except for his boots, they removed his clothes, and his wrists and legs stretched outwards are bound to cabled handcuffs. His body aches, and his mind swims in a paradox of fear.

"Who are you?" Blue Boots beckons.

A few long minutes pass until the blinding light fades.

Blue Boots squints. He sees Randolph and a man dressed in a black suit. Randolph puts on leather gloves, walks up, and lands a heavy blow to his torso. Blue Boots gasps.

"That was for scaring my little girl." Randolph takes another full swing and lands his weighty fist on his face. Blue Boots buckles, and a single bloodied tooth falls to the floor. "That was for kidnapping me."

Randolph rubs his knuckles. He removes the gloves and steps behind Thomas.

"Fuck you, Manchester." Blue Boots spits a mouthful of blood. "I'm a soldier doing my duty. You," he grins, "you're an expired asset. No matter my outcome, you cannot save yourself or your daughter."

Thomas steps up and delivers a brutal blow to his midsection. Blue Boots huffs, knowing a few ribs fractured. Thomas inserts a hypodermic needle into his neck and presses the plunger. Randolph and Thomas walk out of the room.

Thirty minutes later, they return.

By the end of the interrogation, a forbidding reality presents itself, even though the truth does not come immediately. The organization knows everything, even about the safe house in Puerto Rico, which suggests a traitor exists. Thomas agrees. Randolph fights off a growing panic. They still need to find out who hired the mercenaries. Thomas finds himself at an impasse. This attack should have never happened. In his thoughts, he sees the two white birds. He begins to wonder if the family curse has substance.

Thomas tries to revive Blue Boots, but he has slipped into unconsciousness. For the time being, the mole will remain a mystery. Thomas must also assume they have electronically bugged the house. Randolph calls the pilot flying Amanda to Puerto Rico on the encrypted satellite phone and reroutes them to Hawaii. He knows the informant is someone on the plane in case anything happens.

●●

Amanda partially rouses. She hears the quiet roar of jet engines, but her sedated mind cannot discern her actuality. Her partial consciousness experiences the vivid and scary reoccurring nightmare that has haunted her for years.

This episode, similar to the others, begins with her

gazing out across a sunken valley at the wreckage of a fallen airliner. She enters the broken fuselage in front of the massive wings. Moving forward to the cockpit, what frightens her is that there are no seats, portals, or luggage compartments. As haunting, every breath feels laborious. Deep within, she knows she has entered a place of anguish, despair, and suffering. In the distance, a white bird materializes. The wings are not fluttering, yet they soar directly toward her with two reddish eyes gazing into the pulse of her soul. She tries to scream, but no sound emerges, and before she can react, it enters her mouth. Suddenly, a young James Rawlings appears. Like in the other nightmares, he displays a red apple. This time, she can hear his voice. He asks her to take the apple. She tries to reach for it, but her body feels paralyzed. She cannot move her arms or legs or even wiggle her toes. A paradox of fear manifests. A clear and distinct representation of a second white bird emerges within the rind. The difference is that it's flying away from her. It quickly fades, and her father comes into view. She screams. Someone decapitated his head and placed it awkwardly at the apex of a wooden pole.

Extreme turbulence shudders the aircraft. In an instant,

the plane drops rapidly in altitude. Amanda opens her eyes. Her inner sense tells her to grab something, but it's too late. Her entire body goes airborne. Panic divides her consciousness. Her mind spins in contradiction. Could this be part of the nightmare?

●●●

After a playful swim under the glow of the soft moon, they make passionate love. James feels like a fish out of water. Tamara expressed she feels the same way. The following day, she calls a family meeting. While showing off her cigar paper engagement ring, with clear heads, they proclaim their love for each other. Boldly, James asks Frank for her daughter's hand in marriage.

●●

Unknown to Thomas, Blue Boots concealed a GPS tracking device in the heel of his boot. A specialist has infiltrated the compound and dug in within the tree line. In the crosshairs of his scope, he watches Randolph talking on a phone pace around the backyard. The specialist quickly scans the house. He locates Thomas through one of the downstairs windows. He confirms his orders. No survivors and he must retrieve Blue Boots. The specialist steadies himself. As he squeezes the hair trigger, a slight dust cloud vibrates off the hardened and camouflaged barrel. The projectile pierces the window, and a second later, Thomas falls cleanly. Randolph lowers the phone and stares across the lawn. He heard a sound but could not place it. He inspects the house and sees a small hole in the study window. Suddenly, an unprecedented fear ripples. Randolph turns and stares at the tree line.

The shooter watches patiently. The crosshairs painted on his marks forehead. A second later, Randolph falls.

The shooter retrieves Blue Boots from the torture chamber. He feels remorse. They were friends. Before exiting, he hangs Thomas and Randolph's feet first from the pine tree in the backyard. He staples an envelope of evidence relating to his shady business dealings on his chest. Two hours later, the specialist closes the cabin door to the twin-engine plane. He has never failed a mission before, but this one lies heavy. His good friend paid the ultimate price.

As the plane reaches cruising altitude, the small white

box in the rear cargo hold activates. Inside, a heating coil rapidly turns orange and a vile of ignitable fluid breaks open. A moment later, flames engulf the interior. Within seconds, they spread through the cabin, and before the pilot could douse the fire, everyone fell unconscious from smoke inhalation. The plane drops in altitude and crashes in a rural area.

• •

In the few moments where her body begins to float within the interior boundaries of the rapidly descending aircraft, a time and space before actuality merge with the unforgiving truth, Amanda rummages through her past. Specifically, as an innocent adolescent, she saved time in a bottle and cherished the thought that a boy named James Rawlings would love her for eternity. They planted and toiled together in the dirt, growing rose bushes in his mother's garden. How she stole the flower pot containing the very plant he cut and gave to her on her tenth birthday only to drop it off the building a few months later in New York City. The clarity of the picture his mother hand-painted of the both of them holding hands on the exterior remained vivid until finally shattering on the sidewalk fifteen stories below.

Amanda lets out a terrifying scream as her body slams violently against the interior wall of the fuselage. The sensation of paralysis and oxygen deprivation she experienced in her dream come full circle. Her mind grasps the situation. The plane suddenly rolled and initiated an out-of-control descent. She assumes something exploded in the tail section because she can see outside through a rupture above the bathroom door. She wedges her fingers within the portal with all her remaining strength. Combined with the shriek of the flailing engines, the icy coldness of the g-force winds, and her burning lungs, she looks out through the window and comes to peace with the rapidly expanding earth.

Chapter 34

James kneels next to his mother's headstone and places a dozen long stem red roses in the vase. He lowers his head. "Hi, Mom! I'm sorry it's been so long." James looks up and signals Tamara. She kneels and places a single yellow dandelion in the vase. She finger locks his hand. "Mom, I'd like to introduce Tamara, my wife. You were right. I remained patient, and I found my true love. I promise to cherish her for the rest of my life. Mom, I've never been happier. By the way, we're having a baby. Twins. You're finally going to be a grandmother." James kisses Tamara. "Guess what. I live in Texas now, but I promise to visit every chance I get. One more thing! You were right about Amanda and her dad. A couple of months ago, they died tragically. But you knew this would happen, didn't you? I finally understand what you meant by what comes around goes around."

Tamara wipes a tear from his cheek. "I love you, James Rawlings."

THE END

Thank you for reading

BROKEN

From the Author — Matthew Liburdi

CLICK LINK TO VISIT AUTHOR WEBSITE

Hello friends and family and of course, the nice person I don't know who finished reading BROKEN. I'm not asking for any handouts, but as a simple favor, if you enjoyed reading BROKEN, please navigate to any of these sites and leave a review.

AMAZON.com

SMASHWORDS.com

BARNSandNOBLE.com

Then please pass BROKEN on to your friends and family and tell them to do the same when they finish. Your REVIEWS are so important and I thank you all for taking your valuable time to publish them.

Other novels by Matthew Liburdi

CRUMBLING KINGDOM

YA / Family Novel - Suspense - Thriller

DECEPTIVE TIMES

Four-book Action/Adventure series

Deceptive Times 1

Deceptive Times 2

Deceptive Times 3

Deceptive Times 4

WOLLOH

Psychological/Horror

WOLLOH 2 – BROKEN 2 – DECEPTIVE TIMES X5

CRUMBLING KINGDOM 2

coming soon

Made in the USA
Las Vegas, NV
02 May 2024

89413873R00223